THE
SCHOLARSHIP

THE
SCHOLARSHIP

(INSPIRED BY ACTUAL EVENTS)

ALEX R. PRICE

Squaretop Mountain Publishing LLC

Squaretop Mountain Publishing, LLC
P.O. Box 593
Green River, WY 82935

ISBN - 13: 978-1-7332557-5-2

Acknowledgments

I want to give a big thank you to Angela. She has been the best Beta reader that I have found since my literary journey began. There were so many helpful comments that I know my readers won't get lost on their adventure. Thank you to Misty and my many other readers who have helped shape this story. I want to thank those readers who just shrugged their shoulders "Eh. It was okay." I learned that there was something worse than, "It Sucked." Hooray for perpetual learning.

I want to give a big shout out to my editor Sarah, no relation or inspiration to the main character, she has made this book into an amazing adventurous learning tool of moral standards. Without which civilization would be a reckless mess without boundaries.

Lastly, I would like to thank a wonderful person who was the single inspiration for this particular venture and the organizations that thwarted her in rediscovering who she truly is. Your award is on the following page. I know that this book has helped you and I pray that it will help many more who stumble into your shoes.

For the inspiration of this story and the dedication to help see it through, here is #2.

THE
SCHOLARSHIP

Chapter 1

Sarah Menendez grabbed her cellmate's blonde hair, shoved her against the wall and into the corner of the cell. "Get your ugly little punk ass off my bunk," she growled in the woman's ear. A moan escaped the blonde woman as she gritted her teeth to keep from crying out. It wasn't prison, but it was jail, and since Sarah had been a recurring visitor over the past year, she felt that she had privilege to a few things that she called hers, like sleeping on the lower bunk, being first in the shower and having a personal servant whom she selected from the many bodies residing in the women's pod. She seethed when she saw her cellmate sitting on her bed, right after she had made it with the simple blanket that the jail had issued her. Sarah had also confiscated her bunkmate's blanket to use as her own personal pillow since the county regarded pillows as a luxury item and she would have had to buy one if she couldn't swipe one.

Gina was an herbal fanatic and passive to no end. Translated, she was caught growing marijuana illegally and so stoned out of her gourd that she barely noticed that the police had put handcuffs on her wrists. She had just been put into the crowded C-pod with Sarah because the medical ward where she should have been assigned was getting people in who needed more attention than Gina did.

Sarah pressed the blonde head harder into the concrete wall to emphasize her dominance. When she was released, Gina fell to the floor, cupping her head in her hands. It throbbed immensely but she dared not cry out due to the nature of her environment. When everything was stripped from the young women, they resorted to a more primitive social banding. The day room was equal to that of a junior high hallway minus the latest designer clothes. With the lack of direction and a crush of idle time, the young women sought any trivial thing they could to make them stand out as more important than the others.

Sarah spun back to her bunk and straightened the three little wrinkles out of the blanket. She didn't know why she was obsessive about it here. She had barely lifted a finger to clean the house when she was at home with her boyfriend. In jail, it was a way of protecting territory and status, although it was just temporary and intellectual. Here, a neatly-made bed was something to defend regardless of how small, petty and inconsequential it was.

Home was a ratty old trailer on the edge of Pine Bluff, Arkansas. Her boyfriend had bought it for a thousand dollars when his buddy needed cash to hire a lawyer for a DUI. Her mother was three trailers down and dependent upon massive amounts of alcohol to get her through the day. Sarah had sealed away her own chance at freedom when her mother came over in a drunken fit and began beating on her. In her mother's drunken state, she scarcely realized what she repeatedly did, and each time the reason was the same. Her mother blamed

THE SCHOLARSHIP

Sarah for the loss of lifestyle that she had previously enjoyed. Now she was stuck in a broken-down trailer in a neighborhood that she had looked down upon years before.

Sarah retaliated against the beating, breaking her mother's nose and ripping out a chunk of hair, leaving a red patch that began to ooze blood. The fight in her front yard caught the attention of a nearby patrolman who had been sent to investigate a separate incident. In her blind rage Sarah swung at anyone who came within arm's reach, including the patrolman. A glancing backhand to the officer set her up for a possible twenty-five years in prison.

Her attorney shook his head when she wanted to plead innocent. Skeltor Roth was a mild-mannered public defender for the Pine Bluff area. The district attorney was going after Sarah Menendez with fangs dripping for blood. The prosecutor's husband was an officer and anyone who crossed another officer was raw meat that she was ready to run through the grinder.

"Menendez!" a booming voice called out. Sarah glanced around to see who was calling her and if they had seen her discipline her cellmate. "Menendez. Front and center," the guard called out.

Sarah walked confidently to the guard, trying not to show guilt from the altercation just a moment before. "Yes, sir."

"Your lawyer is here to see you," the big man said.

Sarah rolled her eyes at the mundane facts that encompassed her case. Numerous petty crimes that had brought her in for week or a month, only to be released back to the probation officer. This time she knew she would be staying longer, possibly until her child-bearing years were over.

She hadn't given much thought to children. She figured if they happened then they happened, and she would deal with it

3

then. Until that time, she had her sights on parties followed by doing as little as possible. Pizza, cigarettes and Pepsi-Cola were her staples since her high school had released her from their own torture cells three years prior. A couple changes in wardrobe over the past two years sent her from being light to heavyweight in intimidation. If someone looked at her funny, she would offer to sit on their face until they stopped breathing.

Buzzers sounded, metal doors clicked open, and then locked shut behind her as the guard led her to the conference room where her attorney stood waiting.

Sarah rolled her eyes again as she sat in the chair. The guard attached a leg shackle to her ankle and quietly ducked out of the room. Silence enveloped the room in the two seconds it took for Mr. Roth to find his voice. He wasn't a very confrontational man, but he knew his business and stated the facts clearly and plainly.

"Miss Menendez, I have a new option to offer you." Mr. Roth pulled a file from his stack of papers. "It's an intense alternative program that, if completed, will allow you to walk free in two to three years."

"What is it?"

"I'm not entirely sure, but it sounds very promising. It is like a military school, only you are still classified as an inmate until you complete the course." Mr. Roth slid the papers to Sarah for her analysis. "From what I understand, it's a school who seeks out women like you as students. The program is two to three years long."

"You said that already," Sarah huffed.

"Well, you don't have to get snappy. I could have left this on my desk or offered it to someone else. I talked to a young lady who had been through the program and she recommended you for it. She said it is the exact thing you need in your life."

4

THE SCHOLARSHIP

"So, how many screws did she have loose?" Sarah chided.

"This is no joking matter. You could face twenty-five years if you don't take this. If you do, you will get an education and walk free in two to three years."

"What're they going to do? Make me sit up and look pretty?"

"Miss Menendez, if you don't want this, I can certainly offer it to someone else."

"Where's this torture chamber located?" Sarah folded her arms in front of her.

"It is undisclosed."

"What the hell does that mean?"

"It means it is of no consequence to you." Mr. Roth snapped, his patience with this adolescent in an adult body becoming thin. "It doesn't matter where it is. You won't be able to contact anyone until it is done. You can take your chances in front of the judge or you can take this deal."

"What if I don't like the deal after I get there?" Sarah sat up, semi-interested in the discussion, and in the deal.

"If you fail, it is an automatic twenty-five-year sentence. They have a one hundred percent success rate and the program has been in effect since 2009. So, in ten years they haven't turned anyone back."

"Yeah. You can do math," Sarah scoffed.

"Since you don't want it I will…"

The panic button blared in her head. Reaching out, she snatched the paper back from Mr. Roth as he began assembling his files and moving on to find someone else for the deal. "I'll sign."

"Remember, if you fail, you'll get an automatic twenty-five years," Mr. Roth reiterated.

Sarah mumbled under her breath at the predicament she was in. It seemed to be a 'damned if you did or damned if you didn't' situation. A sideways thought crept into her mind: maybe she could escape from this "school." Beat feet to Mexico and find another home that would allow her to live peaceably. Accidentally hitting a cop wasn't cause to spend the nation's budget to root her out of another country. She would need a passport, a plane ticket and some cash or some other means of getting from point A to B. She reasoned that stealing from a wealthy, unsuspecting resident should get her the cash she needed to make her way to a new home, free from persecution. She argued in her mind that the resident would be happy to let go of a couple grand in lieu of saving local citizens hundreds or thousands of tax dollars. Passports could be bought or stolen as long as the individual looked predominantly like her. Once successful, she would be free to start her life anew.

She believed that her situation wasn't her fault. Her mother should have raised her better and her father shouldn't have kicked either of them out of the house when she was fourteen. She might have had a chance to lead a more productive life if her parents didn't have such selfish desires. She cursed under her breath at the hand she'd been dealt. She should be living in a nice house and enjoying life, provided to her at the expense of the rich. Her vote for Bernie was not fruitful, due to the wife of a former president. She knew that the U.S. wasn't ready for a female president. The former Secretary of State had too many skeletons in her closet not to mention the soiled view of her husband. Sarah believed that since Bernie didn't make it, then she was now doomed to suffer under a tyrant's rule.

THE SCHOLARSHIP

She scribbled her name across the pages of the contract followed by the date and initialed where she was asked as the attorney recited what each section was for. Sarah didn't care nor listen. Her loathing toward anyone of authority consumed her mind, discounting anything she heard as babble. She just wanted out. In her mind, she would admit to killing JFK if it meant that she would be able to get out.

Signing the last page with the twenty-first signature, she looked up at the attorney. He now had a pleasant grin on his face. "Thank you." The public defender tucked the paperwork back into his briefcase and slid the pen home in its leather sheath. "You will be well taken care of. I have heard remarkable things about this program. I am almost jealous that I won't be able to watch your transformation."

His sly grin sent shivers up her spine. She briefly wondered what he meant by his last statement and then dismissed the concern. To her, it mattered little what he thought, or what anyone thought. Within a week, she would be soaking up the rays on a Mexican beach and planning her next move to anywhere farther from this little hell-hole town.

Chapter II

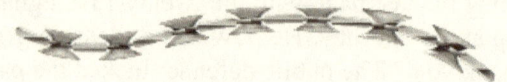

Y ou wanted to see me sir?" Gloria Witcom stood at attention with her toes on the red line just outside Harold Vickery's office. Harold shuffled through some paperwork, signing the bottom of two pages, followed by the day's date. Folding the file closed, he leaned back in his plush, leather chair, surveying one of the best students he had seen go through the program.

Gloria had only seen Dean Vickery's office once before, when she was first assigned to a cleaning detail. Everyone had to meet with him at least once before they started their final phase of the program. She had taken in his certificates of completion: A bachelor's from the University of Wyoming in Social Science, a master's from Stanford University, and a doctorate's degree from Harvard.

Harold had been the first and only dean of the school. The Schultz Business Academy was founded ten years prior when Phillip Schultz had gotten into an argument with Kansas Senator Dillion Walboard over the value of more prisons verses a better rehabilitation system. To prove his point, Phillip Schultz bought an abandoned detention center in the hills of

THE SCHOLARSHIP

Missouri, along with two hundred acres surrounding the facility. Over the years the students, under the supervision of staff and teachers, turned the former prison into a first-class facility filled with classrooms, work shops and offices. The small, sleepy community that relied on the former prison as a major source of commerce was brought back to life with the new rehabilitation program. It had rejuvenated the small town with a better sense of pride, knowing that they were making a difference in the world.

Schultz called in Harold Vickery, the then-superintendent of a Northern Missouri school system to run the school. Dr. Vickery read over the plans and invested a portion of his retirement into the endeavor, then signed on as dean of the school. They found success with the first class of eleven students. Each year they expanded until they had rotating classes of twenty-five students year-round. A sizeable produce export, and a skills center where students were taught everything from auto mechanics to building trades to basic household skills like cooking, sewing and budgeting kept them all busy between sessions of therapy.

The year-round produce supplied the local restaurants, grocery stores, and farmer's markets. A full explanation of how the organic vegetables were grown was given to each customer, along with stories of charity deliveries to senior citizens and the retirement homes. Other revenue was derived from donated vehicles that were repaired and sold to the public, a pet grooming and adoption center, a custom print shop and a coffee shop-deli that stayed busy from open to close. The most significant stream of revenue came from commercial rentals. The school began by buying one dilapidated house to use as a teaching tool for home improvement. Once the renovations were complete, it was sold and two more were bought. Of those

9

two, one became a rental and the other sold to buy a small commercial property. Over the previous ten years the school grew its portfolio to a dozen cash-producing properties.

The purchase of a restaurant topped the business portfolio of the school. Students who showed interest in the culinary arts started in the cafeteria, where once a month they exercised their creative skills to turn an average cafeteria into a four-star restaurant. They designed a menu from scratch, and then bought, cooked and served the food on a budget. The rest of the staff and students were required to write a review of their experience for the culinary students to use as critique feedback in preparation for managing or owning their own restaurants.

"You've been one of our top students at Schultz Business Academy, Gloria," Vickery stated. "I'm not talking about this year. I am talking about over the past ten years running."

Gloria was taken aback. All she had done was commit herself to the program so she could get back to her family sooner. She hadn't seen her three sons in almost a year. The weekend phone calls made her heart ache for their embrace even more. As part of the boot camp section of the program, there wasn't any outside contact, no letters and no phone calls unless there was a death in the immediate family. Even then, students were not allowed to leave.

After the boot camp phase, it was a full sprint marathon straight to the end. There weren't any breaks or vacations. The students were allowed half a day on Sunday for worship otherwise the day was busy with laundry and maintenance of the facility. Gloria enjoyed the fast pace. No one knew when they would finish, only that they would. If they didn't, they knew it was an automatic maximum sentence. Everyone worked as a team but graduated when they were ready. Each student belonged to a team and each team was required to meet

THE SCHOLARSHIP

up a few times a week to discuss and plan the next moves that would allow them to get closer to leaving the school.

A few women found their family within the program and stayed on as instructors and office staff. Counselors and mentors were plentiful as the upperclassmen were required to continually teach those coming through the doors. Even the dean taught a class on communication and problem solving.

Ten years was what Gloria faced if she failed at Schultz's. If she did not finish the program, she would lose all the days she had served in the school and start her sentence from day one at a penitentiary. A decade was far too long for Gloria to even consider. She didn't want to miss out on that much of her sons' lives. This was her primary motivation, and the reason she had done so well at the academy.

"Thank you, sir," Gloria said, still poised at attention outside the dean's office.

"Come. Please have a seat over here." Dr. Vickery stood up from his desk and walked to a small conference area inside the expansive office.

Gloria felt uneasy sitting in the plush leather seat. It was a far cry from the hard-plastic stools she had become accustomed to over the past year.

"I've never seen someone sail through this program as fast as you. I commend you on your accomplishment."

"Thank you, sir." Gloria glanced around the room, taking note of the U.S. Army banner that hung above the dean's head. Seven core values were outlined underneath the Army seal: loyalty, duty, respect, selfless service, honor, integrity, personal courage. It all added up to the acronym L.D.R.S.H.I.P. It was the basis of their mission statement, 'We build leaders to a higher standard.' The statement was painted on each side of every door to instill a sense of growth, accomplishment and purpose.

"Are you ready for the last phase of the program?"

"Yes, sir." Gloria now looked at the stack of files that were neatly placed on the table.

"Since you have the highest marks in your class, you get to pick first."

"What should I look for when choosing?" Gloria asked.

"Most students pick someone whom they feel they can easily communicate with. Some look for the similarities in convictions that they feel they can understand, so that they can better relate to the new student to help them deal with the hurdles that they will face."

"I see. How many applicants are there?"

"There are thirty that make it to this stage. If I remember right, I believe your file was on top when your class came in."

"Why was mine on the top?" Gloria asked.

"The files are ranked from easiest to hardest. The tougher more problematic students are placed at the bottom. Our panel of doctors and psychologists pulled these thirty out of a pool of about three hundred."

"How do the students even get selected?"

"When you finish here, you'll go out and find recruits. You'll work with the district attorney in your area and recommend a few to the program. We look at their cases to see if they would make a viable candidate. This is also part of the program. You will work with them for a year. After that year is up, it's your option to continue. Most of our graduates continue as part of their own charity to society."

"I didn't know that it was so in depth. So, after I finish here, I can go home and be with my family? And begin the recruiting?"

THE SCHOLARSHIP

"No."

"No? Why not?"

"It's required that you move at least five hundred miles away from where you used to live for the first year. This is so that there is less of a chance to fall back in with the same group of people and continue down the wrong road. We found that even after the year was up, most of our graduates stayed away from their hometowns and those that did move back home, began running with a better crowd of people. There are a few we lost track of. We don't know where they are. We do know that they haven't reentered the system. To date we haven't had any of our students get more than a minor traffic ticket."

"What about my sons? When will I see them?"

"When you're settled in, we will make arrangements for your parents to bring them to you. Only your immediate family, as in just your children, can live with you. We want to see you succeed and removing you from your previous environment gives you a better chance at succeeding. It will get you away from the crowd you previously associated with. We will have connections in the city where you move to who will help you and see that you don't fall into a bad crowd. Have you thought about what you want to do once you are out?"

"I really want to start an orchard. I like peaches. My grandmother had several trees and I spent a lot of time with her when I was little."

Harold smiled at Gloria. He was truly inspired to develop a system where honest wholesome food was a large part of their curriculum. Much of the acreage the school owned had been converted to farmland. Students from phase two gathered and prepared the crops for sale to local restaurants and at the farmer's market. The community praised the academy for the transformation of its slumbering economy and the additional resources from food to a print shop and four-star restaurant.

A great emphasis was put on the quality of work and the quality of the products that they produced. The students became a direct representation of the products that the academy put out.

"That sounds great. I'm always glad to hear that one of our students will be producing quality food. Do you feel that you're ready for that type of business?"

"No sir, but I'm going to keep trying until I succeed."

"Good. That's what we like, a diehard attitude that builds the community."

"What's the next step, sir?" Gloria looked at the stack of files apprehensively, wondering who she was going to get as her new student.

"Look through the files. Find one who you feel can really benefit from your knowledge, someone whom you can mold into a productive citizen."

"You said there are thirty files."

"Yes."

"But there are only twenty-five openings."

"Correct. Five of those files won't be offered the scholarship."

"You said that they are ranked from easiest to hardest?"

"We have extras to allow choices for you to match with someone you can identify with."

"And the remaining five?"

"I'm sorry. We are not equipped to handle more than twenty-five right now. It's your success that we are worried about. We want to give you the best option to succeed by giving you a choice."

"I understand."

THE SCHOLARSHIP

"Our success rate is one hundred percent so far. I can't vouch for all of those who completed the academy years ago, but I haven't heard anything negative to date."

Gloria reached out and ran her finger along the spines of the folders. Pinching one at the bottom of the stack, she pulled the noticeably thicker file from the manila tower. "I choose this one."

Concern and worry flashed across Harold's face. He knew the extent of problems that the file contained. He started to protest but caught himself before saying anything. He didn't want to see a star student take on something that she probably couldn't handle. He knew that file to be a very difficult case. He had initially rejected it, but the panel had squeaked it in under the probability that it would not get chosen. "Are you sure you want that one? Maybe one from the top would suit you better?"

"You put all these people in here because someone saw that they had potential. I will not let a little hard work be a deterring factor for someone in need of a hand up."

"I cut that file out, but the panel put it back in figuring that no one would select it. Are you sure you want that one? You have your sons to think about as well."

"I know. What kind of mom would I be if I took the easy road all the time? What kind of message would that send to my boys?"

"I understand. What if this person causes you to fail? Then it would be a lot longer before you'd be home with them."

Gloria sighed at having to deliver the further explanation that anyone who walked through the front doors of the school could be saved from a life of boredom and animosity behind bars. "Whoever this person is, she deserves the effort we put into each student. Once they see and understand that, they will appreciate and value the lessons they learn."

Chapter III

Keep your heads down. Did I say you could look around? This is your P.N.T., personal nap time. You better soak it up 'cause you are going to need it." The female drill-sergeant's voice boomed through the white bus. Black, perforated steel lined the windows, allowing little to no access to the view outside. Even if they were allowed to look, the predawn light wasn't enough to divulge any information on their location.

Farm land stretched for miles across the middle of Missouri. Twenty-five women cowed their heads into their personal bags, afraid of the verbal reprimand along with the possibility of maximum sentences if they did not comply.

Sarah stole a sidelong glance out a small hole in the steel-covered window. Shadowed corn rows flashed by so fast it made her head spin. She figured that the stalks looked to be less than half grown, judging by their height. Beyond was a black soup of fog. It was early summer in the center of Missouri. Rolling tree-covered hills divided the vast fields of corn, wheat and other produce. Sarah pretended to calculate the rows of vegetables as she and her classmates bobbed their heads across the pothole-filled-roads that weaved their way to the academy. She didn't want to predict their yield, just distract her mind from the bone-jarring ride to the complex.

Countless bumps radiated through the heavy, ironclad, former school bus. It jolted its occupants' heads against the hard metal seat backs whenever a pothole passed under its wheels. The driver seemed to purposely align the bus to hit the deepest holes. A young woman directly in front of Sarah whimpered at the unknown they all faced. Sarah had heard her sobs begin just minutes into their three-hour journey.

The ride was mostly silent save for the soft crying of the woman and the communal grunt as the bus hit a particularly large pothole. Sarah breathed a sigh of annoyance from the petty routine. It didn't matter; she would be long gone in a few days. One or two nights were all she figured that she would have to suffer through. Then nobody would have to worry about her any longer.

A pothole jarred everyone's heads against the metal seat backs and a woman near the front rubbed the swelling knot on her forehead. "Keep your damn head down. Cushion that know-nothing head with that fat sausage thing that you call a hand." The 'drill' was more than ready to smash someone's face back down into their bag. Each bag carried seven changes of clothes, one pair of slippers, two pairs of shoes, a set of pajamas and seven stamped envelopes.

The bus's engine wound down as it made several turns through the streets to stop in a halogen-bathed parking lot.

"Keep your damn heads down. Did I tell you to move?" The drill paced to the back of the bus, pushing two of the students' heads down into their bags.

The door opened, and a new male drill voice started in. "You will keep those ugly faces buried in those ugly little bags. You will sit still and listen, or you will pay hell for months on

THE SCHOLARSHIP

end before WE decide to ship you back to the State Pen. Then you can start your sentence. You will not receive credit for any time here."

Sarah listened with growing concern. If she couldn't escape, she could still face twenty-five years in prison. From the underlying tone, Sarah supposed that they could, on a whim, send her to prison just a day before she would graduate. Whatever work was put in, would be lost. It was another twisted turn in her defense attorney's wicked smile.

"You each have a number. I am sure you saw it when you sat down. If you were too stupid to notice it, it is a giant six-inch number painted on the center of the seatback in front of you. If you can't read it, I will help you. I will show you what it is by doing a little math. I will take the number one hundred and subtract the number you are facing. Whatever is left is how many pushups you will do if you cannot read your number." The drill spoke to the group as if they were tiny children in need of a clear and concise explanation.

"When you are told, you will stand up and exit the bus with your bag. There are squares with a corresponding number to your number. You will move to that square with your number and stand with your feet a shoulders-width apart, holding your bag of goodies in front of you. DO YOU UNDERSTAND?"

'Yes, sir' and 'yes, drill' emitted from the beginning students.

"I am Master Drill Ietel. You will address me as Master Drill Ietel!" the man screamed. "When I call on you, you will say 'Yes, Master Drill Ietel.' You will answer questions with 'Yes, Master Drill Ietel' or 'No, Master Drill Ietel.' We will tell you when to wake up, go to sleep, eat, brush your teeth and use the bathroom. If you don't like it, you should have stayed

19

home sucking on your momma's nipple. DO YOU UNDERSTAND?"

"Yes, Master Drill Ietel," came the muffled answer from a more unified voice this time.

"When I say your number, you better be off this bus before I say the next number. Do you understand?"

"Yes, Master Drill Ietel," Sarah said, accompanying the rest of the students.

"Your lives now reside in the drills' hands. You each will have your own personal drill. They will be like your mother. They will feed you. They will clothe you. They will see that you get the necessities of life. Right now, you are nothing. When your biological mother squeezed your bulbous head out, she made the mistake of not choking the life out of you instantly. Now society must suffer your existence. We are in charge of rectifying your mother's mistake.

"WE will see that you are born again. WE will see that you are upstanding, cream of the crop citizens. When you leave here, employers will beg you to work with their teams. But right now, you are nothing. You are not even conceived yet. Your daddy's sperm got lost and impregnated itself."

Sarah gave a slight huff at the intended joke. She agreed that a bit of humor would help the time pass easier.

"When, or rather, IF you finish with phase one, you will be born into this world again. You will be able to attend school and learn more about what life has to offer. If you don't want that, raise your hand right now so we can stop wasting our time on you."

Sarah felt the seat shake in front of her. She heard a few drops of liquid hit the floor. The girl in that seat had lost control of her bladder.

THE SCHOLARSHIP

"You pissed on my floor!" the female drill shouted. "God damn, do you need a diaper? You're going to clean that up, along with the rest of the bus. You flippin' peed on my bus. Are you insane?"

"Number one! Get outside," the male drill said.

The girl in the first row jumped to the command. Like a bolt of lightning struck her, she was out the door before the drill thought to announce the second number.

"Number two." With the same speed, the second girl was out the door.

"Number three." The third girl rose, took a step and plummeted over her two left feet.

"Come on lefty. We're waiting on you. Get your damn feet in sync! Move. Move. Move!" the drill yelled as the woman scrambled to get off the bus. Number Four was next to bolt from her seat, but she didn't bolt like the others. She was hindered by years of channel surfing and an exorbitant amount of calories.

The rest of the numbers flowed out like water behind a damn bursting. The drill skipped over the young woman sitting in front of Sarah and called for number eleven, who sat in the seat to Sarah's right. Sarah's anxiety built to a freak out level but there wasn't anything else she could do. Her number was next.

"Number twelve, get off my bus."

Sarah jumped and did as she was told. She knew that now was not the time to buck the system. She had to wait until everyone was relaxed and not paying attention. Then she would make her move. She would escape before daybreak and be long gone.

Sarah clutched her bag to her chest and shuffled down the aisle, down the steps and out the door. Two more steps brought her to the square where she was to stand with her bag held in front of her.

Before her stood a semicircle of drills. Each had a poker face of indifference. Each wore matching blue fatigues. A blue drill's hat amplified the stern look of each while their immaculately polished boots gave them an air of perfection. The male, Master Drill Ietel, wore regular green, brown and black jungle fatigues. His uniform was pressed, boots shined to a clear reflection and his head shaved. From what Sarah could see of the tall, professional and imposing authority, she assumed that he wasn't cut from the fabric of a criminal.

To her right, she saw a reporter taking photographs of the group as they stood in formation, ready to jump at the next order. Another woman dressed in a business suit shadowed the photographer, tending to his presence and seeing that he didn't get in the way of the proceedings. She wore a blank face just as all the drills did. It was emotionless and extremely businesslike. It reminded her of the blank faces that the Secret Service presented in the occasional photos that she saw of the president. At least the ones she saw on TV anyway.

The bus rumbled away leaving the students and the drills at a face off. A fountain centered in front of the main doors of the building gurgled water over a cascade of rocks before it came to rest in a small pond. Decorative boulders stood as sentinels on either side of the doorway. The male drill sergeant followed the last student off the bus and returned to center himself in front of the formation. During the full minute of silence, Master Drill Ietel continued to gaze upon the line of misfits he and the rest of the drills were charged with beginning their transformations into productive citizens. He studied them carefully, looking for anyone who might pose a problem.

THE SCHOLARSHIP

"Understand one thing right now. You know nothing. You don't even exist. You are not even born yet. Right now, you have been conceived, that is all that you are right now. You are but a blob that we have been given the task of molding into a proper human being. We will teach you everything you need to know. Whatever is in your head, you had better forget it because it got you in trouble and sent you here. If you were smart, you would not be standing where you are today. So, whoever you learned your life skills from, taught you wrong. If they taught you correctly, you would not be standing here. Am I correct?"

Silence answered the Master Drill. Veins pulsed in his head as the expected answer was not returned. "I SAID, AM I CORRECT?" Master Drill Ietel yelled at the class.

"Yes," the class said in unison.

"When I ask a question, I expect an answer. That answer will be followed by a 'Master Drill Ietel.' Is that understood?" he said in a booming voice.

"Yes, Master Drill Ietel," most of the class answered while the rest just answered with a 'yes.'

"Yes. What?"

"Yes, Master Drill Ietel." The whole class said it in unison this time.

"Yes, what?"

"Yes, Master Drill Ietel."

"Yes, what?"

"Yes, Master Drill Ietel."

"That's better."

His stare penetrated the souls of the students as he walked down the line, looking at each one individually. Some returned the look with fear in their eyes, some with a determination to change their lives for the better. Sarah returned a look of

23

indifference. She knew her plan and it didn't include drills, fatigues or combat boots.

"When you walked off that bus you told us that you no longer want to be who you are. You told us you want to be someone different, someone better. You told us that you are ready to pay for your crimes and…" Master Drill Ietel paused, making sure he had everyone's attention, "apologize to society for being completely and utterly useless pieces of flesh.

"Society doesn't want you. You are not worth their time. You chose to be here. You can only blame yourselves. You chose to break the law and you chose to come here. You gave up all you ever had and everything that you are to come here.

"You belong to us now. Under the contracts you signed, we are allowed to do everything short of killing you. If you want to blame anyone, blame those damn sausages that you call fingers." The master drill stepped to within an inch of the obese woman who had smacked her head earlier on the bus.

"What the hell are you crying about?" Master Drill Ietel spat in her face.

"I want to go home," the terrified woman said.

"Oh. You want to go home," Master Drill Ietel said in a soft, condescending voice. "Congratulations! You're here. In fact, I know you're going to love it here. You're going to love it here so much that you'll kiss the pavement two hundred times before you step inside your new home. Drop your bag and get on the ground."

The heavy woman, who had auburn hair that trailed most of the way down her back, set her bag to the side and steadied herself before going to one knee then the other. Putting her hands on the cement she lowered her head down and kissed the concrete. A head-bob later she kissed it again.

THE SCHOLARSHIP

"My god. That is not how you kiss your home. You have to pick that gut up off the ground. The only thing touching the ground will be your toes, your hands and your lips. What's your name?"

"Helen," the woman replied.

"That's not your name! What's the number on the square you were standing in?" Master Drill Ietel asked.

"Four."

"What?"

"Four!" Helen said a little louder.

"Good lord. Are you so stupid that you forgot how to address your superiors? What did I just tell everyone?

"Four, Master Drill Ietel."

"My God. There is capacity to learn. Four, you bend your elbows and lower your face to the concrete. You keep that tire up off the ground. You kiss the concrete and push your body back up. Do you understand?"

"Yes, sir."

"Have you forgotten how to address me again? I am not a sir. You will call me Master Drill Ietel. That is the only thing you will call me. Do you understand?"

"Yes."

"Yes, what?"

"Yes, Master Drill Ietel."

"Whose child is this?"

"Mine, Master Drill Ietel. Drill Hooks." A short woman with strawberry blonde hair pulled tightly back in a bun below her drill hat, stepped forward.

"See that she does all two hundred correctly."

"Yes, Master Drill Ietel."

"You are not children," Master Drill Ietel continued to address the class. "You are babies. Babies are not born with

25

fancy clothes. They are not born with houses, bank accounts, airplanes, piercings, gold teeth, or tattoos."

Whispered grumbles radiated through the line of students. Sarah hadn't listened to much of the explanation that Mr. Roth had given her. She had completely missed the part of tattoo removal being mandatory. Most of the students had several, and one girl exhibited color from her hands to her neck. Sarah was sure that the blonde with pale white skin had plenty more, as her skin tone was optimal for displaying all the vibrant colors.

Helen strained at each push up, only completing twelve. Sarah couldn't imagine the obese woman completing two hundred before lunch. She figured that the woman would die of a heart attack before she hit thirty. Drill Hooks was on the cement with her growling in her ear to finish each one. With the extra strain, Helen let go a burst of methane. The reverberating fart echoed across the front step to the academy. A red-haired woman standing in square number six burst out laughing at Helen's embarrassing act.

Before Master Drill Ietel could say a word, another drill took three large steps forward, stopping an inch from the jokester's face. "You think that's funny?"

"No, Drill."

"It's Drill Hawkins. You must have thought something was funny. You cracked a smile on that ugly little face of yours."

The woman had lost all signs of amusement the instant Drill Hawkins stepped in front of her. "You want to join her, don't you?"

"No, Drill Hawkins."

"What's your name?"

"Lillie Kirkpatrick, ma'am. I mean Drill Hawkins."

THE SCHOLARSHIP

"You don't have a name anymore. You are now Six. Everyone will call you Six until I decide to give you a name."

"Come over here. Set your bag down and come over here." Drill Hawkins drew a square on the cement right before the edge of the pond with a piece of sidewalk chalk. You think it's so funny, you can help her."

The woman's eyes grew wide as the reality of her situation suddenly became clear to her. She stood looking at the pond. "In the water?"

"Yes, in the water. Your mind has been corrupted with garbage. We are going to wash it clean. So, get down and kiss the concrete, Six."

Lillie went to her hands and knees then pushed off to keep her hair out of the water. She stared at it for a moment too long. Drill Hawkins jumped right in the middle of the pond, kicking the water and splashing it in Lillie's face.

"I can do this all day. What are you waiting for?"

Lillie bent her elbows. Nearly submerging her head, she pushed back up. "There's slimy stuff on the bottom, Drill Hawkins."

"That's called algae! Algae need your affection too! Now count down starting from two hundred."

"Two hundred."

"Two hundred what?" Drill Hawkins demanded.

"Two hundred, Drill Hawkins," Lillie stammered. She bent her elbows and plunged her head back into the water. "One hundred ninety-nine, Drill Hawkins," she said as she reemerged from the water a second time.

"You will be judged on team performance as well as your own personal development. You will graduate from this phase only when we decide. There IS a time limit, if you have not grasped the fundamentals of what is needed at that time, you will be sent away for someone else to deal with your incompetence."

Master Drill Ietel continued his lecture with more rules and expectations. Sarah chanced a sideways glance. The number ten square was empty. She scanned the drills and found an empty spot where one had been standing, then remembered that the female drill who road with them in that early morning did not get back off the bus. Sarah figured the drill was likely going to accompany the woman who had peed herself to the wash bay so she could clean it from top to bottom.

"Get 'em inside," Master Drill Ietel screamed. Sarah barely heard the command. She was busy wondering about the woman who never got off the bus. Like a murder of crows on a dead carcass, the remaining drills descended on the new students barking orders and hustling them inside to begin their new lives. Only two students remained outside: one counting up from zero and the other counting down from two hundred, with Drill Hooks and Drill Hawkins monitoring their progress.

Chapter IV

Sarah squinted her eyes against the heat that beat down on the complex from the early summer sun. A gentle breeze struggled to tame the intense rays. Emerging from the air-conditioned building, Sarah's breath caught on the thick muggy air. It was as if she had to chew the air before she could inhale it. Forcing herself to breathe, she plodded to her number twelve square and placed her feet on the painted feet marks.

Three other women stood on their assigned squares waiting for the next instruction. Sarah did her best to keep her emotions in check and comply with everything she was told. She was to wait for her drill outside.

She had gotten a brief introduction to her drill before being shoved from one room to the next where they disrobed her, then issued her orange sweats, boots, shoes, socks and underwear. Like cattle in a chute, they were run through a physical exam, shots and a dietary questionnaire. A barber's chair was next. The barber didn't ask what she wanted; she just trimmed all Sarah's hair to just above her shoulders. Her mid-back length hair was wrapped in a rubber band and tossed in a bin with three other bundles.

"You saving that for something?" Sarah scoffed at the remnants of the locks that had been unfairly taken from her head.

"You signed the paper. Your hair is the property of the school to do with what they please," the large, ebony beautician declared. "Those bundles will go to the Locks of Love Foundation. If you want them back, I'm sure we can arrange that along with a prison sentence."

Sarah didn't feel that her hair was very appealing now, but it was gone anyway so there was no sense in arguing over it. She was shuffled to the next station where photographs were taken of her tattoos, followed by a brief description of the lengthy and painful removal process. In the barracks, she was given a quick rundown of how she was to act, organize her issued belongings and make her bed. A rush through the chow line with only ten minutes to eat left her still hungry, though she doubted that she could stomach another bite of whatever they had slopped on her plate. It seemed that they had intentionally made it inedible.

She followed the first three women out the door and stood with her body straight and her hands locked behind her back, trying to slow her head from the dizzying amount of information blasted on her during the first half of the day. She could see a mountain, or a large hill, ahead of her with a hiking trail zigzagging up one side and down the other. From the top, a long expanse of cable stretched down the slope to an anchored post at the bottom. Ratted lengths of rope were scattered around a field of boulders at the base.

More women emerged and mimicked Sarah and their other classmates. Each stared straight ahead with their own thoughts of what the future was bringing. Minutes later, a flood of puke-orange sweats followed by a sea of blue drill uniforms

THE SCHOLARSHIP

boiled out of the double doors of the barracks. The blue uniforms screamed at them to get in line. Sarah noticed that square number ten was still empty. The scared woman who seemed more girl than adult was not among them. The screaming subsided as each student finally complied, placing their feet in their painted square, their bodies stiff and straight and their hands locked behind their backs.

Master Drill Ietel strode out to the center of the formation and quickly scanned the new class. "The field and mountain you see before you will be your incubator, your classroom. This will be where you get your mind right. Over the next two months, you will be taught how to be a better-than-average citizen. Whoever taught you how to act previously, failed miserably. It is our job to teach you correctly. It is your job to learn. If you don't want to learn, we'll send you back where people are more than happy to tell you what to do and how to act. If it takes you a decade to learn this, then we will know that you are stupid and no better use than a packhorse. For the rest of the afternoon you will carry boulders from the bottom to the top of that hill and send them on the line back down to the bottom. You will repeat this every day until you understand." Master Drill Ietel paced in front of the class.

"Understand what, Master Drill Ietel?" Brenda Anskton asked, from the number one square.

Sarah cringed and almost felt badly for the woman on the end. Master Drill Ietel stepped to the woman, "Until you understand. Do you understand?"

"Yes, Master Drill Ietel."

"Since you're eager to understand you can lead everyone off. Move." Like a swarm of hornets, the rest of the drills flew in to bark orders at their students, motivating them into a run. Each class member hurried to the pile of boulders. New leather

31

boots beat the dust into the air and started the blisters growing on the women's feet.

"Strong and stupid or weak and smart. Which one are you going to be?" Drill Witcom barked at Sarah as she lifted a twenty-pound boulder off the ground. It was the most common phrase of the day as many other drills echoed it to those who didn't seem to put forth their best effort. Before long, Sarah felt that she very well might bust someone in the chops if they asked her that one more time.

Sarah made five trips up and down the hill before they were allowed a ten-minute break. A thirty-gallon cooler was wheeled out by one of the drills, giving the empty canteen that slung across her shoulder a source to fill from. The drill eyed her watch, making a note when each student arrived and departed with a full canteen. If a student lingered too long, she barked insistently at them until they were marching up the trail again.

Sweat poured down Sarah's head, trying to drip into her eyes. She wiped away the perspiration with the back of her hand and then swatted her pants to clean the dust off. The heat from the sun lifted the fine dust into the air, sending Sarah into a sudden sneezing fit.

Several sneezes into the fit, Sarah found herself feeling light-headed from the heat and the lack of oxygen flowing to her brain. Leaning to one side, she caught herself on an elbow. Her vision blurred, and her stomach twisted in a knot. Thoughts of escaping faded to the back of her mind as staying conscious became of the utmost importance.

Her eyes closed as she tried to focus on breathing and eliminating the sneezing fit. Sneeze after sneeze continued to disorient her and she felt her arm losing the battle to keep her upright. A pressure knocked her flat on her back as chilly water washed the dirt off her face. Snorting some up her nose she instantly switched her sneezing fit to a coughing fit. Her eyes flew open looking for the person daring enough to throw water on her.

"Get up. Break's over."

The name 'Witcom' was stitched with black thread on the uniform of the drill who threw the water. Sarah thought she looked to be in her late thirties, possibly forty. The scowl she gave would have melted the concrete except for a tiny hint of something Sarah didn't understand.

Her mind clearing, Sarah struggled to her feet. She gave Drill Witcom as menacing a stare as she could muster. Gloria Witcom gave her own stare back, hoping that all the hours she spent practicing being strong and commanding would pay off. Gloria used to be a pushover, bending to ease the burdens of those around her. The Schultz Business Academy taught her to be firm and decisive on her decisions, a quality that would not have allowed her to enter this school if she had exhibited it before. If she had, she would have already had the discipline to exercise the tough love needed when dealing with all the problems that she had had with her sister.

Sarah cowed her head. She knew that this wasn't the time or place to make a scene. She knew she had to go along with the program and not draw attention to herself. She couldn't risk letting on that she would be gone in a few days. She had to get the lay of the land and understand everyone's routine. Wait for everyone to get comfortable then leave for a better life in some far away country.

"Master Drill Ietel, we're having a problem with dust," Drill Witcom said.

"Get rid of the dust, Drill Witcom."

"Yes, Master Drill Ietel."

Gloria stepped to the hydrant where she had filled the bottle of Sarah's sneeze antidote and turned a two-inch valve. Water sprinklers sputtered to life along the path from the bottom to the top of the hill. She gave a bit of a smirk when she heard several students express their joy at the relief from the dryer-than-normal Missouri heat wave. She knew that too much of any one thing usually ends disastrously.

It wasn't long before the students began complaining about the slippery slope and their struggles to lug the boulders to the top of the hill, only to send them back down on the zip line, beginning the journey again. Animosity built toward the muddy and slippery slope that Sarah and her classmates had to navigate.

"Carry your burdens to the top and let them go. You're either going to be smart or stupid when you get done. If you're stupid, then you're also going to be strong enough to move that mountain," Drill Witcom said to the group, but directed her voice at Sarah. There wasn't anyone else close by. Other drills scattered around the loop screamed at the new inductees as they trudged with each burden to the top.

Some of the students helped each other while others plodded right past. Two students had slipped and twisted their ankles. After being carried back down, they were made to scoot on their butts from boulder to boulder, picking one up and setting it on a nearby bench where another student could grasp it more easily. Their discipline would not be halted due to an injury.

On the downward slide, it had become a slippery mess where most of the women opted to slide down on their butts since they couldn't stay on their feet anyway.

THE SCHOLARSHIP

"I want to see someone puke," Drill Hawkins said in a booming voice. As if on cue, the heavy-set woman struggling up the hill with a boulder, doubled over and vomited.

Sarah saw a slight smile on Drill Hawkins face. Sarah's blood boiled at the callousness of the expression. She flashed a glowering look at the drill.

"Oh, hell no. You did not." Drill Hawkins stomped up to Sarah. She was poised to start a lecture, but instead a whistle flew up out of her hand and into her mouth. A high shrill scream erupted from the bobble. Everyone froze on the trail.

"Everyone, get those rocks up, over your heads," Drill Hawkins bellowed. She was as tall as Sarah, but not as heavy. Sarah noted that there wasn't much fat on this woman. She had the physical attributes of a professional athlete, fast and strong. "Who has number twelve?" Drill Hawkins read the large muddy digits off the front of Sarah's sweatshirt.

Each drill echoed it down the line until it reached Drill Witcom. From the distance, two short whistle blasts announced the acknowledgement of the drill assigned to Sarah. The drills on the uphill side of the track, screamed at the unfortunate half who still held boulders on their trek up the hill to stand tall.

"Keep that boulder above your head. If you can't hold it, you better drop it on that thick skull that's supposed to carry a brain. Maybe it'll knock some sense into you," Drill Harrison screamed at a frail, little woman. The two students who had sprained their ankles were not exempt from this punishment. They were made to hold their boulders over their heads while sitting on the ground. The awkward position proved more troublesome than standing, yet they weren't allowed to move once the long whistle blast echoed across the grounds.

Drill Witcom trudged through the mud up the path to her student who was not holding a boulder yet still had trouble keeping her hands high above her head. The drill's crisp, blue uniform was now spattered with mud. The toes of her boots no longer held a bright pristine shine and she wore a scowl hot enough to melt tungsten.

"What the hell did you do?" Drill Witcom shouted.

"This little girl thinks she can just walk by and mean-mug me," Drill Hawkins explained.

"No!" Sarah balked at the accusation.

"No, what?" Drill Witcom snapped.

"No, I didn't, Drill Witcom."

"Are you saying that you didn't mean-mug her?" Drill Witcom inched closer.

"Yes, Drill Witcom."

"Are you saying that my friend is a liar?"

"No, Drill Witcom. She must have misinterpreted it."

"Oh. I did not misinterpret that." Drill Hawkins glared at her.

"Well," Gloria paused a moment to think. "She might be constipated."

Sarah's eyes rolled ever so slightly. She caught herself and brought about her best poker face to prevent being reprimanded again before the current issue was even settled. Drill Hawkins lifted an eyebrow intent on learning what angle Gloria was getting at.

"When you have an extreme of one thing, you have to balance it out with an extreme of the other. Since she has constipation, we need to balance it out with the runs."

"I see," Drill Hawkins said, eyeballing a now-embarrassed Sarah. With her arms still raised high above her head, she grew concerned that the remedy they were concocting was something she would not want to endure. Her thoughts of being doubled over on the toilet did not set well with her.

"I'll talk to the P.A. and see if she can prescribe something for that constipation," Drill Witcom suggested.

"When will those laxatives kick in?" Drill Hawkins asked, her anger subsiding only slightly at a possible solution to Sarah's defiance.

"First thing tomorrow morning," Drill Witcom said.

Drill Hawkins nodded her agreement then picked up her whistle, blowing three sets of two.

Chapter V

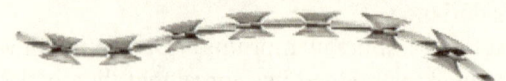

Sarah's muscles rippled with pain from the countless trips up the mountain and back. Technically, it wasn't considered a mountain: it was only six hundred and twenty-seven feet in elevation from the base to the summit. Regardless, the steep terrain made it a formidable obstacle, and the boulders made the climbing torture.

The class staggered through the barrack doors, slumped from the exhausting, meaningless work of trudging a twenty-pound rock up the hill only to send it sailing back down on a zipline. The drills had mangled and thrown their dinner in the trash due to their student's lack of hustle. Some grabbed what they could ate the slop anyway. Sarah could only find bits of a sandwich that she pulled out of the garbage pail. By the time she came back around to the table after foraging for a meal, everyone had already eaten except her and the overweight woman. The escape attempt she planned didn't account for her complete exhaustion from packing boulders all afternoon. She still forced herself to observe what she could and make mental notes of it.

THE SCHOLARSHIP

Their clothes were drenched and muddy from the afternoon's activities and the students discarded them into their laundry bags, showered, changed into their night clothes, and then stumbled into the army style cots. The luxury of anything other than hot and cold running water was stripped from their lives. Their cots were simple, strong and served their basic purpose. Everything, including daily chores, was designed to be manual and hands-on in order to give them a sense of what luxury was.

Drill Flemings turned out the light and sat at the end of the army-style barracks reading a textbook and taking notes under the single desk lamp. Sarah wondered briefly about the laxatives remark, but she drifted off as sleep claimed her.

****

"Get up, number Twelve," Gloria yelled. Her voice was loud enough to raise the dead. The other twenty-three students were ripped from their exhausted slumber as a dozen drills turned over bunks spilling bodies onto the floor. The clock above the door read a few seconds after midnight. "Everyone, get up and get outside."

Groans echoed through the barracks as some women pulled on a clean set of sweats then their socks and boots. Most had fallen asleep wearing a fresh pair of their numbered sweats and had only to tug on their footwear.

"Faster, you digits. You're just numbers. You haven't earned a name yet. If you want a name you can call yourself Leech," Drill Hawkins bellowed at the rest of the group.

Drill Witcom focused her attention on Sarah. "Come on, Twelve. You look a little constipated. That's alright though.

We have a cure for that. Get your boots on and get in formation."

Sarah tugged her boots on and hurried out into the cool, crisp, night air as a change in weather brought lower temperatures southeast from the Rocky Mountains. Flood lamps lit up an area the size of a football field with a dirt track around the outer edge. Several drills herded them out the doors like cattle out of a corral, while the remaining drills stationed themselves outside to prevent their students from straying. Hurrying to her personal square, Sarah placed her feet in the foot outlines, locked her hands behind her back, stared straight ahead and waited.

Looking out across the field, she saw two vehicles with identical trailers. The guessing game commenced in her mind as to the nature of the torture that would soon commence. Sarah stared at the arrangement knowing that she would find out very soon. She already regretted her lack of self-control from the previous day.

The green lawn stretched one hundred and forty yards before meeting the far end of the field where Drill Dawson sat in the Ranger ATV waiting for the education to begin. Drill Dawson had run this gauntlet before, and she remembered the pain that her stubborn pride had inflicted on her and her class when she was in boot camp. It was her fault for sneaking oxycodone into the facility. She was caught and tried to blame another girl and she paid for it dearly. This very same lies and integrity drill broke her on the first day. It took her exactly eighty-four times across the field, carrying the fifty-pound plate of lies, before she told the truth and asked for forgiveness. She still had to revisit the lies drill two more times on account of others in her class taking shortcuts or pawning their work off on others. In the first days of boot camp it was hard to tell

THE SCHOLARSHIP

what the rules were and the amount of attention that they had to pay to each minute detail.

"Welcome to the first lesson of your core values for everyday life. Doing what you say and saying what you mean are vital in everyday business and everyday life. If it's a handshake, then it's a binding contract. If you agree to something, then you better see that it is done." Drill Witcom paced the ground in front of the class. "If I say that I will burn all the fat off you, then I will have you doing calisthenics out here in the grass until you don't have an ounce of fat left. When you don't have anything left, we will fatten you up again just to do it one more time. That's how thorough we are and that's how thorough you will become. You will learn to over-compensate on everything you do. When you do that, you will find a freedom that few in this modern world will ever know."

The word freedom echoed in Sarah's mind as Drill Witcom said it, only she imagined a far different method of attaining it. She rolled her eyes imaginatively, and not in reality, out of fear that one of the drills would catch her. She watched Drill Witcom out of the corner of her eye. She knew something was up and it wasn't going to be good for her. None of this would be good. Not until she was beyond the razor wire and across the border. Then she could breathe easier. Her blood boiled inside her and all she wanted to do was rip this goody-two-shoe woman's face off as she spouted off the benefits of transformation.

"This is your home. There will not be any lies in this house or in you. This is the first step in becoming an honorable woman. You will leave here honorably, or you won't leave at all. You have a limited amount of time to graduate from here. I suggest you use your time wisely.

"In front of you is a collection of plates. They are full of lies. They are the lies that men have told you. They are the lies that your family has told you. They are the lies that your lawyer has told you."

Sarah rolled her eyes again thinking about the sly little smirk that her public defender had given her when she signed the papers. He knew what was in the papers. He should have told her the extent. She might have thought twice about this punishment if he had.

"Most importantly, they are the lies you tell yourself. If you want to be old and grey when you get back to society, turn around and go crawl back in bed and we will ship you back to prison," Drill Witcom said in a voice so powerful that it challenged any who considered the idea to toss it aside.

"Get those ugly little feet back in that box," Drill Hawkins screamed at the petite woman on the end. "Oh, hell no, you are not backing out on this. I did not get up in the middle of the night to watch you go back to bed."

Sarah turned her head toward the commotion. Tears streamed down number twenty-four's face. Her body trembled with fear. She stared wide-eyed at Drill Hawkins.

"Get back in that ugly little square." Drill Hawkins pointed to the yellow painted footprints inside the number twenty-four square. The girl, barely a woman, went by the nickname of String Bean. Brynlee Lynn Kasper had a love of garden vegetables and a consciousness of other living creatures. This, coupled with her thin-as-a-rail frame, didn't make her seem the type of person who could survive a severe boot camp. Several misdemeanors, followed by a grand theft auto on a rogue decision to see her boyfriend across the state, landed her a scholarship to the toughest business school in the country. A school that only a specific group of people could ever be eligible for.

"The lies you believe about society, about this facility, about our goal here are all sitting on those plates over there. When I blow this whistle, you will run to the trailer in front of you, pick up your plate of lies and take it away from your home. Take it to the far end of the field and put it in your designated square. If the trailer is not down there, you will stand with the weight high above your head until the trailer arrives."

"How many times, Drill Witcom?" an older woman who appeared to be in her early to mid-thirties asked the authority figure.

"Did I give you permission to speak, Sixteen?"

"No, Drill Witcom."

"Then why did you open that big ugly trap?"

"I wanted to know how long we will be doing this, Drill Witcom."

"Until I bloody say you're done. Do you understand, Sixteen?"

"Yes, Drill Witcom."

"Good, you can sound off every time the last member of your class crosses that ugly yellow line at midfield. Do you understand?"

"Yes, Drill Witcom."

"Does anyone else have any issues? No? Good," Gloria said, without giving anyone a chance to respond. She lifted the whistle to her lips and blew the shrill noise through the night air.

Twenty-four students pounded dirt as several drills screamed orders for faster movement. Shouts taunted the students to hustle by comparing them to their elderly

43

grandmothers. Sarah ran within the pack of criminals, hiding among the numbers and trying to use them as a buffering zone to keep distance from the drills. She made her way to the far side of the trailer to pick up her plate of lies. Written on the steel plate in large letters was the word 'lies.' In smaller letters, we're common phrases that she had heard many times. *You are worthless. I should never have been born. I'll never amount to anything. You sicken me. How'd you get so fat? I'm ugly. You're a waste of air. You'll never be anything without me. You're stupid. I'm stupid. You'll always fail. You'll never matter to anyone. No one will ever believe you. No one cares about me.*

Many of these phrases had hurt Sarah in her past. She heard them numerous times in school, especially in the junior high. Her classmates were ruthless. Some used their imaginations to concoct elaborate derogatory names while others simply called her a whore.

The students quickly grabbed their plates of lies. Sarah balked at the immense weight and confusion spread across her face as she watched others, even String Bean, pull their plates off the trailer with mild effort. She looked at the others who seemingly had little trouble lifting their plates and charging across the field. She pulled on the handles again. She moved it, but she still couldn't pull it off the trailer.

"What's the holdup number twelve?"

"It's heavy, Drill Witcom."

"Is it heavy, or are you weak? Pick it up and get moving," Drill Witcom barked.

Sarah heaved the heavy plate off the trailer and started for the far end of the field.

"You must love those lies," Drill Witcom growled at the students again. I don't see anyone running to get rid of them.

THE SCHOLARSHIP

These are all the lies that your boyfriend has told you. 'I'll love you forever.' 'Trust me. You won't get pregnant.' 'I promise to take you to dinner next week.' What about the lies your family has told you. 'I'll pay you back.' 'Just call if you need anything.' How about, 'Your dad may not be your father?'"

Drill Hawkins paced through the group like a strict schoolmarm tending her class. "Does any of this sound familiar? How about, 'I ain't that boy's daddy.' Any of you been told that? I know someone has."

"How about the lies you tell yourself?" Drill Witcom stepped through the group as they hurried to the far end with their twenty-five-pound plates of lies. "How about, 'I won't get caught?' I'll bet every one of you thought that." Drill Witcom found her way back to Sarah. "Because of your constipated face yesterday, we added an extra twenty-five pounds of laxatives to help with your problem," Drill Witcom growled at Sarah.

Sarah scowled at the trick. She was beginning to realize that the drills were more cunning than she had first estimated. They presented the lesson so intensely that it left precious few seconds for her to evaluate and form a plan of escape. She focused on the trailer in the distance, but still tried to look for a week spot in the chaos disguised as a school.

Drill Hawkins ran ahead and climbed atop the trailer waiting for the first students to reach the platform. "Put those ugly plates in your assigned square. Pick up the integrity plates and get your ass back down to the other end. Come on Three, move it. My grandma can move faster than that. Why are you taking your time?"

The students hurried to drop their plates. Drill Hawkins paced back and forth atop the flatbed trailer. An evil glare penetrated the defiant students. Weaving and stepping around

45

each other, the students found their assigned square, set the iron plate down and picked up two halves of a disc. Each half was carved out of aluminum and polished to a shiny smooth finish. The grips were comfortable and easy to grasp. The contrast in handling the two different teaching instruments was like night and day. While the Plate of Integrity was easy, its counter, the Plate of Lies, was anything but comfortable to carry. The grips were like coarse sandpaper. The outer edge of the weight was razor-thin and if left to rest against the skin would rub a hole right through the student's tender flesh. The bulk of the mass, along with the additional twenty-five pounds in the center left Sarah feeling awkward and off balance.

"Come on Twelve. That constipation on your face is still there. I'll bet that fifty or sixty of these will loosen you up." Drill Hawkins stared down at a face filled with defiance. Sarah muscled her way through the first round of the lesson. The dread engulfed her when she realized that this was only one of the proclaimed fifty-plus trips. She heaved the iron plate up onto the flatbed trailer then grabbed the aluminum discs that were set just above the square. She ran back across the field to catch up with the others, crossing a faint line that was painted across the middle of the field. "Two," a voice called out next to Sarah as she hurried back to the start. She had been the last one to cross the center line. Helen was even ahead of her due to her lighter, twenty-five-pound steel disc of lies.

It was Sixteen who called out the repetition. She was a soccer mom type with the beginning hint of bingo wings. Sarah thought perhaps the woman had been in the military before when she saw how Sixteen had ripped through the staging of her bed and arranged her clothes in lightning speed. She put away all her assigned clothes neatly, just as the very loud drills described.

46

THE SCHOLARSHIP

Sarah later heard that her name was Rome and verified that she had been military. Drug use had earned Rome a dishonorable discharge, and her continued use and a sale to an undercover officer earned her a short stay in jail. After her release she vandalized her cheating boyfriend's truck, giving her the opportunity for the scholarship to Schultz's and the counseling options that it contained.

Quality counselors were expensive in Rome's hometown. The ones she could afford shuffled her from one counselor to the next to tell her story from the beginning again and again. The progress she had expected was non-existent and she dropped out of the sessions due to the high turnover rate of the counselors. She didn't see the point of continuing when she felt little to no progress. She sometimes felt that she needed counseling just for seeing the counselors. Due to the sheer number of times she had to start over, there was no time for the deep therapy she needed to unravel her original problem.

Twenty-four women raced back to the start. The trailer that they had all placed the Plates of Lies on raced back ahead of them and parked at the end of the track. If it was anything like the day before, Sarah knew that they would be in for a long night on little sleep. Her anger built at their pushy authority. She knew that the reason for this exercise was to break a person down and get them to submit to a different way of doing things. She knew that for the time being, she would have to play along.

She found her assigned square, set the aluminum discs down and picked up the fifty-pound plate. Turning, she tripped over number eleven and crashed to the ground. The edge of the plate dug deep into her middle as she fell on top of it.

"Watch where you're going," Sarah barked, after regaining a bit of the air she had lost due to the collision. She looked up into the terrified eyes of a young Hispanic woman. A tattoo of a hand with an 'M' in the palm adorned her neck.

"Perdón," the young Hispanic woman said quietly, and then hurried to do as the drills ordered. Sarah wasn't afforded a chance to rip the woman's head off due to the haste of the situation that they were all in. It would have to wait until they were released to go back to sleep or to use the bathroom or some other task. She knew that this abuse couldn't last forever. They had to stop at some point. It was the clock that they were up against, a clock that ticked away at every second of their freedom. If she didn't figure out how to escape, she knew that she would be in for a long stint in jail. She didn't trust that they would hold up their end of the bargain. She was convinced that they would let her go so far then send her back to prison on a minor technicality. It was better to just escape and disappear into the future. She would be doing a whole lot of miserable time if she didn't figure out how to break out of their ritualistic torture.

"Get off the ground, Twelve. This ain't no time for a nap. Move it." Drill Hawkins paced atop the trailer, screaming at any student who did something just the slightest bit out of what was expected. Sarah heaved her plate up off the ground and continued carrying the monstrosity down the field. The drills stood scattered across the field like large boulders in a river, daring the water to move them.

"To keep your house in order you may have to physically pick up that liar in your life and haul their butt out the door. This is training for that day. This will make you strong in the mind and the body." Drill Witcom paced midfield as the women ran back and forth carrying one plate, then the other. "Come on number four, pick up those pontoon feet and move out."

THE SCHOLARSHIP

Helen Whetherstein was the largest and most overweight woman to walk through the doors of the academy. She stood just short of six feet tall and tipped the scales at three hundred thirty pounds. She was winded when she reached midfield on the first go-round. Even with an extra twenty-five pounds, Sarah still felt she should have been able to outpace Helen. Helen had been a habitual pot smoker and dealt the substance as well. An exorbitant electric bill triggered an investigation that found her with dozens of plants and all the makings of a small illegal dispensary in Colorado. She was in the business with her boyfriend, who had stepped into the shoes of a buddy's distribution system when he was extradited to Georgia on an old assault charge.

Her boyfriend had kept her supplied with plenty of edibles and constant reminders that he was in charge of her, whether it was a verbal reprimand or a physical one, but he was gone now. He skipped town and left her holding the bag. Out of the assumed love, she covered for him and took all the blame. She was facing five to ten years before the scholarship was presented to her. It was explained to her that it wasn't easy but those who accepted the scholarship became new, strong independent women. While the authorities collected the evidence to convict her during her year-long wait in jail, Helen had reached a point when she realized that she needed to change, and the scholarship was her opportunity at creating a better life for herself.

Her only regret was that she had to have all her tattoos removed. She didn't mind losing some of them, but others represented good memories of her father who had treated her so well growing up. He had died as a victim of a snowy wreck in a severe winter storm that claimed several lives. Her father had been one of two truck drivers killed in the fifty-seven car and semi pileup. One of her tattoos was a portrait of the two of them on a hiking expedition in Yellowstone when she was just fourteen. She had lost him two years after that trip.

For years, she craved guidance in helping her fill in all the gaps that were left vacant from her father's passing. She stumbled through the last years of high school, became depressed and substituted a healthy diet with comfort food. Now she viewed this scholarship opportunity as a way to drastically change her life, both physically and academically. The program was explained in detail to her, along with the possibility of a bachelor's degree in business management. The scholarship's degree and the opportunity of eating healthier and shedding pounds sent her into an almost euphoric state and she eagerly signed on every line that was presented to her.

Sarah glowered at all the hustle, feeling that everyone was intentionally making her look bad, especially when she came to a trailer next to, or just behind, the overweight woman. The only positive side of the extra weight that Sarah carried was that she didn't have to hold the weight above her head by reaching the other end too early. She was happy about that. She focused on keeping her mind strong and fortified against any weakness that she might encounter in herself when dealing with the ritualistic breakdown from the drills.

Chapter VI

Sarah rolled out of bed at the hammering of a trash can lid. The academy incorporated a bit of old school into the daily routine. In fact, it was all old school. There was nothing in the facility that resembled the twenty-first century except for lights, running water and security cameras. Each student was required to wash all their own laundry by hand, along with the mandatory, ceiling to floor barrack cleaning. All the dishes and kitchen equipment were washed by hand. The general maintenance did not incorporate a power tool among the vast assortment that were kept in the maintenance rooms.

After the 6:00 A.M. revelry, a shower and inspection, they were allowed to eat. Then it was off to various appointments, from individual counseling sessions to tattoo removal to small group therapy where they talked about the issues that caused their lives to become so out of control. Sarah rolled her eyes and passed whenever her turn came to discuss what had been bothering her. She disclosed little when it came to her past. The fear and embarrassment about what she had done shamed her into silence.

To let that information out was more than she could imagine, not to mention the repercussions that would ensue afterwards. It had been her fault and she didn't want to discuss what was safely tucked away and blocked from her memory. It was in the past and had no bearing on the future. The thought of going to jail for it was more than she could bear. She would slit her own throat before she would tell anyone her secret.

From her peripheral vision, she watched and catalogued everything she could into her brain. She memorized the layout of the facility, all the out-buildings and the distances between each. She observed the behaviors of each drill on how they walked, spoke and conducted business. She memorized the basic routines of the academy and the times of chaotic function which seemed to come in waves. At first the chaos was in the afternoons. Stretching and physical training were appetizers and lugging boulders to the top of the mountain was the main course.

Fern Sillman sat next to Sarah during their noon time meal. "Isn't it great that we get a chance to be reborn?"

Sarah maintained her poker face of indifference through the first week. She calculated every bit of information she let in or out. Fern, number seven, was a textbook bible-thumper in Sarah's eyes. Every solution Fern offered incorporated massive amounts of prayer. With that much prayer, Sarah wouldn't have been surprised if the food levitated off the table and into her mouth. On two occasions she had been cornered into a one-sided discussion of how Jesus will save everyone's soul if only they open their hearts. The perpetual optimism made the hair stand up on the back of Sarah's neck every time she heard the wiry woman's voice.

"What did you do to get sent here?" Fern asked.

Sarah ignored the question.

THE SCHOLARSHIP

"I'm glad you and I are here for this. We'll become lifelong friends and praise God for all the wonderful things he has given us."

Sarah rolled her eyes at the ridiculous claim. She tried to scoot away from the insistent do-gooder, but Fern inched twice as close.

"I was sent here by God to help tend his flock. Bring the heathens of the world back into the light of God."

Sarah sighed, "Good luck with all that."

"I know. It's such a huge burden. That's why I need your help." Fern leaned a little closer. "We have to do it from outside the fence." Sarah's interest perked up and all her senses fired to double speed.

When Sarah didn't shy away, Fern continued, "Tomorrow night, when the moon is black, we leave." Fern focused back on her food, taking a few bites of the average, cafeteria-style food.

Sarah thought the food tasted better today or it could be that the blandness was overshadowed by the excitement of an escape.

"You have to run three hundred yards in thirty seconds," Fern whispered.

"Are you kidding me?" Sarah whispered back in surprise. "Only Olympic athletes can do that. This ain't Rio and I don't see a torch."

"You have to. That's the only way."

"I'll pass."

"You have to. It's our only way to get out and save the Lord's children."

"God don't exist."

Fern gasped and looked at her table mate. "He does exist." A look of horror came over her face and she was shocked to think that anyone could think otherwise. "You are here. That means that God has a plan for you. He wants you to teach people about God and all the wonderful things that he brings into this world."

"Seven. You need to leave me alone."

"Beware he who lurks in the shadows. He is of bad intentions and can't be trusted. He must be destroyed."

Sarah hurried to finish the last of her food so she would be allowed to leave the table. They had to ask permission to move on to the next task, just like school children. She turned on her chair and sat at attention with her tray on her lap. Fern ambled on in her one-sided conversation about the glory of God.

"Number Twelve, go." Drill Abernathy said. She was Fern's personal drill and seemed to be one of the nicer, more lenient drills. Sarah turned her tray in and started on the next task on the list, washing dishes. Every student received a chore, and the chores alternated so that no one could complain that one student worked less than another. As many times as the kitchen had been cleaned, one would think it to be a hospital. The drills observed the painstaking task of moving all appliances, cleaning the kitchen and then replacing them after every meal. Permanent scuff marks were worn into the ceramic tile.

The cooks were second phase students brought over to prepare the meal and point out what needed to be cleaned, which was everything, regardless if it was used or not. The cooks would point to imaginary dirt and complain that twenty-four hours of dust had been allowed to collect on the pots and pans. Therefore, they were not acceptable to cook in and must be cleaned.

THE SCHOLARSHIP

Evelynn Shoenstine, number two, joined Sarah at the sink to help wash the trays, followed by the pots and pans.

"Did you get saved by Jesus?" Evelynn asked.

Sarah rolled her eyes. "God, I hope it's not by her."

"She is some piece of work, isn't she?"

"Yeah. She is," Sarah agreed, trying to keep the small talk to a minimum.

"She supposedly stole a large amount of cash from several churches and handed it out like Robin Hood. She said she was helping God's children."

"So, God didn't take too kindly to his money being stolen?"

"When they caught up with her, they found her in a brand-new BMW, handing out cash to the homeless. "You've got to be seriously unhinged if you think you can pull a stunt like that off. Any smart criminal would leave the state or the country."

Sarah just nodded her head and continued to wash everything that she knew would come under close scrutiny, but her mind drifted to thoughts of escaping. She wondered if Fern was serious or if she really might be looney. If it was going to happen, then now seemed to be the time. Her classmates were immersed in the program, trying to prove themselves capable of changing their ways and coming out the other side a better person.

Fern praised God continually, stating that the work he did was miraculous, and endlessly repeating "credit should only be given to Thee." At times, Sarah wanted to hurl at the thought that someone or something could be given credit for not doing anything. The more someone talked of the glory to *Thee*, the more bitter she became. Sarah figured it was her duty to balance out everyone's light with the darkness that consumed her. She tried not to let it show and composed herself with

55

indifference, but she couldn't help wondering if anyone noticed.

Thinking back to the few years she attended high school, she remembered loathing the favoritism and praise that her high school classmates received. They binge drank, had sex parties, consumed or injected multitudes of different drugs, yet they still drove new cars, received scholarships to the top schools along with praise for their involvement in the churches and community.

Her own father disgusted her the most. After returning home from a two-week training session in Houston, he suddenly kicked her and her mother out of the house. Their divorce was quick and final, leaving Sarah's mom with little more than the state minimums. Sarah watched her mother turn to drugs and alcohol as her father's career flourished through the ranks of the city, from police officer, to detective, to chief of police.

"Move it children. It's past time that you need to be on to your next appointment." Drill Hawkins strode through the kitchen to double-check the cleanliness of the station. Glancing behind a stainless-steel counter, she suddenly ripped it out into the aisle. "Get a mop over here. You missed a spot." Sarah moved to grab a mop, only to find that the redhead Lillie Kirkpatrick was already on the move with a mop in tow. Sarah grabbed a scouring pad and stood by ready to remove any difficult stain.

Drill Hawkins moved through the rest of the kitchen, inspecting any little blemish she thought she could find. Sarah pushed the counter back to its place after the floor was clean while Lillie marched the mop and its bucket back into storage.

"Put that away," Drill Hawkins yelled at number four, pointing to a bucket of cleaning supplies. Helen grabbed the

THE SCHOLARSHIP

bucket and stored it in the utility closet. "Get outside and get in formation," the drill snapped.

Six women rushed outside to stand in their respective squares, joining the eighteen others who already stood outside waiting for the next instruction.

"You children signed into this program because somewhere in your life, you failed, or someone failed you. Regardless, it is your responsibility to navigate your life according to the rules of this country and its respective states. Living life is challenging, but not that difficult. If you want easy you shouldn't have signed those papers to come here. You should have squashed your time and been happy with three hots and a cot. Let the taxpayers feed, clothe and house you for your entire sentence." Master Drill Ietel paced back and forth, as usual.

"As some of you may have guessed, we have incorporated the seven core values that the U.S. Army uses to train young men and women into soldiers. You learned about integrity your second day here. Now we will discuss duty and how it is vital to your everyday lives. During this lesson you will listen to the stories and apply it to your own lives. You will think of the best way to serve your country.

"You have already started serving. Those of you who had your hair cut saw that it was tied up and set aside. Your hair was donated to the Locks of Love Foundation. Some of you may have noticed that in your contracts. Cancer patients all over the U.S. will be thankful for your donation. What else will you do to serve your community?"

"Master Drill Ietel, I don't understand what you mean by serving our community. How does a business school teach community service?" Brenda asked.

Master Drill Ietel strode up to the student and squared off in front of her. "Community service isn't just picking up trash on the side of the road. Do you understand?"

Brenda returned a blank stare, still not understanding what he was talking about. "No, Master Drill Ietel."

"Community service involves everyone from the President of the United States all the way to the chain gangs in Texas cleaning up the roadways." Master Drill Ietel turned and continued to pace back and forth in front of the class. "Even the waitress at the last restaurant you ate at was conducting community service. The waitress provides you with a pleasant dining experience; you reward her with prompt payment of the bill and a fair tip. A car dealership sells you a car. They provide you the service of transportation and you provide them a service that allows them to buy food and take their family to the movies. This is what business is about, providing fair exchange for community service. Some exchanges are not made with cash, they are made with time, effort and, sometimes, blood. Community service is anything that enriches the lives around you as well as your own. Your reward may be a paycheck, a smile or a monument that stands the test of time."

Master Drill Ietel stopped and stood at the center of the formation. He looked over the students as they stared at him or straight ahead. "Group, attention." The class snapped their feet together with their hands fisted at their sides. Master Drill Ietel snapped a salute to Drill Walker to take charge of the class then marched off to the side, turned and stood watching.

A long awkward silence followed after Master Drill Ietel walked to the side. Neatly trimmed grass covered the circle surrounding the flag. Three spotlights hid amongst the

THE SCHOLARSHIP

boulders illuminated the flag at night, just as it had in the early hours of day two.

"On the word 'move,' you will fall out, and then fall in next to the three logs lined up in the field. You will face east with the log next to your right foot. One through Eight on the first log, Nine through Thirteen on the second and Eighteen through Twenty-five on the third." Drill Walker paused to see if there was any hint of incomprehension.

Since the second day they had held formation at six in the morning and run the flag up the pole. In the evening they repeated the process in reverse, bringing the flag back down when the workday was done. Sometimes that was at 7:00 in the evening, sometimes 10:00 or 11:00, or even later. It was whenever the drills felt that the day's lesson was learned. If a punishment was not fulfilled by midnight, it started over the next day with ten percent more work added, along with the next day's chores and duties.

Sarah regretted being tricked by her attorney. Her muscles ached from days of work, yet there wasn't any pay. She wasn't ready for another day of lessons that involved strenuous activity. Going back to prison seemed like an increasingly better idea.

"Move!" Drill Walker bellowed.

The moment of silence had ended. "Get over to that ugly little log!" Drill Witcom screamed in Sarah's ear. The rest of the drills followed suit screaming at their student to hurry. Three logs were set up with twenty-four pairs of numbered gloves, one for each student. Nearby was a mass of additional logs.

A scramble for the logs ensued. Sarah continued to stay in the middle of the pack and do only what was necessary. She liked that buffer area to help shield her from an assault

59

from the drills. Her habit of watching the rearview mirror after passing a patrol car clung to her here. She didn't have a car anymore, yet she still kept track of who was where and who was the biggest threat. All twenty-four drills screamed at their students to move faster. The adrenaline exploded in each person as the fear of disobeying or disrespecting a drill seemed worse than death.

Drill Walker waited for the students to stand at attention next to the log as ordered. "Put on your assigned gloves then stand back at attention. Quickly. We have things to get done today." Drill Walker took charge of the group. "In this exercise you'll learn that it is your duty to do your part to help your family and community. Everything you do from this day forward will be to build a better life for tomorrow.

"Get those gloves on and stand next to the log." Drill Hollister growled at her student when she had fumbled with them, dropping them three times.

"It's important to learn that everyone gives their all to help with the overall goal. You don't get a choice to sit on the porch and watch your family member do all the yard work. It's your yard too. You need to be out there doing whatever it takes to make your house look better, function better and be more enjoyable when the workday is done.

"Everyone, face to the east with the log on your right side. If you can't see above the ears of the person in front of you, move forward until you can. We want the short numbers in the front. If you're the shortest person in the group, get to the front." A short minute of hustle later, the students were aligned, shortest to tallest. "All odd numbers, except number nine, will step over the log so you are on the opposite side.

"Someone dumped these logs here last night. They are in the wrong spot. They need to be moved a quarter mile over by the fence. It is your duty to clean up this yard and make it a better place for you and others. On the word 'move' you're going to reach down together and lift as one unit. You're going to carry each of these logs over to its corresponding yellow flag on the far side of the field."

Drill Walker stood in front of the students, looking for any objecting faces. "Do you understand?"

"Yes, Drill Walker," the students said in unison.

"Move."

The women, dressed in their orange sweats, lifted the logs up onto their shoulders and began the quarter mile trek to the yellow flags. After the initial moans and whispered complaints, the women settled into the morning team chore.

"Now, for your listening pleasure," Drill Hooks called out over the megaphone, "everyone here has a duty to make our communities a better place to live. Everyone from officers of the law to school children belong to this community. Therefore, each one contributes to making this a better place to live in. These are a few stories of people doing their best to make their communities better.

"In Carleton, Missouri, Officer Gene Taylor, a forty-year law enforcement veteran, was responding to a disturbance call. He found a mother and her teen daughter arguing. The girl wanted to end it all and ran out onto the tracks in front of a freight train. Her mother couldn't get her off the tracks. Officer Taylor grabbed her and pulled her off the tracks only a second before she would have been hit.

"It was Officer Taylor's duty to serve and protect. He protected the mother from a million 'should-haves.' He protected the train conductor from a thousand nightmares. He protected his community from what would have been a very sad day. That is his duty to his community. That is the oath he swore when he took that job."

Nearing the scattering of yellow flags across the field, Drill Hawkins instructed the placement of each log near a small flag numbered one, two or three. Two dozen yellow flags were scattered out across the grass-covered field. Drill Flemings checked her paperwork and instructed which numbered log went to which flag. "Number one goes here. Number two at this flag." She paced a few strides away and instructed the third log to its future home.

The students took a breather to quickly gulp some water before they raced back across the field to the tangled pile of logs.

The second trip underway, Drill Hooks started in with another story. "Forty-seven-year-old Charles Kinsey is a behavioral therapist in Miami, Florida. While at work he noticed that a twenty-four-year-old autistic man had gone missing. It was Charles' duty to track him down and bring him back. Charles found the young man sitting down in the middle of the street. While talking to him and trying to convince him to come back to the assisted living facility, a confused bystander placed a call to the authorities about a suicidal man with a gun.

"Officers arrived, and Charles pleaded with them to understand the situation. He told them that the autistic man did not have a gun, that he was holding a toy truck. He continued to try to reason with the police while he complied with their orders to lie on the ground and hold his arms above his head. One officer shot at the autistic man but missed and hit the therapist in the leg. No other shots were fired, and the autistic man was returned to the assisted living facility.

THE SCHOLARSHIP

"Charles served his duty to his community by staying with the young man and reasoning with the officers, even at the cost of being shot."

The students carried the logs in silence until Drill Witcom echoed her voice across the two dozen students. "Officer Taylor did his duty by saving the mother from a million regrets. He saved the train conductor from a thousand nightmares and he saved the community from a sad and mournful day.

"Charles Kinsey stood next to a young man who didn't have the cognitive skills to understand the severity of the situation that he was in. He faced that duty even at the cost of getting shot.

"You have a duty to your communities. That duty is to become an asset and not a liability. In your business classes you will learn the difference between an asset and a liability. For those of you who can't wait to start learning, an asset is something that gives to you and a liability is something that takes from you. We will teach you how to be an asset to your family and your community. We will teach you how to believe in yourself, to believe in your community and to believe in your family.

"The community you join after your release from here will welcome you with open arms as they will know that you have instilled within yourself the values that will make their community brighter and a wonderful place to visit. In return, you will enjoy the fruits of your labor by being asked to attend events and functions. You will be asked to help troubled teens because you've already been down that road. When you do this, it will lift your spirit and give you a sense of accomplishment and belonging.

"When you have someone comeback and say thank you for enriching their life by your actions, you will be filled with such strength that these logs will feel like balloons. It will make every ounce of crap that you've gone through in the past worth every precious breath you take in the future. There will always be lows and highs in your life. Some of you have already experienced a low in your life that makes this boot camp a walk in the park for you. Some of you have yet to learn how low your life can go. Either way, we will be here to teach you how to handle what is thrown at you and come out the other side in the best shape possible."

The students walked in silence as the drills guided the three groups to drop their logs next to their corresponding markers. Several more stories about officers, veterans and good-hearted people accompanied the final trips to transport the logs from one side of the complex to the other. A sense of duty was well illustrated for the students to draw off of. Sarah rolled her eyes at some of the stories. She didn't know these people. They didn't know her either, so what did it matter? She was stuck listening to the happy joy that others got, and that she was deprived of. Every smiling face deepened the scowl she held inside.

The constant running and exercise had left the students physically and mentally drained. Having to always be on your guard to appease the drills became exhausting work. Learning how to sound off when directed, march a certain way, organize and dress their bunks so that they were exact copies of the next bunk. The daily group and individual therapy sessions became daunting. Sarah built a wall to block any of their theories of expected behavior from encroaching on her sanity. She knew what their game was. She knew that they wanted her to understand that what she did was wrong and to say sorry for

64

THE SCHOLARSHIP

backhanding the cop in the face as she hammered blow after blow on her mother. She felt she was justified because of what her mother did to her.

Sarah felt pressured to say something constructive, yet how could she and be sincere about it when she was the one who was wronged? This injustice had caused her to commit a despicable act which she vowed to take to her grave. The therapists wanted to hear those cookie-cutter responses, 'I'm sorry for what I did.' 'It won't happen again.' They didn't have a clue what she had been through and if she told them, who would they believe? Certainly not her. She was in the system and not worthy of anyone's acknowledgement, trust, or time. She had already been labeled and discarded as trash. To her, the academy was a program that pretended to do the right thing all in the name of glory, God and society. It was a way to attempt to do the right thing. Feeble or not, an attempt was an attempt and counted as a win in the eyes of society. Sarah was certain that selected students were chosen to give rave reviews on how their life has benefited from the program, no doubt greased by a favor or two from the establishment.

Prayer seemed to be the only recourse to be absolved of one's sins. She heard plenty of prayers throughout the night along with the whimpering and soft cries of loneliness and despair. She listened to her classmate's whisper prayers of strength, prayers of understanding and prayers of forgiveness.

To Sarah, God didn't exist, therefore prayers were a useless waste of time and thought. Everyone proclaimed that God was merciful, yet she wondered how he could be merciful and allow so much hate to run rampant in the world. Hate was familiar to her, and had visited her many times with the mask of love, and the hunger of lust.

Chapter VII

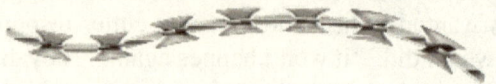

The following day was met with more barely edible food, though it was clear that an emphasis was placed on calories and not taste. The day's events hadn't been announced yet, but Sarah was sure it would involve back-breaking manual labor.

She took a seat at an empty table and hoped that no one chose to sit next to her. The fault in her plan was that there were only eight chairs to fit around each of the three tables for the twenty-four students. She knew that such close proximity would result in a conflict. The one person that got on her nerves more than anyone was the bible-thumping Fern.

"Oh, good. I am so blessed that you reserved a seat just for me." Fern set her tray down next to Sarah. She lowered her voice to a whisper: "I'm leaving tonight if you want to go, too."

Sarah's hearing became very acute. She didn't reveal any interest at the thought of being free from the overly intense moral makeover, but in her mind, she was screaming for a way out of the business prison camp. It might work for many in here, but it wasn't going to work for her. She set her mind that they would not break her. Society had made her that way and

THE SCHOLARSHIP

she was determined to make society pay for what they had done.

"It takes at least two people to escape from here. I have studied the cameras and the angles in which they point. I know their timings and that the night shift usually falls asleep at 2:00 A.M., after they file the daily reports. All reports are due in by 2:00. After that, there is radio silence. With such a small group to look after, they commonly take a nap for a couple of hours."

Sarah didn't acknowledge the slightest understanding of the plan in case someone was watching. She didn't want to alert anyone to the possibility of an escape. "Rice again?" she mumbled.

"I know. This sucks," Brenda Anskton said, as she set her tray down two seats away from Sarah's right. "At least they could give us some potatoes. They are legal to grow and eat you know." Brenda had been caught with a sizeable amount of pot that she and her boyfriend had tended. Her prosperous Mormon family couldn't bear the thought of their only daughter going for a lengthy prison sentence and had hired a prominent attorney to see that she received something much less substantial.

Brenda stood in the number one square and seemed to understand her mistake, now seeing that recreational pot in Utah will likely never be legalized, even if it became accepted nationwide. Her lawyer painted a picture of a reluctant participant even though she had originally brought up the pot-growing idea to her boyfriend. Brenda claimed to have parted ways with him, but Sarah was more inclined to believe that she would rebel just to spite her parents as soon as she was free to make her own decisions again.

Sarah had grown up with a girl named Belinda, who went to church every Sunday due to her parent's strong Christian

67

faith, and then drank like a fish every opportunity she got to balance out their strict, and sometimes unfair, standards. She believed Brenda to be that type of person. For every good deed Brenda did, she balanced it out with something that was equally negative. Her negativity reached a zenith when her parents forced her into the music program at their local school and persuaded her to work hard for the number one chair.

Brenda did all that she could to please her parents, including gaining the coveted first chair. Then, in retaliation, she sold a sex tape to the dark web of her losing her virginity to the very flute that gained her that first chair. Her mind reeled at the secret knowledge of her escapade when they mounted that trophy inside a glass case and labeled it: "The flute that stole the show. Washington D.C. National Recital, 2014." Her parents had become purposefully ignorant to the influences Brenda was tempted by and pretended that their daughter could never do such a thing. Each day they prayed that they would receive their loving daughter back to sit with them in church once again. They might have thought differently of the flute if they had known its other credentials and the nine hundred dollars' worth of alcohol it bought for a high school party when Brenda sold the video.

She met a dropout during her first semester at a coveted Utah university who invited her into his group of stoner friends. The short year they were together, they amassed a fair-sized business through their illegal herbal products. This led to a mass arrest, picking up all but two of their regular circle.

Sarah gave a slight nod thinking that some potatoes would be a good switch from the rice. She didn't care for the rice, but Fran Thibodaux, number twenty, gobbled it up after dumping some black pepper to the mix. Black pepper was the only pepper she could get her hands on. Coming from Louisiana, she was accustomed to the spicy food in the South and regularly put hot sauce in most of the dishes she was served.

Sarah shoveled in the barely edible food, knowing she had to eat it because the drills would yell even louder if she didn't have the energy to complete the work to their satisfaction. Also, she would need extra energy for an escape if the opportunity presented itself.

As the rest of the students filled the chairs and fed their stomachs Sarah thought about what Fern said. Escaping tonight would be great, yet she had reservations about trusting someone she barely knew. It could end disastrously, but it could also end with her living it up in Mexico.

"Does anyone know what happened to number ten? I know she was on the bus, but I haven't seen her since," Heather Smith, number thirteen, asked.

"I overheard the nurse say that she was pregnant," Ulyssa Vence chimed in. "We were in the same pod back home before coming here. She had been in there several months, getting rolled over and over for some technicality and the judge's month-long vacation. There was no way she could have been pregnant before she was arrested."

"Sounds like someone's getting some action on the inside," Heather whispered the conclusion that everyone else assumed.

****

Sarah sat outside the counseling room. Every other day they were to have a one-on-one meeting with their drills. Her meeting usually resulted in Drill Witcom asking questions and Sarah returning a vague answer, if she answered at all. The door opened to a neatly dressed and groomed drill Witcom. The only thing that was glaringly out of place was her puffy and moist eyes.

"Come on in Twelve. We can discuss what ails you or we can sit here in silence for the next half hour," she said, with a slight crack in her voice.

Sarah paused at the comment. A half hour of silence was not expected when Drill Witcom tried to reason an answer out of her. She took her usual seat in the hard plastic and steel chair and noted that nothing about this place was comfortable. The Army bunks they slept in had steel frames and stiff-as-a-board mattresses. Everything else was similar in discomfort, just like being in jail. At least in jail, the guards treated you better and they didn't make you build the jail that you were housed in.

Drill Witcom was noticeably upset about something. She was quiet and indifferent to Sarah being there. Sarah fidgeted in the chair waiting for Drill Witcom to say anything. Gloria held her clipboard up like a shield, almost as if she were hiding behind it. The usual endless babble that spewed from the drill's mouth usually annoyed Sarah to the point of wanting to pull her hair out, but she didn't say anything this time.

From morning to night, it was chores, hauling logs or some sort of work that filled the pockets of the owner with cash. Sarah was sickened at the thought of all this free labor that the facility was getting. She sat in the chair and waited for the onslaught of questions to begin. Drill Witcom sat rigid and agitated opposite her in the room. A camera in the ceiling focused on the center of the table to record anything that might be said or done.

Sarah's poker face became a mainstay of her attitude. She maintained her resolve not to be broken by this woman or the system she was tricked into signing up for. They didn't know what she had gone through. She wouldn't be a burden on anyone if they would just shove her on the other side of the border and say good riddance.

Drill Witcom usually sat watching Sarah, but this time her mind was elsewhere. She was distant, drawn up inside herself like she was fighting an internal battle. When Sarah glanced at her, she thought she could see that Gloria was about to burst. Like she wanted to let her own feelings out. Like she had to release something, or it was going to explode.

Most women who volunteered for the program were selected because they were willing and open to changing their lives. The questionnaires and counselors were meant to weed out those who didn't crave a change in their lives. Gloria figured that somehow Sarah had bluffed her way into the program but couldn't figure out why.

She knew something was locked deep inside Sarah, something that was the key to unraveling her whole attitude. Something that, if found, would free her emotionally and spiritually. She doodled on her notepad scribbling a thought unrelated to Sarah. Prying herself back to her job, Gloria glanced at Sarah as she considered a possible motive for the stubborn woman's unwillingness. She sized Sarah up like a prize fighter would an opponent and wondered how many rounds it would take to finally break through and understand what was really eating at this young woman. That revelation would have to wait, because today Gloria was too distracted by her last phone call. It had sent her mind into a mix of distorted emotions.

"Well, our time is up. It was good listening to your silence. Maybe next time we can try for another thirty minutes of meditation." Drill Witcom flipped the psychology around, gaining her the subtle win over the obstinate student. She opened the door and waited for Sarah to exit. "Back to the square. We have more work to do." Sarah walked past the table and glanced down at the clipboard. "Appendix" and "emergency surgery" were scratched across the top of the folder. The remaining space was filled with a prayer scratched a hundred times over, pleading for God to watch over Gloria's son.

****

Sarah knew this day would be more brutal than the previous as soon as a shovel and a heavy iron bar were dropped on the ground next to the yellow flag labeled '12.' Where each flag had been placed, the women were to dig a hole eighteen inches in diameter and four feet deep to place a tall post in. Sarah found the dirt soft for the first foot, then hit solid rock, as did most of the other women. A shovel and an iron bar were the only tools available. The heat from the sun made the work harder. The few lucky ones, who hadn't hit rock and completed their holes early, were made to help the others toil at the impossible sub-surface. Taking turns breaking the rock and fetching fresh water for those who were running low, the class worked as a team to complete each hole.

Sarah was the last to receive help as she had dug deeper into the rock than anyone else. Ulyssa finished digging her posthole and helped with another before coming to aid Sarah. The two women took turns beating at the rock, making an inch progress at a time. Fern visited each woman after her own easy dig, refilling their canteens at the direction of the drills.

"God has blessed us with a wonderful day, don't you think?" Fern held the bucket up for Sarah and Ulyssa to refill their canteens. Her strawberry blonde hair reminded Sarah of a girl she popped in middle school for calling her a whore. The girl went home with a fat lip but didn't seem to learn her lesson. She still rattled off names at Sarah with the backing of her friends. Seven against one was not the odds that Sarah would care for in any situation and she tried her best to avoid any and all contact with that vindictive mob. She also remembered that the one counselor that she felt close to in middle school had gone on maternity leave the last several weeks of the year. The following year the woman had been transferred and left Sarah without any refuge.

Sarah looked at Fern and wished she could pop her in the mouth, figuring that one good smack would swell her face to limit her speech for a few days. She reasoned that others would praise her for that as well, but it wasn't worth the twenty-five years she would face if she did. She had seen more than a few cringe at the sound of Fern's voice. Though it would have been justified in her classmates' eyes, the consequences for whacking Fern would be too steep.

"Fern," Ulyssa said, "I think they wanted some water over there."

"Oh. Heavens me. I shall take care of them right away." Fern picked up the cooler of water and started off where Ulyssa had pointed. "The Lord's work is never done."

Ulyssa and Sarah stared at the woman as she hurried off to fulfill God's work. "That woman is a straight-up crazy," Ulyssa said, relieved that the gospel conversation had temporarily halted.

Sarah smiled in agreement, yet she still wanted to escape and believe that Fern might be sane enough to pull that off. It was time that they leave. As soon as she was on the other side of the fence, she would ditch the religious fanatic and chart her own course. Actually, the fence wasn't the real obstacle; it was the cameras and the personnel watching the screens who would alert the roving guard that they really had to worry about.

Chapter VIII

Sarah woke in the middle of the night. She lay on her bunk listening to the other women breathe. Springs creaked as a body shifted in sleep. The glowing exit sign at the end of the barracks, along with the hall light coming through the windows at the opposite end illuminated the room enough that one could find their way to the bathroom without stumbling over another bunk.

A pop in an ankle joint sent an alarm to Sarah. She opened her eyes to find Fern standing above her. Fern quickly put a finger to her lips and waved her out of bed. Picking up her boots, she followed Fern, walking quietly through the shadows. The night watch was absent from her desk. They opened the door just enough to slip out, making only the slightest shuffling sound. Down the side of the building, they clung to the slim shadow that the yard light provided on the wall. At the corner of the building they stopped.

"We have to wait for the cameras to cycle away from our path."

"Which way do we go?" Sarah whispered.

"We are going to the back side of that shed," Fern pointed. "Wait there for thirty seconds then run as fast as you can for the fence."

"Which part of the fence?"

"That darkest part over there. I stashed a shovel there last night, so we could dig under the fence and not be seen. The ground dips down there and we'll be out of sight of the cameras while we dig."

"You go first, and I'll follow." Sarah instructed. She didn't feel comfortable with Fern telling her what to do. They hadn't had much time to plan their escape and Sarah didn't like that she knew so little about it, but she also desperately wanted to get beyond the fence and away from the concentration camp.

"No. You must go first. God has spoken to me and said that you must go first. You are much faster and stronger than I. You must go first and start digging the hole. I will wait for the next clear opportunity to follow."

Sarah nodded her understanding. She was stronger than Fern and it made sense since she could dig faster than most. As long as she didn't hit any rock, it would only be a matter of a few minutes and they would be off in the jungle of the growing corn field.

Fern stared at the cameras as they rotated automatically from one side to another. "When I say go, run to the back side of the shed and wait. Peek around and I will wave you off to run to the fence. I will follow on the next cycle and we can be free of this place."

Sarah gave a nod in understanding. Her muscles were sore from the previous day's digging, but they were charged with adrenaline now and ready to make a run for freedom. Fern placed a hand on Sarah's shoulder and watched the camera swing away from the path. With a shove and the word 'go,'

THE SCHOLARSHIP

Sarah was off like an Olympic sprinter. Her boots pounded the asphalt to the corner of the outbuilding that housed all the tools and lawn equipment. Rounding the corner of the building, she skidded to a halt in the loose gravel and backed up on the side of the shed.

She gasped for breath as the sprint and excitement pushed her heart to its limits. Calming her breathing just a bit, she eased around to look back for the next signal. In the barely-lit corner of the building she watched as Fern held up her hand for Sarah to hold her position. Sarah tried desperately to control her breathing. The paranoia that she might be heard caused her to hold her breath only to exhale loudly a moment later. She strained to listen into the night for any sound that might indicate a possible roving guard. All she could hear was the thumping of her own heart.

Fern's hand was down waving frantically to run. Sarah wondered how long it had been signaling while she was distracted trying to catch her breath. She bolted for the fence where a slight drop in the slope would shield her from any cameras that might swing that way. It was nearly two hundred yards to the fence. She had to make it to the drop, and then she could crawl the rest of the way to the fence where Fern said that she had hidden the shovel. Her legs didn't tire as they might have otherwise. Too much was at stake. The race for freedom surged energy through her blood and carried her legs faster and farther than what she would have thought possible.

The edge was a stone's throw away. She could see the dark shadow that she could hide in to catch her breath and wait for her accomplice to catch up. Three more strides and she dropped over the edge and slid to a stop. Panting loudly, she turned and peeked back through the grass to see the progress of her escape mate. She searched the back side of the outbuilding. Nothing. Her eyes turned to search the corner of the barracks and didn't find a soul. She wondered if Fern had sprung one of her fragile ankles and was now lying in the middle of the field, unable to complete the journey.

"She's not coming." The normal-volume voice sounded like a thunderous boom in the still of the night. Sarah spun around to see that Drill Hawkins stood only thirty paces behind her. She was dressed in blue sweats and had her hair pulled back neatly into a tight bun. Sarah's hope turned to disappointment then to dread as the implications of an attempted escape struck a terrifying fear of twenty-five years into her mind.

Sarah's breath caught. She couldn't breathe as she waited for Drill Hawkins to ask her to put her hands behind her back and be hauled off to jail. "One of the things you will learn here is loyalty."

A click of a door latch sent Sarah spinning again. Drill Witcom stepped out of a small, black-as-night pickup. An electric-powered Chevy truck sat on the dirt road that encompassed the compound just outside the fence. The silent running vehicle was optimal for their nightly patrols. "I am loyal to Drill Witcom and she is loyal to me. I would just as soon send you back to prison, but Drill Witcom argued that it wouldn't do you or society any good. She sees something in you that no one else can fathom. I think she's wasting our time with you."

Sarah looked at Drill Witcom standing on the other side of the fence. "She might have been out checking the perimeter for those who want to escape," her drill said.

"No. I think she was trying to escape. You can see it written all over her face. That mean mug, yes, I can see it even

THE SCHOLARSHIP

in this black night. The anger at being deceived and the embarrassment at being caught."

Sarah stewed in silence at how right Hawkins was. She was definitely embarrassed and angry. She resolved to remain silent and not let anyone break her no matter what or how much extra they forced her to do. A full minute ticked by in the black silent air.

"I think we should haul her in and send her back to prison, but she's your student Drill Witcom." Drill Hawkins turned to her comrade, awaiting a decision.

"That was some of the fastest running I've ever seen. It was as if the devil himself was on your tail ready to claim your soul," Drill Witcom said, as she approached the fence.

A shiver ran up Sarah's spine at the thought of having her soul claimed by anyone other than herself. She had separated herself as much physically and mentally from other people as she could. She would rather use people and push them aside like she would have done with Fern, but Fern beat her to the trick. Fern led her into a trap intended to make her look good and Sarah look like a fool.

"I think that either Sarah wanted to test our security system or that she wanted to come out to help patrol as well." Drill Witcom walked up to the fence close to where Drill Hawkins stood. Drill Hawkins eyed Sarah like a vulture getting ready to feast. She burned to see Sarah sent away. In her mind Sarah would be a career criminal.

"If she wanted to patrol with me, she would have asked." Drill Hawkins folded her arms in front of her chest. "I think she would have climbed this fence if we were not here."

"Well number twelve, were you trying to escape, or did you want to patrol with Drill Hawkins?"

Sarah glanced over her shoulder to see if Fern was coming to the rescue. Without any notable sign she turned back to the drills. "I wanted help Drill Hawkins with the patrols."

"I don't believe her," Drill Hawkins huffed.

"I think she could prove it to you. If she can keep up with you on the rest of your patrol, then I think what she says is true."

"Are you going to patrol in those?" Drill Hawkins looked down at Sarah's unlaced boots. "I would say that they are a poor choice if you were to try and chase someone down."

The chirp of crickets echoed through the night as Sarah sought an answer for the problem. "When you circle back by the barracks, she can quickly change them out with her shoes and continue with the patrol," Drill Witcom offered.

"Alright then. Could you please tell our watchdog that it was a false alarm and to light up the backyard?"

"I will." Drill Witcom crawled back into the patrol vehicle and silently rolled down the perimeter to the front gates.

"Well come on. Let's make sure the perimeter is secured. Don't disappoint me. If you can't stay ahead of me, I'll see that they ship you out faster than you can sneeze."

"Yes, Drill Hawkins. I won't disappoint you, Drill Hawkins."

Sarah and Drill Hawkins started off together in a fast, ground-eating run. "You know that those cameras are 1980's technology. They are up there to fool you. We saw you coming and waited in the most likely spot where you would try to go over the fence. We know that you're not stupid enough to go under. There's four feet of concrete you'd have to dig under, then through solid rock. You know the stuff you dug through yesterday. Or was that the stuff rattling around in your head? Hard to tell which one is more dense."

THE SCHOLARSHIP

Sarah glowered at the insult but kept up the fast trot just a few strides ahead of Drill Hawkins. She intended to break Drill Hawkins off and make her wish she wouldn't have invited Sarah for a run around the campus, even if it killed her.

Chapter IX

Sarah was exhausted, but pride wasn't going to let her show any weakness to the drills or to any of the other students. She had a reputation of being tough and she wasn't about to let some kooky drill sergeant wannabes break her down. Throughout the morning she did as little as possible to rest and recover from the half-marathon that she and Drill Hawkins had run in the early hours of the day. Each lap around the field was nearly two miles and together they pounded out seven of them before the revelry trumpet sounded and a drill crashed through the barracks with a stick and a trashcan lid.

Sarah thought that not being jolted awake from the trash can was the only benefit from the morning run. She headed straight for the latrine to organize the disheveled mop atop her head and to change into a fresh set of clothes. Fern swung wide of Sarah, knowing that Sarah could plant a fist or an elbow at any unsuspecting moment. She knew that her safest place was closest to a drill, yet she tried to act nonchalant about the trick that she had played on Sarah. Sarah couldn't tell if it was a deliberate trick to get rid of her or if the woman was just that crazy.

THE SCHOLARSHIP

The morning stretches and workout were like a cooldown after the pace that Drill Hawkins had put her through. She had almost collapsed on several occasions but forced herself to keep pace with the drill. She was relieved to hear that the morning would be spent in group therapy. After the run she could barely stay awake and had to be nudged a couple times by one of her classmates to keep her from sleeping.

****

"What do you think Drill Hawkins?" Felicia Gonzales flipped through Sarah's file, making notes at various points as to the progress of the student.

"I know she was trying to push me as hard as she could, "Hawkins answered. "She wasn't going to back down. Not from me. She has the determination of a stubborn bull."

"Looks like you ran her six foot under. She looks like I feel," Drill Knight, said referring to the summer cold she was recovering from.

They looked at the closed-circuit television and watched Sarah sleep in the chair as the group shared their thoughts and feelings about life. The counselor roused her at times to answer a question and keep her semi-engaged in the conversation. "I think you're right Drill Witcom. I think she is hiding something so personal that she would rather die than let it out."

"What do we do about it?" Drill Witcom asked, twisting a pencil in her hands.

"I don't know." Felicia closed the file and set it back on the table.

"We know that she tried to escape." Drill Hawkins looked at the confirmation nods of Drill Witcom and the counselor. "We know that she was at least persuaded by number seven."

"I agree." Drill Abernathy turned her chair to face the counselor and Drill Hawkins. "Seven is a definite instigator. It seems she would throw you under the bus, and then pull you out in the nick of time just to be the hero."

"Remember, Twelve is vindictive by nature. We will have to watch her like a hawk so that she doesn't get a chance to retaliate," Felicia added.

"Maybe we can help her retaliate in a positive and constructive way." Drill Hawkins grinned a devilish smile. The only thing she hated worse than a bad seed was one that smiled at your face while stabbing you in the back.

"How?" Drill Witcom asked.

"Tell her to be explicitly truthful in our next exercise. Maybe we can kill two birds with one stone," Drill Hawkins answered.

****

"Today's lesson is about respect." Master Drill Ietel boomed his loud voice, jolting Sarah out of a standing slumber. "Respect is a core value that you will need if you are going to navigate life successfully. You need to have respect for your superiors as well as your subordinates. Respect is probably the most important value you could ever learn. All the other values tie into it. Loyalty ties into it. You can't be loyal to another without having respect for them at the same time. You have to respect the decisions of others and perform your duty to whatever task you are assigned. You have to respect the less fortunate when sacrificing yourself for the benefit of others.

THE SCHOLARSHIP

Integrity is the respect of doing what is right both physically and morally and when you hold personal courage at its highest level you have respect for yourself."

Master Drill Ietel paced back and forth in front of the students. He executed his speech flawlessly and with perfect precision. After describing the basics of the task, he turned it over to the drills to move the students out to the next exercise.

A mile run around the compound in a tight formation brought them to a pit filled with muddy water. As the students gathered around the pit, they observed a narrow-elevated path that wandered like a maze through the stretch of brown mud. A junction split the path and gave the option of a longer, more crooked path, or an easier, direct path that included a gap where the walker would have to jump over an open space.

"This exercise will teach you to trust in your fellow student." Drill Witcom paced in front of the group as she explained the course and the implications of failing. "If you fail to navigate the course, you and your partner will pack boulders the rest of the day. If you succeed you will be allowed to use the washing machine to wash your clothes."

A cheer went up from the students who had for most of two weeks washed their own clothes by hand. A washing machine was now seen as a coveted prize and greatly cherished. Every task on the compound had been reduced to manual labor to instill a sense of gratitude for the simple luxuries of daily life. The washers were old, with hand cranked ringers that squeezed the water out of the clothes and back into the fifties-style washing machines, but they were still a glorious prize compared to a galvanized tub and a washboard.

Drill Abernathy paced behind the students. She stopped behind Fern and whispered to Drill Hooks. "Number Twelve doesn't trust anyone. She has a lot of animosity toward everyone here. I wouldn't be surprised if she purposely gave the wrong directions just to see someone take a dive off the path into the mud."

"I hope she doesn't, but I agree. She is very vindictive. There may be more than mud in the water. Leeches are common in these parts," Drill Hooks said.

"I'll tell the P.A. Make sure she has tweezers and antiseptic ready. Once those things get their jaws on you, it's a son-of-a-bitch to get them off. Ya' almost have to pull the skin off with them."

Fern stiffened at the mention of wrong directions and even more at the mention of leeches. She was rapidly approaching the point of hysteria over being directed by someone other than the Lord. Drill Witcom instructed the commands in a demonstration with Drill Zefon. Drill Zefon blindfolder herself and stepped to the command of Drill Witcom.

"Three steps forward."

Drill Zefon paced three average steps forward at Drill Witcom's command.

"Turn hard right."

Drill Zefon turned ninety degrees to the right.

Drill Witcom had instructed her to go down the shorter, more direct path. She gave her several more commands inching her toward the cavernous void. "Two heel-to-toe steps forward."

Drill Zefon complied.

"You're right at the edge. Now leap."

The class held their collective breath, waiting to see if Drill Zefon would make the leap or plunge into the muddy water. Drill Zefon leaped the chasm with grace and ease. Applause went up from the class as everyone took their next breath of relief. She continued as per Drill Witcom's commands and completed the task without getting wet and muddy. A cheer rang out for the accomplishment.

A string of students made it through the course with only one who mixed up her left from her right and walked off the edge, falling face-first into the mud. Sarah followed the directions from number seventeen, Jennifer Daniels. She gave Jennifer a hug for expertly delivering the flawless directions. Now it was Sarah's turn to give directions. The drills pulled the fake number out of a hat to see who was going to be the next contestant in 'direction-misdirection.'

"Seven," Drill Hawkins announced.

Fern swallowed hard. Her anxiety shot through the roof. She hadn't anticipated Sarah to still be here. She was sure that she would be carted off for having tried to escape. Now, Sarah was in control and Fern had the blindfold on, completely at the woman's mercy.

The course made several turns until a T in the path offered a choice of right or left. Sarah would have to tell Fern either right to navigate the void or left to wander the extended maze. A person could step over the open space which simulated a leap of faith, with only a slight hop. If they hopped far enough and in the right direction, they could greatly shorten their commute from one side of the mud to the other. Multiple students had turned their charges left, opting for the longer path and avoiding the leap across the muddy waters.

Fern stood at the starting line presenting a false front for the rest to see. "I praise the Lord that he will see me safe across this pit that is filled with the devil's creatures. I know that Jesus will guide my feet to the safety on the other side as he has guided me to avoid the devil's temptations."

Sarah smirked inwardly. Drill Abernathy double-checked the head gear and tightened the chin strap on the Fern's football helmet. Drill Abernathy aired up the interior cushions to make a snug fit for Ferns slender face. "You can do this Seven. Remember to listen carefully and do as you're told. This is a trust exercise as well as a respect exercise. If you respect someone then you also trust them, just like they trust you." Drill Abernathy gave her a pat on the shoulder and squared her up with the start of the platform.

"I trust in Jesus."

"I don't think Jesus can save you from gravity!" Lillie Kirkpatrick yelled from across the pond.

"Five heel-to-toe steps forward," Sarah began.

"Don't worry Seven, it's only six feet down and you have a soft landing," Brenda Anskton chimed in. She was the only one so far who had mistaken her right from her left and now was covered in the white mud.

"Two more," Sarah added. "Good. Now turn directly to your right."

Fern did as she was told.

"Four heel-to-toe steps forward." Sarah paused, waiting for Fern to comply. "Turn hard left. Five heel-to-toe steps forward." Sarah watched as her previous night's accomplice navigated the course.

"Two more. Turn hard left." Fern started to relax a bit. She had navigated three corners successfully.

"Four heel-to-toe steps forward."

"God will see me through this obstacle. I have total faith in his grace. *I will instruct thee and teach thee in the way which thou shalt go: I will guide thee with mine eye,*" Fern preached, not realizing that she wasn't quite square with the walkway. She had turned a little too far. With her growing confidence she took four heel-to-toe steps and stopped. Her feet were close to the edge but did not overhang enough that she could feel it.

THE SCHOLARSHIP

"Turn hard right." Sarah struggled with her mind, wondering if she should allow Fern to walk off the end or try to keep her on the course like a good girl. Hauling boulders up the mountain wasn't appealing but the chance to extract some revenge made it seem worth the price.

Fern turned and waited for the next command. "Two medium strides. You're lined up well. You can take two medium length strides."

Fern tilted her head toward the sky and raised her arms as if she were about to begin her walk across water. "And the LORD shall guide thee continually." She stepped out with her left foot and landed it solidly on the platform though it was dangerously close to the edge. Her right foot followed, and didn't find anything but air.

Gravity pulled Fern down over the edge. Air ripped around the helmet that protected her face and head as she accelerated into the pit. Panic engulfed her as if she were falling into the pits of hell. Her slender body made a big splash as her arms flailed for something to grasp. She found two feet of water and another foot of shoe-sucking mud to cushion her fall.

For a brief two seconds, Fern had disappeared into the muddy, cream-colored water. Her emergence was slow as the bottom tried in earnest to suck her back down. She fumbled through the water, reaching for anything solid. Her arms swung wildly, grabbing at the surface. A gasp of air, along with some of the gritty water left her hacking hard, trying to exchange the dirty water for life-giving oxygen.

The panic for air subsided while the panic over the leeches engulfed her mind. Swatting at her own body, she mashed any little tickle that her mind thought was a leech.

"What are you doing?" Drill Hooks asked.

"Leeches!" Fern screeched as she ripped her top off pulling the helmet and blindfold with it.

"There's no leeches in there," Drill Hooks said.

Fern paused to look at Drill Hooks, then at the blade of grass that she had ripped from her stomach. She looked down at her bare skin. A black sports bra still covered her chest, and dozens of blades of grass clung to her exposed skin. "Drill Abernathy said there were leeches," Fern tried to explain.

"There are," Drill Abernathy admitted, "in the creek over there, just outside the fence. Drill Hooks filled this pit three days ago. There aren't any leeches in it."

The roar of laughter elevated the spirits of many who had become increasingly annoyed by the overly-radical, religious fanatic. Fern finally gained her feet and pulled the blindfold completely off while still coughing up bits of inhaled water. Her humiliation was cemented in now. She felt that she would never be looked upon as anything but a joke.

Accepting a hand from Heather, she pulled herself back up onto dry ground. The warm summer sun beat down, offering its best to dry the wet and soggy woman. Drill Abernathy escorted her back up to the start line where she would have to begin again until she completed the exercise successfully.

This time Sarah tried her best to give accurate instructions, but Fern had lost any hope and confidence in her classmate's directions. Sarah was satisfied with the one plunge and was equally happy to haul boulders up and down the mountain. Fern fought to control her composure. Her thoughts of God slipped to take a back seat as the heckles from the group caused her own vanity to muscle its way to the front of her mind.

"Where was Jesus? How come he didn't come to save you?" shouted number thirteen, Heather Smith.

THE SCHOLARSHIP

"Maybe he thought she was too self-righteous and asked that she be taken down a notch," Lisa Fairbanks volunteered.

Sarah gave spot-on directions after the mishap, yet Fern didn't listen and either turned opposite or over-compensated for the intended directions and subsequently fell off three more times. Her anger flared more each time she had to start over.

****

"You did that on purpose!" Fern blasted Sarah, when they were out of earshot of the others.

"Yeah. You set me up. How else would they know the exact place to wait for someone to try an escape?"

Fern fell silent, stewing over the trick that Sarah had played on her.

"You're a real piece of work. You know that, right?" Sarah added.

"God will give me vengeance," Fern said defiantly, before angling off to walk by herself.

"Yeah. Well, karma's a bitch," Sarah said just loud enough for Fern to hear but no one else. She lifted her boulder higher on her shoulder and quickened her pace to leave Fern even further behind.

Chapter X

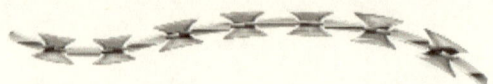

Sarah replayed the events in her mind from the past twenty-four hours: From the escape attempt to a midnight marathon to intentionally walking Fern off into the mud. Walking her off the platform was all she knew she could get away with. The rest of the events she considered bonuses. It seemed that the drills were really rooting for her and she had even caught a few of them wearing mischievous smirks when Fern took her third dive off the path. Maybe they didn't like seeing someone be set up the way Fern had done to Sarah.

Soft snoring became the crickets of the barracks as Sarah lay awake for most of an hour that night before the call of nature enticed her to climb out of bed. It took several moments to convince her muscles that the need to move was more important than the need to rest. Silently screaming at her arm to do something, Sarah flung the covers off and sat up in her bunk. She was happy that they didn't have bunk beds, otherwise she might have acquired several lumps on her skull by now due to the way she shot up in the morning when she heard the trash can. Jumping up and falling on the floor did not hold the same allure as drinking a fresh cup of coffee would: a simple pleasure that she would give anything for now.

THE SCHOLARSHIP

Quietly sliding into her shower shoes, she shuffled to the latrine. She wondered why the drills called them shower shoes when the rest of the world knew them as sandals or flip-flops. Pushing the door open she walked to the second stall and lazily opened the door to step inside.

She found herself sitting on the commode dozing off. She felt relieved and a bit satisfied from the day's activities and thought that she might finally fall asleep easily now, instead of tossing and turning trying to determine what the drills would throw at her next.

The early morning run left her exhausted, but the short naps during group counseling and an easy afternoon with little physical work allowed her to recoup some of her energy. Her sweats were beginning to hang off her hips, made noticeable by the constant barrage of reprimands to pull them up. She thought about Helen and how much she was slimming down along with most of the other students. If nothing else, Sarah thought that one good thing was gaining a healthier body through this God-forsaken program. She still loathed the positive attitude, but it was more tolerable than having to deal with Fern. As tired as she was, she still felt an increase in energy. She felt better, yet she yearned for a day to just sleep.

A rumor circulated that the coming Sunday might be one of those days, a day with a preacher coming in to administer faith and healing through prayer. Sarah didn't believe in God, but the additional downtime would be welcome. She wondered how an almighty God could let havoc run wild on this planet. How could he let people suffer at the hands of someone else or themselves or nature?

Sarah's head thumped against the side of the latrine wall jolting her awake. She had fallen asleep sitting on the toilet. With barely the energy to finish her business, she stood. Pins

93

and needles engulfed her legs in pain making any movement excruciating.

Opening the door to the stall, she looked up to see Fern charging her with a stick in her hand. Sarah put an arm up to block Fern's attack, but failed to stop Fern and staggered back on legs that were not ready to move. Ferns eyes were wide with vengeance and her muscles tensed to extract blood.

The brazen-hickory broom handle had been broken a couple of days before, and Fern had stashed it and then spent time honing a sharp point on it. Now she clutched it in her right hand and stabbed at Sarah repeatedly. Sarah toppled backward over the toilet and landed hard against the wall.

She didn't cry out. She was too stunned to react or call for help. Fern gritted her teeth and continued to stab her victim as fast as she could work her muscles. She stabbed at her shoulder sinking three, one-inch-deep wounds then hit bone after barely penetrating the skin. Sarah focused on the wooden shank and the fist holding it. As it came down for a fourth damaging blow, Sarah pushed Fern backward. The sharp end of the shank sank into Sarah's leg. She grabbed Fern's wrist and dug her fingernails into the skin, causing her to release the weapon.

Sarah went from sleepwalking to immediate shock. She didn't hear any sound at all, but suddenly realized that Fern was screaming. If she had been screaming the whole time, Sarah couldn't say. Sarah pulled a knee up into Fern's crotch and knocked her off balance then stuck a foot in her stomach and shoved. Fern stumbled backward across the latrine, losing her footing and falling on the floor. She rolled with the momentum and lunged again for Sarah.

Sarah had barely regained her footing and emerged from the bathroom stall when Fern tried to claw at her eyes. Sarah grabbed both wrists with a vice-like grasp. Fern jerked to get

94

away and bumped the broom handle that was still embedded in Sarah's leg.

She screamed and released her hold on Fern. Fern immediately grabbed the handle and jerked it out. Blood poured out of the open wound, soaking the sweatpants Sarah had been sleeping in. Fern lunged again trying to stab down on Sarah's neck. Sarah pushed the dagger aside. Two big arms enveloped Fern from behind. Sarah looked up to see Helen's face.

Helen squeezed the air out of Fern until the shank clattered to the hard tile floor. She backed Fern out of the stall, turned and hauled her out of the latrine. Sarah watched as Helen walked effortlessly carrying her squirming payload. Brenda and Lisa rushed to assist Sarah. Brenda grabbed Sarah and helped her to lie down on the tile while Lisa grabbed a stack of paper towels out of its holder and knelt next to the spreading red pool, placing the towels on the gaping wound and applying pressure.

Drill Zefon burst in, followed by Drill Witcom, who was still in her sleeping attire. The drill's barracks were on the opposite side of the building in a different wing, which accounted for their delay in arrival. They drills summoned the in-house nurse, who brought a trauma kit and rushed to Sarah. She first checked Sarah's alertness and then quickly turned her attention to the blood leaking onto the floor. Students lined the door and the hallway trying to get a look at what had happened. After seeing that no more help was needed, the drills ushered the gawking students back to their bunks and reminded them that business as usual would commence at zero-six-hundred and that sleep would be pertinent to their success. Then the drills returned, lining the door and hallway where the students had been.

95

Drill Witcom stayed to oversee the care of her student and sent Brenda and Lisa back to their bunks to join the others. A wheelchair was brought into the latrine to carry Sarah to the infirmary.

"What happened?" Drill Witcom asked.

"I don't know. She just came at me."

"Why?"

"I don't know." Sarah flinched as the nurse stabbed her with a needle, giving her a local anesthetic to numb the area around the hole the sharpened broom handle had made in her leg. She didn't want to appease the drills any more than she had to.

"Tell me what happened," Drill Witcom said.

Sarah sighed, reluctant to verbalize what was apparently obvious. "I was lying awake in bed. I knew I was tired as hell, but I couldn't go to sleep. I had to pee because you guys make us drink a quart of water every night. I got up and went to use the bathroom. Fell asleep on the toilet. Woke up. Finished and walked out, then was attacked. Does that about sum it up for you?" Sarah said in a condescending tone.

"How did she come at you?"

"I don't know, like she was going to kill me. I doubt she wanted to start a book club first."

"Stop being cynical. Tell me more details about the attack. Which wound did you get first?"

Sarah sighed again. She knew what Drill Witcom wanted. She wanted to know if it was instigated or provoked. "I couldn't sleep. I went to the bathroom. I fell asleep on the toilet. I woke up. I opened the stall door. She came at me with a wooden shank. She stabbed me three or four times in the shoulder. I pushed her off. She stabbed me in the leg. I kicked her across the room. She or I screamed, I don't know which one of us did. Maybe it was both of us. I don't know. She came at me again, trying to scratch my eyes out. I grabbed her wrists then let go when she bumped the stick that was still stuck in my leg. It fell to the floor. She picked it up again and came at me. Helen grabbed her around the middle and hauled her out of the room. That's when you showed up."

Drill Witcom didn't like the answer, or at least the condescending way that it was presented. Drill Zefon stayed in the infirmary with Sarah as Drill Witcom left to meet and talk with the superiors who would be arriving shortly. Sarah heard muffled voices outside and assumed that Drill Witcom was telling other drills what had happened. A male voice sounded in the hall and the same muffled reply repeated.

Dean Vickery entered the room and stood next to Sarah's bed. "How are you doing, young lady?"

Sarah rolled her eyes. "I'm leaking all over the damn place. How do you think I'm doing?"

Dean Vickery was taken aback. He hadn't expected so much hostility from a victim of an attack. Sarah was shocked to see him in anything other than a suit and tie as was his usual dress, but it didn't stop her from lashing out. The jogging clothes that he wore seemed alien to his personality, just like Drill Witcom's sweats and her hair draped down to her shoulders. "I'll check back in on you after a while." The dean quietly left the room, embarrassed by his unwelcome concern.

The resident P.A., Anna McKieel, grinned as she set up her tray to stitch the wound on Sarah's leg. The wounds on her shoulder had stopped bleeding and likely only needed a couple stitches after cleaning. "He's a good man. Try not to be hard on him. He's like the dad that many students here never get to experience. He really cares for all of you and wants to see you succeed."

"Well he don't need to come barging in here. I don't need any father-daughter bonding time. I've had more than I can stomach."

"Next time you see him, be nice. He really is a good guy." Anna said. Sarah was about to let go with another tongue lashing when Anna unceremoniously stabbed a needle into her flesh and prevented the outburst.

After the short cooldown and less-than-gentle treatment by the nurse, Sarah thought about the woman's words. She was right, though Sarah tried hard not to admit it. She felt she might have snapped at the pope if he had walked through the door. "I'll think about it," she finally said, gritting her teeth against the pain that the local anesthetic had not fully relieved. She didn't want to come off as being kind-hearted.

"What's going to happen to me now? Are they going to kick me out?" Drill Zefon hovered over her using a small digital camera to take pictures of her wounds, both before and after McKieel finished suturing them closed. The pictures would be used in the assault charges that would be filed against Fern.

The P.A. glanced up at Sarah then back at her work. "Not likely, if you were only defending yourself as you say. By the looks of this wound and the ones on your shoulder, they would support that evidence. You'll be restricted to this room for a day, then minimal duty until I feel you are ready to resume the race of the rabbits. It'll probably be about a week.

"You see, we are all about helping people stand back on their own two feet. I..." McKieel paused to peer into the open wound. She stitched together a section of tissue with dissolvable stitches. "...take care of the physical aspect of it and the drills and psychiatrists take care of the mental aspect.

98

THE SCHOLARSHIP

I think my job is easier. If I wanted to dive into the human mind, I would have been a brain surgeon."

Sarah rewarded her with half a smile at the intended pun. "Will I have to do anything during the day?"

"I have heard some things about you. I recommend you get some sleep while you can. Even here gossip travels. The worse the news the faster it travels."

"Really?"

"Yup. This news will hit the state news channels before the morning rush hour. It'll look like a big blemish on the academy's face for a while, but it'll pass, and we'll be back to business as usual."

"Will they say my name?"

"No. We are on a strict confidentiality notice until you reach phase two. The founders made it that way intentionally to help give the program and students the best restart possible. You know news media, anything to attract and sell. They're a business, and businesses run on sales."

Sarah grasped the concept and suddenly felt ashamed about snapping at the dean. She looked up at the ceiling, feeling the eerie sensation in her leg as the PA stitched it back together. Grey dots on the ceiling became her only entertainment as she tried connecting them in random patterns to create obscure images. There wasn't any TV in sight. No way to distract her from the boredom that she knew would overtake her. "If I have to be in here for however long you say, what is there for me to do? I'm going to get bored as hell sitting here. I'll probably get up and start pacing the floor."

"Well, there aren't any TVs, nor computers."

"Are there any books?"

"No, but I could probably find you a pad and pencil or pen," The P.A. mentioned. Maybe you could write a letter to

99

someone. We can't disclose where you are or send it to them before you finish phase one." Anna tugged at the string and snipped it with a pair of scissors.

"I don't have anyone to write to."

"Maybe you could write to yourself."

Sarah huffed. "Right. How the hell would that work?"

"I don't know. Maybe you could write a letter back in time to tell yourself not to make a dumb mistake. Hell, I would do that." Anna suggested.

"You would?"

"Yeah. If I could tell myself just one thing not to do, I would tell myself what the seven minutes in heaven was all about and I might not have gotten set up with the nerdiest boy in my whole class. Yet, when I think about it, I got to kiss the now ninth-wealthiest man in Kentucky."

"Ninth-wealthiest?"

"Yeah, he was a nerd, always fiddling with computers. I heard he invented a program in college, got a bunch of money from that and then flipped it into the markets and cleaned up even more. Now he owns a couple wineries in Kentucky and a few businesses in Silicon Valley."

"Sounds like you're a stalker," Sarah chided.

"No. When I hear his name mentioned, I pay attention."

"Anna, the stalker."

"No." The woman turned a little flush around the gills. "I'm not a stalker. I was set up."

"How old were you?"

"It was a middle school field trip."

Sarah knew the P.A. was embarrassed and more than a tiny bit of her enjoyed it. "It sounds like you were his first kiss. Did you make it memorable for him?"

"I guess. I don't know."

THE SCHOLARSHIP

"If you were his first kiss, then I would bet that he thinks about it." Sarah wondered if she was qualified to give advice to those who had puppy-love flings in middle school. She thought of her first kiss and the alcohol breath that came with it. She turned her head to vomit but managed to swallow it back down. She suddenly didn't want to talk anymore. The past resurfaced and almost made her lose her dinner. It was yet another part of her youth that was robbed from her, the innocent feelings and emotions of what most everyone else had and she craved. Those years were long gone. She could never get them back, no matter what they had been like.

"You okay?"

"Yeah. Just the sight of you pulling on that string got to me a bit," Sarah said, side-stepping the real reason she felt nauseous.

Chapter XI

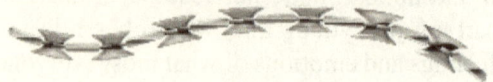

Fern was arrested for her assault on Sarah and transported back to jail. She would not see the light of day for many years to come. A general peace overtook the class. Laughter, joy and enthusiasm replaced the gloom of uncertainty that once hung over the compound. Students began to look forward to each new challenge. The counselors were on overload trying to write down all the new and revealing facts coming in their doors. Most of the facts shaped up to look like an easy sweep to launch the students to the next phase.

The students were selected for the scholarship based primarily on the fact that each demonstrated a desire to truly turn their life around. Sarah remembered that early questionnaire when she was still in the county jail. She gave them what they wanted to hear. She shed a few crocodile tears to appease them, not thinking that anything would materialize out of it. The judge and prosecuting attorney signed off on it leaving the standard maximum sentence hanging over her head. Sarah thought the interview was another tactic to evaluate how many years she would get for accidentally hitting a cop.

THE SCHOLARSHIP

There was talk of restitution to pay but the officer was familiar with the program and convinced the department to waive any grievances if she completed the program. He was one of the many good-natured officers who believed in building their communities for a brighter tomorrow.

Sarah became more engaged in the program after the attack, although she had to stick to the sidelines for almost two weeks until the P.A. released her to gradually get back into full physical momentum. They started her off on the mountain by having her carry an empty net at first, then a small five-pound rock.

When she snuck a full-sized boulder up to the top, they deemed her capable of continuing but allowed her to progress at her own speed for a couple more days. Sometimes they even blocked her path to purposely slow her down or pulled her aside for a mini-counseling session, giving her a small break from the boulders.

Three weeks into boot camp, the dills divided the class into teams according to their offense and personality. Sarah now wore green sweats with the number twelve written front and back in large numbers.

"Over the next several days, you'll begin to learn what honor and loyalty are," Master Drill Ietel addressed the students as they stood in colored squares painted on the ground that matched their uniforms. "I say begin because you will continue to learn about these throughout your whole life. You will learn how to be loyal. You will learn how to honor those around you. You will learn how to recognize these values and cherish those who are loyal to you. You are now part of a team. Your team will either graduate together or fail together. If one of you refuses to learn what is necessary here, your teammates

103

may vote to cut you loose, at which time you may be leaving the academy to resume your sentence in jail.

"You will help each other, defend each other and do everything in your power to see that you and your teammates graduate. Over the next several days you will bivouac out here. You will forage for materials to make a shelter. You will develop a system for obtaining a reliable source of fresh drinking water. Dehydrated meals will be provided, but you will be responsible for cooking them.

"Each team will have a flag that must never touch the ground. If your flag touches the ground, you will lose half your provisions. If it touches again, you lose all your provisions. If another team has something that you need, you will have to negotiate for the trade or battle to take it for yourself."

Sarah looked out across the field. In the far reaches of the green pasture she could see four different flags, one for each team. She caught the meaning of the game: It was survival as well as diplomacy. She didn't want to be on the short end of the stick. She wanted to have the upper hand for once.

Sarah leaned slightly toward Three. Faireuza Williams was wiry fast and could run circles around most of the other students. She was feisty and her hot temper landed her in the academy for beating up her former boyfriend when he wouldn't stop disrupting her video game. A stupid reason to argue with him, and one that shouldn't have necessitated a hospital visit.

"Go get our flag," Sarah whispered. "I'm going to get the blue flag to use as leverage."

Faireuza gave a slight nod of her head. Sarah leaned back and listened to the rest of the rules and conditions.

"You'll need to use your heads, your wit and your physical strength to last the next several days. If there is an

104

THE SCHOLARSHIP

altercation, it will be settled in the ring. You will have a chance to face off one-on-one with your opposing team. Bartering, stealing, challenging and diplomacy are all on the table as a means to acquire what you need to survive.

"You are not allowed to hit another student except in the ring and only when wearing the gear provided. All other rules of the academy apply." Master Drill Ietel centered himself in front of the teams. "Class. Attention." The teams snapped their feet together waiting for the next command. "Begin," Master Drill Ietel said, in a booming voice.

Sarah didn't hesitate. She blew past everyone who stood frozen in formation wondering what to do. She was twenty yards ahead before shouts of concern rose from behind her. Sprinting with all her might and a slight winch from her recovering leg, she made a bee line for the blue flag.

From the corner of her eye, she saw the dark skin of Faireuza, a former high school track athlete, sprinting for their own flag to secure its safety. She took a split-second to glance behind her and see the rest of the class desperately trying to catch up. Her team raced for their flag and the jumble of supplies that lay on a pallet behind it. Ripping the blue flag from the ground with one hand she eyed a stainless-steel pot.

She stole another glance behind her and saw a blue number nine sweatshirt below the determined face of Elizabeth Reardon. Elizabeth was from a prominent family in Virginia, but the blue that she wore signaled the problems with meth that took control of her life. Now she was a mere two yards behind Sarah and closing on her heels. Sarah wanted the stainless kettle but lacked the opportunity to grab it with Nine this close behind her. Instead, she reached for the handle and knocked the kettle into the path of her pursuer.

Elizabeth collided with the shiny pot and tumbled to the ground. Sarah raced on to her own flag as the rest of her team arrived to defend and congratulate their hero. Sarah raised the trophy over her head to show the initial triumph. Her team gathered around and patted her on the back, cheering their good fortune.

"Okay good job everyone. We have a lot to do before dark," Faireuza said, taking the lead to organize her team. "Let's see what we have. Twenty-one and Fifteen, take that tarp and stretch it out to see how big it is. Eighteen and Twenty-two, go through the rest of the pile and see what we have."

"They're looking at us." Sarah gestured to the group of women from whom she had stolen the blue flag.

"Let them look. We have something that they want. So, we have control over them. We can use it to trade for something. First let's see what we have and what we need." Faireuza turned to the supplies piled on their pallet: tools, rope, copper tube and assorted other items including a case of bottled water and a first aid kit. Sarah took the flags to the far side of their work area and planted both of them firmly in the ground.

She joined her teammates to help organize their supplies and make a plan on how best to utilize them. For tools they had three shovels, an ax, and a piece of flint decorating the ground. Sarah knew that their only source of water after they used up the bottled water would be the mud hole that was used for the respect lesson. Their water bottles would run out soon leaving them to drink only muddy bug-infested water.

She thought back and enjoyed reminiscing about that glorious day when the crazy stick figure, Fern, fell into the muddy water over and over because she tried to second-guess Sarah's directions. She knew that, somehow, they were to make that muddy water safe to drink.

106

THE SCHOLARSHIP

She looked across the field to see that the other three teams were sorting their items as well. The drills milled around to observe and referee when needed. They weren't to take sides or offer advice, just to provide safety to the students. Of course, the students were expected to take care of their own minor bumps and scrapes.

Two blue shirts approached their camp as Sarah's team discussed what kind of shelter they could build with the tarp. Sarah nudged Faireuza with her elbow. The team turned to the advancing party and stepped out to meet them.

"Twelve. Three." Elizabeth nodded to the women. Her blue sweatshirt and pants were now stained with a bit of green grass and dirt.

"Nine. Thirteen." Faireuza returned the acknowledgment.

"Well, it seems as though you have a bartering chip." Elizabeth shifted her weight from one foot to the next. She peered past the six women in green to size up the possibility of stealing the flag back and to see what goods they might have or lack.

"That we do, thanks to number twelve here." Drill Hooks and number nine's drill, Drill Douglas stood to either side of the group, ready to step in if the women turned to throwing fists instead of words.

"That was a genius move," Elizabeth said, following the rule of always offering a compliment.

"You are fast yourself. A few more yards and we wouldn't have a bargaining chip." Sarah smiled politely. She had gotten a thrill from the simple challenge and a bigger one from the success of it.

"Would you care to do some trading?"

"That would depend on what you have to offer." Faireuza kept her guard up looking for any hint of deception.

"We invite you to come take a look," Elizabeth said.

Sarah and Faireuza glanced sideways at the rest of their team to see if there were any objections. Seeing none, they ventured forward together. The other four remained close to their pile of scraps to guard what would be the necessities of life over the next several days. Twelve and Three walked a short distance behind the pair from the blue team, in case there was a trick play somehow. They wanted to be able to race back to their camp to defend what they did have.

"Do we want to trade?" Sarah asked.

"No. Not without consulting the rest of the team," Faireuza replied, in a hushed tone. "This lesson is about loyalty and honor. We need to stick to those values. Especially within our team."

Sarah nodded, then walked in silence the last little bit, taking in every little detail of the blue team's supplies to assess what they could possibly use. The blue team had done the same as Sarah and her teammates. They had all their stuff laid out to take inventory and develop a plan to utilize it. She saw a wooden water barrel, which she thought would come in handy if they could figure out how to turn the mud pit into a fountain of life. The barrel would be invaluable in storing water.

The blues had a scattering of galvanized pipe of various lengths, a smaller tarp, several lengths of timber, a pile of firewood, two stainless pots and the same assortment of tools and single case of bottled water that Sarah's team had. "What looks good?" Sarah asked.

"Definitely one of the pots, since we don't have one. We're going to have to boil water somehow."

"Okay. So, what do we pick?" Sarah said, eager to get on with the construction of their shelter.

THE SCHOLARSHIP

"We'll talk it over with the team. Just memorize what is here and we'll discuss it back at our camp," Faireuza said.

Camp? Sarah never thought of this event as camp, yet it fit every definition. She had never camped before. Her parents had never taken her, nor did she have any friends who would invite her to go with them. She had only seen movies and television where camping was mostly glamorized. She felt that it wouldn't have been this challenging, this soon. The image of camping was one that the fire was already started, and the food was already sizzling over the flames. She hadn't a clue how to start a fire, let alone how to do it without a lighter or matches.

"Do you see anything that you could use?" Elizabeth asked.

"We'll discuss this with our team and get back to you. Thank you for the opportunity to consider a trade." Faireuza spoke first, to prevent Sarah from committing to something that the rest of the team might not be ready for. She nudged Sarah and turned to walk back to their camp.

"Should we go and see what the other teams have to offer?" Sarah asked after they had distanced themselves out of ear shot of the blue team.

"That's a good idea. We'll discuss it with the rest of the team."

"What do we have and what do we need?" Faireuza asked her team, when they were together again.

Lisa Fairbanks stepped to the circle. "We have a large tarp that we can use to collect water if it rains. It has a large hole in the middle. We have nine two-by-fours that we can use to build the framework of a shelter, maybe a tent. We have a couple of large, clay pots. About twenty feet of rope, again we can use it for the construction of a shelter. We don't have any pot to boil water in. We have…"

"Our main objective is to build a shelter and create potable water. What kind of shelter can we build?" Faireuza asked when Lisa's pause lasted a little too long.

"How about a teepee? The tarp has the hole for the smoke to go out," Jensen Michaels offered.

"We don't have anything to make a fire." Samantha Owens complained. Samantha had once lived a lavish life, until her father lost his business and turned to drinking. Then they moved from the suburbs to the other side of the tracks, into a trailer. She was another woman who finally decided to fight back against a verbally abusive relationship, and ended up in cuffs after leaving her boyfriend with a bruised eye and a bruised ego. He had a high-priced lawyer and she'd had a public defender, fresh out of college.

She wanted to return to the lavish lifestyle that she had grown up with and latched onto the first guy that flashed a persona of status her way. As in many cases, everything was bliss for the first several months, and then the subtle belittling began, which escalated to the all-out bad-mouthing. Samantha felt trapped. She didn't want to go live with her father in a run-down trailer, so she endured the abuse. One day, for some unknown reason, she snapped and tried to scratch his eyes out.

After several months of sitting in jail while the attorneys and judge tried to make up their minds on what to do with her, she was offered a scholarship. She had heard of boot camp jails before, but this was different. This was described as more of a school than a boot camp.

Growing up she felt at home in a school and always did her best to be the top student. School was somewhere where she felt alive, where there was always a new challenge around the next corner. The rewards she received in school and the near straight A's she pulled on her tests resulted in shopping

THE SCHOLARSHIP

trips with her father for clothes and jewelry. She was also on the cheer team and had trophies from her swimming competitions.

When she got into trouble, her lawyer was approached by a former Schultz student who showcased the benefits of the Business Academy, along with their outstanding results of one hundred percent completion by all who had entered the program. The prosecutor agreed with reservations. He insisted that the maximum sentence should be given, without any appeals if she should fail. The judge agreed to the maximum sentence but kept in place the option to appeal the conviction.

"We'll find a way to build a fire even if we have to rub two sticks together. What's everyone's background? City? Country? Suburbs?" Faireuza asked, clearly taking charge of the situation.

"City." Jensen Michaels and Faith Nixon called in unison.

"Suburbs," Samantha said.

"Outer space," Galaxy Thorngood said. The shoulders under the number twenty-one sweatshirt hunched as the rest of her team stared inquisitively. "That's what everyone tells me. I don't socialize well. My mom tried to take my game system away. I freaked out and hit her. My game system was my world. I could be anyone I wanted to be. I just didn't want to be myself. I felt that my mother was ripping my world apart, because my world was a virtual one. It had no bounds. I lived in that world that fed me the connectivity that I craved.

"I didn't want to face the real world because it was depressing and sad. Everything on the news was about shootings and bombs."

"Where did you live?" Faireuza asked.

"I don't know." Galaxy was truly perplexed.

"Tall buildings or short buildings?" Sarah asked

111

"I don't remember. They say that I had spent three years in my room."

"Did you see anything when you came out?" Sarah asked.

"No. The sun was so bright it hurt my eyes, so I kept them shut."

"What about when you were younger?" Sarah prodded further.

"That's it. I just don't remember."

"Well, it sounds like we're all sluggers. We punched our way into this academy," Faireuza explained. "This is a school. This is a time for us to learn, to grow and to overcome the obstacle before us. We are faced with no water, or rather a limited supply. We have to show the drills that we can survive. Isn't this all about learning something and being tested?"

Samantha's ears perked at being tested. She felt that she was one of the few who looked forward to the tests that they had at school. Her high was one of comparing herself to others and out-shining them. "So, why don't we hit this one out of the park? If they want a shelter, we'll build a mansion."

Faireuza look around the group and watched the slight nods coming from her teammates. "Okay then. A mansion it is. How big of a mansion can we build with what we have?"

All the women surrounded the heavy plastic tarp. Four teammates grabbed a corner and stretched it out while two climbed under to lift the tarp. The thick canvas tarp was too heavy for only two women to hold up for more than a few seconds, but it gave them a rough idea what they could do with it.

"We can all fit, though it might be a little crowded once we bring the tarp down to the ground," Sarah said. She indicated that the tarp could be used as the walls of a tent that

THE SCHOLARSHIP

they would fashion using the scraps of lumber for the supporting structure.

"It will have to work for now. We are going to be running out of daylight before we know it." Faireuza and Sarah stepped to the center of the tarp and let it fall down around them. "Does anyone have construction experience?"

"I do," Faith Nixon volunteered. "I helped my father build sheds in his spare time. Do we have nails and a hammer?"

"No," Lisa said. "Think any of the other teams have any?"

"The blue team don't. Maybe the red or yellow teams have some." Sarah picked up an end of the rope, toying with it as she waited a response and thought of possible solutions.

"Eighteen and I will go have a visit with the red and yellow teams, see if we can do some negotiating. Sarah, I think it is best if you stay close to the flags and keep them safe. If we can't trade for anything, we will have to use what we have. So, to save time, try to figure something out." Faireuza and Jensen went off to check with the other teams. Sarah turned to the materials on the ground and picked up a stick of lumber, seeking the hidden message on how their mansion should be assembled.

Chapter XII

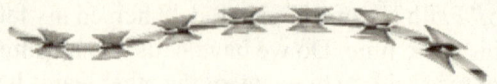

Screams echoed off the hill as the students faced off inside a circle painted in the grass a short distance from the blue team's camp. Two opponents, Sarah and Elizabeth, faced each other within its outline. They wore air-filled helmets and carried inflated gladiator jousting sticks.

Two days had passed and the last of the good water had disappeared that morning. There was a desperate need to get a stainless pot for the green team. They had nothing to boil water in. The clay pots had holes in them and any plug that they tried failed to hold as they boiled it over the small fire. And the fire had all but consumed their supply of firewood.

Elizabeth landed the first blow to the side of Sarah's head. Sarah shook it off and became more attentive at keeping her guard up. Blow after blow was traded with no real hits. Sarah knew that it would become a game of who outlasted who. The big, inflatable jousting sticks wouldn't do any real damage, but the weight and bulkiness of them could tire out the best athletes surprisingly fast.

"Come on. Come on," Sarah's team yelled, doing their best to encourage her. Sarah ducked a wild swing and countered with one that made Elizabeth wobble on her feet as it struck her knee. Sarah attacked the knee again, trying to bring Elizabeth to the ground. Once on the ground it would only take two more consecutive blows to the body to claim victory in the duel.

Sarah knew she would be in for a slug fest. Elizabeth wanted to fight Sarah as a personal challenge, as well as to try for the large tarp and their flag, which the green team still possessed. Sarah's team was hoping for a stainless pot to boil water in and the wooden barrel to store it, once it was purified.

Elizabeth protected her knee at a cost of taking a blow to the stomach and a couple more to the head. She always knew she was hardheaded and now was as good a time as any to prove her reasoning. The women sucked their own spit in over their mouth guards, trying to retain all the water they could. Sarah took a blow to the side and countered with one on her opponent's face. She quit trying to attack the knee and aimed for Elizabeth's head. One good blow and it would be over.

Sarah swung and swung at the blue team leader, but she wasn't going down. They broke apart and circled each other, catching their breath and evaluating their next moves.

Faireuza and Jensen's trip to negotiate for more means of survival revealed that the red team was hoarding some nice long bits of timber and a few sleeping bags that could be used on the chilly nights. Shivering around the fire was burning up their fuel way too fast, and now they had just enough fuel to last one more night. Huddling close to the fire was not what the green team had in mind.

First, they needed to secure the blue team's pot and barrel to be able to scrape by. The freeze-dried rations were hard to choke down without water. They had to get one of the pots soon. The pressure was on for Sarah to win. If they lost, they could very well shiver into oblivion before morning. Nights

115

during the summer were usually warm in Missouri, but any cold front that comes through would be enough to send a person into hypothermia.

Elizabeth lunged at Sarah. Sarah side-stepped and landed a blow to Elizabeth's back, knocking her off balance. Sarah dived in to finish knocking her down. Drill Zefon and Drill Hooks countered the two sparring opponents, watching for the two consecutive blows or any hits not made by the jousting sticks. Elizabeth saw the blow coming and rolled out of the way to escape the defeat.

Cheers and blasts of encouragement rang out from the students as their team members battered each other to win a vital piece of gear. The red and yellow teams weren't quite as loud and had one person who didn't seem to be enthusiastic at all. Harley Whittaker, number eight, stood with a blank face, watching the battle.

Back on her feet, Elizabeth feigned a swing, which Sarah moved to block. In that moment Elizabeth spun around and landed a blow to the back of Sarah's head. Sarah fell to the ground. A blow landed on her back.

"One!" Drill Hooks announced.

Sarah spun out of the way as the second blow connected with dirt. A third blow came down and landed on her shoulder.

"One!" Drill Hooks called again.

Sarah tossed her jousting stick to the side and grabbed her opponent's when it came down with another blow, holding it firmly and pulling Elizabeth down on top of her. She clenched the jousting stick and shoved the blue uniform off her, sending Elizabeth sprawling a few feet away. Sarah spun on the ground, landing the end of the jousting stick on Elizabeth's head and knocking her face back into the dirt.

"One!" Drill Hooks called.

THE SCHOLARSHIP

Elizabeth spun out of the way and came up to her feet, diving for the discarded stick. Sarah lunged and shoved her back on the ground, pinning her belly down. She quickly brought the balloon up and down twice in the middle of Elizabeth's shoulder blades.

"One. Two!" Drill Hooks called. Drill Zephon blew the whistle. The challenge was over. Sarah rolled off Elizabeth, panting to catch her breath. Her mouth was dry as the rationed water had not been enough to keep her system hydrated. Sarah's team came to her side to help her back to her feet.

The blue team helped Elizabeth to her feet. She squared off with Sarah and offered a hand. Sarah took the hand and said, "You're a tough bird. I'd hate to come across you when the gloves are off."

"Likewise." Elizabeth spat a little bit of blood and grass out of her mouth. One of the blows had caused her to bite her lower lip.

"Twelve. Nine. Report to the infirmary to get checked out. Then back to your camps," Drill Zefon ordered. "Nine, when you get back, you'll deliver the items to the green team."

"Yes, Drill Zefon."

Jensen escorted Sarah to the infirmary to get her bumps and scratches looked at while the rest of her team prepared to boil some water.

****

The firewood ran out part way through the night, but they had some water and a hot meal to tide them through until morning. The makeshift teepee clattered to the ground during a small storm that blew through. The green team propped the canvas up the best they could until the morning sun shed

117

enough light to see what they were doing. Sarah was cold and sore from the previous day's activities and the impromptu teepee repair in the middle of the night as she and her team wrestled with the canvas structure. As they worked, Helen Whetherstein and Harley Whittaker approached the green team's camp.

The contrast in size of the two women was staggering. Helen had slimmed down dramatically, but would still be considered obese. Harley was barely into the triple digits. Her shy and reserved demeanor allowed her to go unnoticed much of the time.

Faireuza nudged Sarah. Sarah turned to see the two approaching and stood like a sentry next to Faireuza. Drill Witcom was nearby, silently listening for anyone who might get out of hand. Drill Douglas finished checking one of the many fire extinguishers stationed amongst the camps in the event of a fire and then stepped over to the meeting.

"Three. Twelve." Helen acknowledged the two.

"Four. Eight." Faireuza nodded to the two women.

"We want to challenge you," Helen started.

"Challenge us?" Sarah scoffed. "There is no way that I would challenge you. I'm sore to the bone and haven't slept much last night. There is no way I would have a chance against you."

"Not me. Eight wants to challenge you."

Sarah looked at Eight. Her eyes were cast down to stare at the ground just in front of her feet. Sarah laughed. "No. No. That's ridiculous. I would kill her. I'm afraid if I move too fast, she might just faint. I admire your courage, but I really don't think it's a good idea for your sake."

"Are you sure you couldn't use some warm sleeping bags?" Helen asked.

118

THE SCHOLARSHIP

Faireuza and Sarah froze in their tracks and turned back to the two women.

"I believe you're out of wood. It's going to be colder tonight. Sure you couldn't use a few sleeping bags?"

"We'll discuss it with our team and get back to you." When the two leaders of the green team turned around the other four were standing right there. From their eyes, Faireuza already knew the answer. She turned to Sarah and asked, "Do you feel up to it?"

"Yeah. I can do that. How hard could it be? I can just push her down and tap her a couple times to end the challenge. The only thing that would be damaged would be her pride."

"Okay. We have the blue flag and when we win this round, we can have control of more key items that will ensure our success at this," Lisa observed.

"Is there a chance that we'll lose?" Faith inquired.

"Not really. She can't weigh more than a hundred pounds. I'm almost twice that," Sarah said.

"Do we go for it?" Faireuza asked.

"Yeah. We should," Jensen said.

"Anyone opposed?" Faireuza inquired. Silence befell the small group. "Okay. Then we shall."

The green team turned toward the two women dressed in yellow. "We accept your challenge. What are the terms?"

"Everything we have except our flag against everything that you have except your flag."

Sarah was shocked by such a high wager. They gave pause to reevaluate their decision. "Whoa. Wait a minute. Everything? Why not just a few sleeping bags?"

"Are you going to feel guilty if you take everything from us?" Helen asked. "If you do, you can always give back what you don't want and call it charity. It's a good business practice," Helen assured them. Harley continued to look at the ground with an occasional glance at the women dressed in green.

Faireuza breathed a sigh of relief. She didn't want the women to freeze, so the option to give back some of the prizes sounded appealing. Faireuza shook hands with Helen and Sarah with Harley.

****

"Go." Drill Abernathy said as she and Drill Sanders flanked the opponents.

Sarah was semi-relaxed watching Harley, who herself seemed totally relaxed and off-guard. She continued to look at the ground. Slowly she raised her baton out in front of her and dropped it to the ground. The baton fell, angling toward Sarah. It struck the ground and bounced. The top fell forward as the bottom came up. A quick step and Harley's foot connected with the bottom end of the baton. The quick snap of her leg, like a field goal kicker, launched the jousting stick up, hard.

Sarah didn't have time to move. There was nothing she could have done except be wary of this shocking surprise in a small package. The baton impacted her right eye. The force from the kick caused the baton to burst one of the airbags inside it as it stopped suddenly bouncing backwards off Sarah's face and landed on the ground at her feet.

Sarah toppled backward, landing flat on her back. Her body bounced slightly, almost coming off the ground again before gravity pulled her down and hugged her close. All the cheers died out. Not even the yellow team cheered. They hadn't cheered from the beginning. They had all stood with poker faces waiting for the outcome of the match. Harley calmly walked over and picked up her baton. She stood over Sarah's limp body and tapped it twice on the side.

"One. Two," Drill Abernathy said. Drill Sanders blew the whistle. Drill Abernathy rushed to Sarah's side, checking her vital signs. Drill Witcom brought up the first aid kit and a bit of ammonia brought Sarah back to consciousness. In her foggy haze she struggled to make sense of what had just happened.

Harley waved Helen to come into the ring. Helen pointed to the sky. "See those clouds above? Those clouds usually precede a storm. None of us are anywhere near prepared to deal with what is coming."

"Don't you see? The drills have set us up to fail if we couldn't put the puzzle together. There are enough materials for everyone if we all work together. We all have pieces of the puzzle. If we put it all together, we will have what we need to survive this challenge. Blue team, you have a stainless pot to cook in. We have a simple filter to screen off the large bits of mud. Green team you have a huge tarp with a hole in the middle. That could be used for a chimney. You also have the stainless pot and copper tubing that can be used to create drinkable water."

"Wait. Wait." Elizabeth was puzzled. "How do you know what we have in our camps?"

"I went through each camp last night to see what you had. No one has enough to survive what is coming," Harley said.

"I'm a light sleeper. You couldn't have gotten into our camp without me knowing. I tossed and turned most of the night because I was cold and couldn't sleep," Brenda said, as she looked at her fellow sisters in red.

"I know. When you rolled over, you pushed the flag over and it leaned against number two."

"There's no way you could have…"

"Check the top of the pole. I put a small square of duct tape on top," Harley said. Her personal drill, Drill Walker, grinned from ear to ear because she had watched the whole thing the night before, with the aid of night vision goggles. Sarah was sitting up now and listening. Drill Witcom was by her side, steadying her. "Green team, there's one on top of yours, too."

Faireuza jerked their flag down to look at the top of the pole. A simple small square of tape lay neatly displayed on the brass cap that covered the end of the pole. She looked back at the tiny little woman in the ring, the one who had knocked out their toughest member from eight feet away.

"Nine." Harley turned to the leader of the blue team. "I put one in your left shoe." Elizabeth ripped her shoe off to find a square of tape placed inside. She looked back at Harley for an explanation of how that could have happened. "You have very ticklish feet, which made it difficult to put the shoe back on. Drill Walker wanted to stop me, until I told her what I was doing. Five was there too."

Elizabeth looked at Drill Walker, who was doing everything she could to keep from busting up laughing. Embarrassment and shame came over Elizabeth and her team. The knowledge that someone had been in their camp and could have taken anything that they wanted was an insult. Leaving a humiliating mark and not taking anything seemed worse than if they had.

"Do we want to work together and be warm and dry tonight?" Helen asked. All the students gave a nod. "Okay. Red team and green team, I would like you to pick a spot for a shelter. Pick somewhere where the water won't flood us out if it's a heavy rain."

122

THE SCHOLARSHIP

"I can put together a water purifier. It's kinda like making a still," Heather Smith said.

"How do you know about stills?" Helen asked.

"My pappy taught me how to make one. You boil the water off and condense it in the copper tubing. So, we will need a stove and an icebox."

"We're fresh out of those." Elizabeth's condescending tone struck a wrong chord with many in the group.

"Nine, do you want to try saying that with a little more enthusiasm?" Drill Douglas chimed in.

"We're fresh out of those, but we can find something else that will work." Elizabeth looked at Drill Douglas for a slight nod of approval.

"Okay. The yellow team will split up to help anywhere an extra hand is needed. We have enough sleeping bags for everyone except two people." Helen announced.

"Why are we lacking two sleeping bags?" Galaxy asked.

"Probably because we're expected to have two guards on duty throughout the night," Sarah said, regaining her feet with the help of Drill Witcom and Samantha Owens. "You've got a heck of a kick number eight."

"Sorry. I think I might have kicked it harder than I intended," Harley said trying to look small and back away.

"How did you do that?" Sarah asked.

"I have a black belt in taekwondo, and I was a college soccer player."

"Ladies, we need to get things going unless we want to sleep in the rain tonight." Helen brought the attention back to the major obstacle that they faced: preparing for the storm.

Chapter XIII

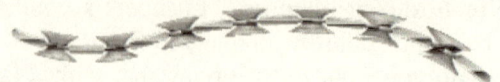

The class stretched the canvas across the grassy knob. Axes and shovels dug into the field to remove an eight-inch-wide strip of sod. The women worked together to stack up the pieces of sod to create four walls. This was the result of a suggestion from Ulyssa, who reminded them that pioneers who settled across the prairie often used it to build the walls of a shelter. The idea to use the sod for the walls was agreed upon by most of the class. They layered it like bricks, overlapping and interlocking each piece to form a sturdy wall. Once all the sod was gone from what would be the interior floor of the shelter, they stripped it from the ground nearby.

The downside of their shelter location was that the walk to the porta-potty was now a bit longer than the centralized location of the original setup. The yellow team brought all the sleeping bags from their camp and stacked them nearby. Teams of every color flag worked feverishly as the storm clouds started to roll in. The yellow and red teams had most of the firewood that had been provided by the academy, along with a couple sections of triple-wall chimney pipe.

THE SCHOLARSHIP

They decided that they would make two V-channels to capture and direct water to the water barrel from the canvas tarp roof. The empty plastic water bottles from their starter case were cut in half and used to make gutters to funnel the rainwater from the roof to the water barrel which was positioned just inside the wall. A crossbuck saw, a roll of duct tape, a small paring knife and a pair of industrial scissors rounded out the simple tools they were given to make all these elements work.

The blue team constructed a fireplace using mud, the clay pots from the green team and wooden boards taken from the scattering of pallets. Two openings on either end of the fireplace allowed it to be fed from either side and for some of the heat to radiate out in the rectangular dwelling. Two-by-fours framed the small doorway where two members of the red team were fitting a tarp to the opening.

The ceiling, barely six feet high on one side and five feet on the other, provided a slope to channel the water to the taped bottle plumbing. Lumber was tied together and stretched across the top of the shelter to support the tarp.

Many 'excuse me' and 'sorry' statements were exchanged as the women continually bumped into one another. Tensions came and went quickly, as they all knew that the urgency of building the shelter was priority. Each team leader continually called for patience and hustle at the same time, stifling any outbursts quickly and moving to finish building the shelter before the rain started.

"Alright. Let's get that tarp up!" Faireuza called. Several women stood inside the dwelling, ready with several sections of sod. Stretching one edge of the tarp across the top of the wall, the women stacked the sod along its edge to hold down the canvas on the prevailing wind side. The lumber frame was

125

nestled into simple notches in the sod wall, and with the help of the wind, the tarp blew over the anchoring row of sod in a neat fold, just as the first drops of rain began.

"Boulders! Get those boulders up. We want this thing looking like a castle," Elizabeth called. Women scrambled to add weight to the edges of the tarp. The yellow team grabbed armloads of sleeping bags and hauled them into the sod house. Elizabeth and Heather assembled the chimney and shoved it through the hole in the middle of the tarp. The hole in the canvas was still much bigger than the stove pipe. Rain and wind were going to get inside if they didn't figure out a way to seal it.

"What do we do about that?" Sarah asked Elizabeth.

"I don't know."

"Do we have enough duct tape to tape it closed?" Faireuza asked.

"No." Harley held up the nearly depleted roll of tape. "We used most of it on the bottles."

"Do we have excess of anything else?" Sarah asked. The women close to her looked around for anything that might not be in use.

"What if we use the tarp from the door?" Evelynn offered.

"Then what will we use for the door?" asked Galaxy.

Silence befell the crowded chamber. Eyes darted around in the dimming light to search for a solution. "We'll use one of the sleeping bags. Two people will have to be on guard at all times anyway… so why not just make it three?" Faireuza said. The group nodded and mumbled their approval. "Pull that door down and let's see what we can do with it."

"What do you have, Eleven? What are you looking at?" Helen asked, as she hunched under the low ceiling.

THE SCHOLARSHIP

Maria held up the small blocks of wax. "I find these smashed in the ground earlier. I don't know what we can do with them."

The rain and wind increased, letting its presence be known. The first drops of water began to trickle into the bottle funnel and gradually make its way to the freshwater barrel.

"It's going to be really dark in here in a minute. How will we work then?" one of the women mumbled, and a few of them exchanged worried glances.

"I know what to do," Helen said. She took a short board and stabbed it into the wall, anchoring it into the sod and creating a shelf. "Scoop out a handful of mud and bring it over here." She pulled out the scissors she was carrying in her pocket and cut a short length of rope hanging from the tied lumber above her head.

Maria was baffled by the request but complied anyway. Helen took one of the blocks of wax and cut a slit in it with the edge of the scissors, stuffed the rope deep into the cut and mashed the block of wax back together. She then trimmed the top of the rope and set it on the shelf. "Okay. Put that mud around it, but don't get any on top." Helen walked to the fireplace where the blue team had just gotten the fire going. Light flickered across the dirt floor of the shelter. With a sliver of wood, she lit the end of the stick and carefully walked it over to the improvised candle.

A moment of holding the flame to the waxed rope, the wick caught and began to spread light across the interior of the shelter. "Four, Eleven, you are goddesses." Brenda said. A cheer went up as congratulatory pats on the back accentuated the gratitude.

"We need someone to go up on the roof to put the tarp on. Someone light on their feet," Faireuza called out.

"Number eight, where you at?" Elizabeth called.

"I don't think Eight is very light on her feet. I think Twelve can attest to that." Stacey Adams volunteered the wholesome humor at the expense of Sarah's ego. Laughter filled the room as the storm complained outside.

"Eight, are you ready?" Elizabeth asked.

"Yes ma'am," she said, eager to be finished with the project so they could settle in for the night. The class looked tired, but in good spirits as the final piece of the puzzle was ready to be put in place.

Sarah, Evelynn and Jensen escorted Harley outside to hoist her up on the roof. Helen stayed close to the chimney to hold up the boards in case they wanted to buckle due to Harley's added weight. Harley kept the small tarp tucked neatly under her arm as she stepped gingerly on the boards supporting the canvas roof. A hole had already been cut in the small plastic tarp, just a bit smaller than the diameter of the chimney. Smoke filled her face as the wind shifted one way and then the other. She held her breath and shut her eyes as the acrid cloud passed across her face.

Kneeling on the two-by-fours, Harley set to work fitting the tarp over the hole. She tore the hole a little to allow it over the end of the triple-wall chimney pipe. Quickly, she wrapped the tarp and pipe with two and a half wraps of duct tape, creating a seal to keep the weather out. Tossing four ropes over the edge of the building, she then placed four rocks given her at each corner to hold down the tarp. On the ground below, Sarah pulled the rope to stretch the tarp out so it wouldn't flap in the wind as the storm picked up its ferocity, then lined what she could reach with a few more rocks around the edge of the tarp.

THE SCHOLARSHIP

"C'mon, Eight, let's get inside." Sarah commanded as she hammered an anchor into the side of the sod house and tied the rope to it while Faireuza and two others did likewise to the other ropes. Eight stood on the edge of the building ready to jump the four feet to the ground.

A flash of light ignited the night sky, blinding anyone who happened to be looking in its direction. The air exploded with sound instantaneously and shook the earth. The tingle of electricity ran up Sarah's leg. She was looking at the ground when the lightning hit. Her senses dulled instantly from the explosion, but she still saw Harley fly through the air and land thirty feet away. Sarah looked to see vapor rise off of the woman as her body lay on the rain-soaked grass, lifeless and unmoving.

Sarah screamed, without hearing her own voice. Her numb and tired muscles ceased to exist and were replaced by dread-fueled motion. Sarah lunged for the tiny woman.

"No. No. No. Eight! Eight!" Sarah screamed. She smacked Harley's still face, almost brutally. "Wake up, Harley!" Raindrops spattered off Harley's lifeless eyes.

As they heard Sarah screaming Harley's name, a sense of alarm radiated throughout the crowded shelter. Students poured out of the tiny entrance and gathered around their downed colleague. Drill Hooks rushed up from just a few steps away. She took one look and her face drained of any color. She keyed the mic on her radio. "I have a student down. I have a student down. I need an ambulance and the paramedic kit."

The radio squawked back asking for more information. "Number Eight, Harley Whittaker was struck by lightning. One student is already performing CPR on her!" Sarah had checked for a pulse and then immediately started with chest compressions.

129

"I've called for the paramedics. They're en route," came an answering voice over the radio.

Sarah continued the chest compressions while Faireuza breathed into Harley's mouth. The rest of the students stood by, watching and murmuring among themselves. Sarah repeatedly rocked her straightened arms as she pushed against the tiny woman's chest.

Wails, gasps and whimpers began resonating through the small crowd. "You two, run and grab a stretcher from the infirmary," Drill Hooks barked. "The rest of you, do something to block the rain here."

Several students rushed inside the shelter and emerged with a half-dozen sleeping bags and stretched them out close behind Sarah and Faireuza. Sarah didn't notice that the rain had stopped assaulting her back: she just kept in rhythm with her friend, pausing only long enough for Faireuza to give a breath of life.

Drill Hawkins bolted out the back door of the barracks, running towards the group with her feet barely touching the ground. She moved like a demon was hot on her trail. Her form wasn't graceful, but her purpose was all-powerful. She carried an AED in one hand and an emergency trauma kit in the other. The mud caused her to weave slightly as she raced toward the group of women.

She slid to a halt and knelt next to Faireuza. "Keep going," she said to Sarah and Faireuza, as she ripped through the trauma kit, pulling the scissors from the assigned pocket. She cut up one side of the large number eight on Harley's sweatshirt. A split-second pause from Sarah's compressions and the sweatshirt was off, exposing Eight's skinny body. Two more snaps of the scissors and her sports bra pulled aside exposing her bare chest to the elements.

130

THE SCHOLARSHIP

Drill Hawkins quickly assembled the AED and hit its start button. Sirens split the night air like that of the now-distant thunder. The flashes of red and blue lights struggled to reach through the onslaught of pouring rain from the advancing ambulance.

"Get back." Drill Hawkins commanded.

Sarah and Faireuza scooted back as the voice commands and beeps from the box warned of the life-saving shock that was but a moment away. Harley's body lurched in the mud as the electric jolt contracted all the muscles. The muscles relaxed and her body sagged back into the mud again. Several women pleaded for the ambulance to hurry while others cried to the heavens for the return of their sister.

"Harley!" Sarah clutched her hands in the muddy grass waiting. Tears rolled down her face, mixing with the slowing rain. Faireuza sat back on her heels. She couldn't utter a word, only stare at her classmate in horrified shock. Again, the box told everyone to stay back, and again, electricity coursed through Harley's body. Her arched body defied gravity and then sank back into the mud after the electricity cut off.

Drill Hawkins stabbed her fingers on the woman's neck to check for a pulse. "I've got a faint pulse. Keep breathing for her."

Faireuza pushed one breath into Harley's lungs and then Harley vomited. Drill Hawkins rolled her to her side to keep her from inhaling her own stomach contents. The ambulance had turned off its siren and was following a trail of drills scattered along the path that led to Harley. Each one flagged the boxy vehicle toward the terrified crowd. The automatic four-wheel-drive kicked in when a tire spun in the soft grass covering the soil, but the driver had a bit of cowboy in him and didn't shy from the possibility of getting stuck. The dual tires

131

on the rear axle bobbed over the uneven ground, making steady progress to the small crowd.

"There's no pulse!" Drill Hawkins cried out. She rolled Harley onto her back and listened for the prompt from the box.

"Perform chest compressions." Sarah immediately jumped back to her task of trying to restart the woman's heart.

"Check for pulse," the machine ordered. The ambulance arched a turn close to the gathering, stopping with the back doors just past the group. Drill Hawkins checked again for a pulse. "No pulse," she called out.

"No pulse. Stay clear," the red box ordered. Sarah and the others sat back on their heels, waiting for the shock to be delivered. Harley's body clenched again and then relaxed. *"Check for pulse."*

"I've got a pulse," Drill Hawkins said as the EMT knelt in the mud next to her. Faireuza gave two last puffs of air to the woman as the EMT wrenched open his bag and pulled out an Ambu bag to place over Harley's nose and mouth. The students standing guard swapped positions, still holding the bed rolls up to shield the life and death struggle from the returning onslaught of rain.

The EMTs quickly packaged up the fragile little body and slid her onto the gurney, then into the bright interior of the ambulance. A few short minutes later, the red and blue flashing lights began their steady descent to the pavement, then out of sight. The rain began to hammer down harder.

Like a group of penguins, the women stood close together with their backs to the wind and watched the flickering red and blue lights disappear into the storm. The temporary sleeping bag shelter now hung about the women's heads and shoulders as they watched their friend vanish into the night. Worry and dread hung on every woman's mind. There was nothing that

132

THE SCHOLARSHIP

they could do now: It was out of their hands and into those who were trained for emergencies like this. And into the hands of God.

Drill Hawkins had been handed a poncho though it would do her little good. She was already soaked to the bone and mud covered her uniform from the knees down. "Everyone to the barracks. We'll talk about this inside."

The students started for the warmth and comfort of the large building. One person stood out from the rest and stood firm, like a large oak tree. Helen looked at the small deflated group. "No, Drill Hawkins."

Fire ignited under the blue hood of the poncho. Before Drill Hawkins could utter a word of authority, Helen continued: "I'm going back in this little shelter. I'm going to stoke the fire, collect some water, dry off and pray for my sister.

"This lesson is about loyalty and respect. If I give up now, I won't learn the value of either. If I go into the barracks, I'll not have any respect for myself. I believe in this program. I believe in every moral fiber that it teaches. I don't want to miss out on one ounce of what I can learn.

"Drill Hawkins, you taught us integrity, doing what is right legally and morally. Legally, I should do as you say. Morally, I cannot. I'm not going to disrespect my sister or this program. I'm going to stay the course and finish. I will not let anything influence me away from doing what is right."

Helen turned and ducked her large frame through the tiny door. Sarah looked at Drill Hawkins, who stood like an expressionless statue. Sarah had a growing respect for the drill, and the no-nonsense way that she handled business, but she knew that Helen was right. They couldn't let any obstacle dissuade them. If they did, it would be the same as drugs, alcohol and violence pulling them back into a vicious cycle.

Sarah stood up straight, defying the downpour. "Drill Hawkins, with all due respect, Four is right. I need to do what is right, also." Sarah walked through the rain and ducked into their little building. One by one the students ducked inside the shelter. The orange glow grew atop the stovepipe as the wood was piled into the clay pot fireplace.

Drill Hooks waited next to Drill Hawkins for a long moment. Water dripped off their rain gear and onto the saturated ground. Drill Hooks stepped forward and ducked inside the small shelter.

The students shuffled quietly through the crowded space, settling into the most comfortable spots they could find. Sarah and Helen tended the fire from either side of the fireplace. Several stopped to stare a moment at the drill who stood just inside the door. Drill Hooks quietly embedded a camera into the wall next to the ceiling. She adjusted the lens to capture a large swathe of the students activities, who were now settling into place and reaching out for each other's hands. She ducked back out and sloshed to Drill Hawkins.

"They've got to be the best students that this place has ever seen," Drill Hooks said. Drill Hawkins blinked at the unusual comment and looked at Drill Hooks for an explanation. "I can't think of anything else we could do to teach them what they just learned right now. I think they got this."

Drill Hawkins stared across the dimly-lit field. Fear and horror from another dark night kept her frozen in place. Drill Hooks looked upon the face in the limited light from the complex field lights, recognizing the faraway look she had seen before. She had learned that gentle coaxing was necessary to bring Drill Hawkins back to the present.

"Come on. Our little sister is going to need all the prayers she can get." Drill Hooks nudged her colleague's arm and walked with her back to the barracks.

Chapter XIV

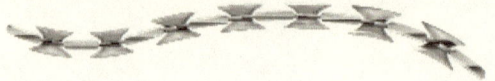

Vapor rose off the field as the first rays of light stretched over the eastern horizon. It was the second morning since their sister was blown off the roof by the lightning. All night they prayed together, holding hands in the cramped shelter. They constantly tended the fire and took turns drying their clothes on a makeshift clothesline.

The dehydrated packs of food were brought out and distributed among the students three times during the previous day's drizzle. They spent their day alternating between basic personal hygiene, eating, mending their shelter and praying. The drills watched from their security control room and observed the loyalty of the group. The subtle bickering had melted away as they tirelessly awaited news of their sister.

A shrill whistle pierced the quiet serene landscape. Drill Abernathy ripped the tarp off the simple wooden frame opening. "Get outside you digits." Whistles and garbage cans blasted the air like a horribly out-of-tune orchestra.

Sarah and her classmates jumped from the clatter. Another corner of the tarp ripped open as Drill Witcom pulled

THE SCHOLARSHIP

the boulders off the edge and allowed bright sunlight to blind those still struggling to pull themselves out of a slumber.

One by one they emerged into the bright, warming rays. Chaos engulfed the disoriented class, like that of their integrity lesson. Clothes were tugged on, feet were stomped into boots and laces haphazardly knotted.

"Move your asses," Drill Hooks screamed. "Get over to the field. Find your number and plant your feet in the square."

The drills stood on either side of the path corralling them and ushering them to their doom like ancient natives driving herds of animals off cliffs for slaughter. Each one yelled for the students to make haste to their assigned square at the end of the field.

Sarah raced across the field, struggling into her sweat top, much like the rest of her classmates. Two days in a cramped little shelter left their muscles complaining and sometimes refusing to work. Many students hobbled, gripping a cramped muscle as they approached the station they were instructed to go to.

Crude boxes numbered one through twenty-five were waiting for them on the damp grass. Numbers ten, eight and seven were omitted, as the class had now shrunk by three people, one of whom they all prayed would come back to them soon. Sarah quickly found her square and looked at the plate of lies at her feet. "*Great. Another lesson on integrity. At least I get the small plate this time*," she thought. She stole a glance down the line of women. The fifty-pound plate was placed in front of Helen. Sarah thought it must be from her disobedient claim of sticking to the moral fibers of integrity instead of the legal fibers of rule and law.

She stood in her square at parade rest, her eyes locked forward and her ears tuned to the next command. She heard the

137

last few sounds of feet shuffling through the grass to find their spots.

"Group, attention." Drill Abernathy stood a few paces in front of the line. "At ease." The students returned their hands to the smalls of their backs and stepped sideways with their right feet. "It seems we need another lesson on integrity. You are the students. You will listen and heed our commands. Somehow this lesson was forgotten."

Sarah rolled her eyes. Everyone knew it wasn't forgotten, but just like some parts of society, those who have authority can make their own rules as they see fit. Sarah began tuning out when it became apparent that they should have been good little soldiers and done what they were told instead of doing what felt right. "So much for morals," she mumbled under her breath. As Drill Abernathy droned on about following orders, Sarah wondered about trying to escape again. Could she dodge the cameras and outwit the drills? Could she slip out over the fence and get away? Could she make it to Mexico or further? Would she even be able to carve out a decent life there if she did make it?

"When I say 'move,' you're going to pick up that ugly little plate and you're going to lift it up over your head. You're going to hold it there until you are told that you can put it down. When I call your number, you will turn and carry that plate over your head to your drill. If you drop it, you will have to start over. Do you understand?"

"Yes, Drill Abernathy," the students said, almost in unison.

"Ready. Move," Drill Abernathy snapped at the students. Sarah bent down and grabbed the plate of lies and heaved it over her head. She stood waiting for her number to be called. She knew that even a five-pound bag of flour would become heavy if held over her head long enough. Twenty-five pounds would shorten that wait time considerably.

"Four!" Drill Abernathy called out Helen's number first. She held the plate proudly over her head, turned and marched it to the other side of the field. One by one Drill Abernathy called their numbers straight down the line from number one to twenty-five. She paused five seconds before calling each number. "Twelve," Drill Abernathy called out to Sarah. She turned to see all the drills lined up on the halfway line. All those who preceded her were now standing in front of their drill. Their plates were still held above their heads, except for Helen who held her heavier plate at her waist.

Sarah tried her best to fake the pride that others seemed to be exhibiting as she carried the plate of lies above her head. She stopped at the line like the rest of her classmates and looked ahead into Drill Witcom's eyes.

"You did well out there," Drill Witcom began. "I'm impressed with your initiative. The respect you have for Eight and Four is commendable. You made a very honorable decision when you consider the harsh consequences. You chose to stand by your friend and the morals she believed in. I'm proud of you. You're doing well and I can see that you're going to accomplish a lot here. I know you have it in you to do something to prove to the world that you're worth every bit of effort we, and you, put into your education." Sarah nodded her head. "When Drill Abernathy gives the command, you'll lower the plate and we'll finish carrying it to the other end together."

Sarah nodded and breathed a sigh of relief. It didn't appear that they would be running laps carrying the plate back and forth like their first night in the barracks.

"You look like hell warmed over," Drill Witcom said. Sarah smiled at the compliment. She never thought that phrase

139

could ever be a compliment, but after the last several days of learning and accomplishing what they had, she was happy to wear the 'hell warmed over' look.

"Plates down," Drill Abernathy called. "Hand one side off to your drill and finish together."

Together the drills and students hauled the plates to the far end of the field and stacked them neatly in their storage crate.

They were ordered to assemble back in their teams facing their shelter. They watched Master Drill Ietel pace back and forth, looking at the lumpy sod house. He called Twenty-one and Four into the sod house, along with their drills. Moments later they reemerged and stepped back into formation. "Class, attention!" Master Drill Ietel barked.

Dean Vickery stepped to the front of the formation and took charge after returning Master Drill Ietel's salute. "At ease."

Dean Vickery scanned the dirty faces and disheveled hair of the class. Worried faces mixed with hopeful eyes and sober attitudes stared back at him. "I make it a point to be here during this part of the program. It always amazes me how a group of students can fall apart or come together as one. I almost didn't make it today because I was waiting on some news to come in. Eight had a rough go of it, but she is awake. I talked to her this morning."

A sigh of relief radiated through the formation. Whispers to the Lord could be heard as smiles and tears of joy transformed many long faces.

"The doctors say that she will make a full recovery, but it may take a while before she's released. We don't know if she will come back here or have to go to prison. They might even give her a chance to reclass. We're talking with the board to

THE SCHOLARSHIP

see what the best course of action is. We have our best people on this and want her to succeed the same as we want all of you to succeed. We have even called in one of the best doctors in the U.S. to consult and oversee her injuries.

"It appears that your prayers were heard. To that, I'd say that you have learned the concept of loyalty and you will honor her by continuing that loyalty from here on. You have all learned so much in the past several days. I want to commend all of you on your achievements. I've seen a change in this whole class both as a unit and as individuals.

"One thing we haven't seen before is a sod house." Grins spread across the class at the acknowledgement of their innovation, doing something new and unique that was recognized as a success. "It's a novel idea and one that proved very effective over the past couple days. It appears that you made it work and were able to gather water from the rain and from boiling the muddy water from the pit. One thing I want to point out is that this is a school that teaches business. When you see an opportunity, grab it with all your might and keep it for yourself until you're established. After that, be sure to donate to your favorite charities. Twelve, you did just that. You saw an opportunity to secure a valuable item and you took it.

"That's what business is about, finding opportunities and capitalizing on them. If you know someone who is hungry, feed them and they will pay. Find something that someone wants and offer it to them at a fair price. Just like Sarah saw value in obtaining what someone else wanted. Her team was able to negotiate for a couple of key pieces of equipment just for taking the initiative to obtain a desirable object.

"Eight and Four put all the puzzle pieces together. They understood what was going on. Four saw what it would take for all of you to succeed and she wagered everything her team

141

had for the opportunity to be heard and it paid off. As long as you keep standing back up, learning from your failures and keep driving forward, I guarantee that you will be successful and happy.

"Not everyone will be a multi-billionaire and not everyone will live under a bridge. Most of you will be somewhere in the middle. One or two might end up with a penthouse suite and a few of you might have to live under a bridge for a while. Either way you will be successful as long as you don't give up.

"Our policy is not to graduate you until you have the skills to be successful. If you do find yourself living under a bridge, you can be confident that you won't be there for long because you'll always have your classmates who can help point you toward another opportunity and give you the encouragement that you need.

"I want to commend all of you for a job well done. As a reward, we've brought in a few modern washing machines to help you clean up your acts." Smiles and whispered cheers rippled through the formation. "Our job is to show you that how you lived before doesn't have to be your future. You can rise above those influences from your past and create your own future. That's why we put so much emphasis on the seven core values.

"We're not here to make soldiers of you. There are other organizations that do that. Many of our graduates opt to join the military, and they do exceptionally well there. We're here to give you the tools and encouragement to live full and productive lives without having to look over your shoulder every day. However, discipline is a key ingredient to success. You will need discipline to be at work on time every day. You'll need discipline to run a business and you'll need

142

discipline to keep your families organized and healthy. We are not here to tell you what to do. We are here to partner with you to make you better. We want you to leave here and only come back to volunteer or for the annual picnic, which has some amazing food, by the way. We let our top culinary students cater the event, so it is in your best interest to make time every summer to attend. It also gives previous graduates a chance to network and connect with some good talent from graduates and soon-to-be graduates.

"After you complete the boot camp section, you will not be told what to do. You will be given suggestions. It is your job to evaluate and choose the correct path for you. There will be many decisions that are wrong. There will be many decisions that will be correct. It is your job to think about the consequences down each of those roads before making that decision. You can think about them right now, when you're staring at the ceiling at night or sometime in the future. For example, you can make the decision right now that you will not ever key your cheating boyfriend's car."

A snicker rumbled through the class. Dean Vickery continued, "You're better than that. You can make that decision to get up every morning and greet the day with enthusiasm. You can make that decision to have an omelet three days a week. You can make that decision to say no to your friends when they want you to go out. You can make those decisions right now and hold them so close to your heart, so when those moments of temptation come, it will be easy to say "no." It will be easy because you made that decision right here, right now to be the person that you want to be. And if your friends chastise you for sticking to the path you set for yourself, or start frowning at your success, then question if they are actually good friends in the first place. If they can't be happy that you are trying to succeed, then they don't need to be in your life.

"Our country has a wide expanse of opportunities for you. You can own a restaurant and serve amazing bar-b-que ribs. You can invent the next iPhone and give Apple a run for their money. You can be a dedicated mechanic to a boss who treats you well and makes sure you are paid on time every time. This country needs smart people as well as skilled people, but everyone needs to know a little bit of how to run a business. From the skills we teach you here, you can run a multibillion-dollar company or your own family's budget.

"Think of the world as a giant frozen lake. Parts of that frozen lake are flat and smooth, while other parts are riddled with cracks and lumps. The part that is legal is the flat smooth part where you fall down, get up and fall down again, until you learn to skate well. Then it becomes more fun and you get to enjoy gliding along with grace and style.

"The law is your boundary. Sometimes it's a big sign that says, 'thou shalt not kill,' and sometimes it's a tiny line in the ice that says, "it is illegal to use a lasso to catch a fish." The students chuckled at the absurd law.

Sarah wondered what ridiculous person drafted that law and why, while Dean Vickery paced in front of the formation. He looked thoroughly pleased, like a father watching his children after they scored the game-winning point. "It's a real law in Tennessee. Look it up. We have a hot breakfast for you. After which the drills will have more instructions."

"Sir?" Helen asked.

"Yes, number four?"

"Can we send a picture of our shelter along with a get-well card to Eight?"

THE SCHOLARSHIP

"Absolutely. I don't know if she'll recognize you. You look like some tribe from the Amazon, all covered in mud."

The hot breakfast of eggs, sausage and waffles was highly cherished after close to a week of bland, dehydrated food. By taking the simple luxuries away, like a hot meal or an automatic washer, the school had taught each student to be grateful for what most had previously considered basic necessities.

The sod house was disassembled, and the sod put back in the ground. The tools were put away and the women washed their clothes, not by hand, but with the automatic washers. They erected clothes lines to let the warm sun and gentle breeze dry their clothes.

Chapter XV

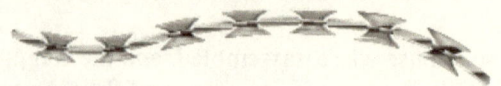

It was Tuesday, and the second day of their week-long, selfless service run. The teams alternated between picking up roadside trash and volunteering at the soup kitchen, the animal shelter or the senior citizens center. The long lesson on giving back to society was drilled into each student and cemented in place with the appreciation from those that they helped.

Sarah dipped the ladle into the pot of beef stew dozens of times as the line in the Salem soup kitchen seemed to keep endlessly growing. All morning her team had helped the kitchen staff prepare the multiple pots of food to divvy out to those struggling to rebuild their lives. Jensen Michaels stood next to her, rationing out bread to those holding a tray.

Jensen and Sarah pined over the little boy who flashed them a sincere, flirty smile just before he hid in his mother's pant leg. "He is so adorable." Jensen said.

"I know," Sarah agreed. "He has such a wonderful smile."

"Thank you," said the young boy's mother.

"I sure like that one-sided dimple," Jensen said, as she placed two slices of bread on the tray for the mother and son team.

THE SCHOLARSHIP

"Me, too. You are so adorable." Sarah reached a hand out to tickle his cheek. "Oh, my gosh. Look at those blue eyes. Have you ever seen such blue eyes, Eighteen?" Jensen didn't respond.

"Eighteen?" Sarah looked over at her teammate.

The loaf of bread she carried was now smashed inside her fist. Her hands shook with a mix of fear and anger. Her eyes stared straight ahead at the man standing at the end of the line. "Eighteen, what's wrong?"

Jensen dropped the bread and picked up a knife from the serving counter. She moved toward the end of the counter, pressing her palm hard into the hilt of the blade.

"Eighteen, no!" Sarah scolded her friend and teammate, but Jensen continued around the end of the serving counter.

Afraid for her friend, Sarah took two quick steps, wrapped Jensen in a bear hug and trapped her arms. Then she hauled her through the kitchen door. "Fifteen. Three. Can you go on the serving line please? Drill Simpson, we need your help."

Faireuza and Lisa jumped to the task as Drill Simpson sped around the prep counters to aid in wrenching the knife from Jensen's hand.

"Jensen Marie, stop it," Drill Simpson ordered.

Jensen immediately quit struggling. She looked at Drill Simpson, then at the blade still clenched in her hand. Horror overtook her and she immediately released the knife. Crumpling to the floor, she almost toppled Sarah on top of her as her center of gravity buckled. Her hands flew to her face. "I'm sorry."

"Shhhh. You're alright," Drill Simpson said, in a soothing voice.

"Did I hurt anyone?" Jensen cried between sobs.

"No. You didn't." Drill Simpson talked softly to Jensen.

"Did anyone see?"

"Only Twelve and myself."

Jensen nodded her head still hiding behind her hands. Light sobs continued as Jensen broke down on the kitchen floor. Drill Witcom came to kneel at her side as well and Sarah took a step back to allow them room. She looked out the window at the line of people waiting to be served.

"What happened? What did you see?" Drill Simpson asked.

"I saw him. I saw his face. Like in my nightmares when he attacks me. I must have had a nightmare flashback or something."

"What's he look like?" Sarah asked.

Drill Witcom waved Sarah off, but Jensen answered anyway. "He's got a goatee with a little bit of grey. He has green eyes and his head is balding. I dug a nail deep into his skin next to his left eye. His friends laughed at him for being small. I didn't know what they were talking about until they each took their turn. He got angry when they made fun of him and beat me instead of them until I passed out. When I woke, he was on top of me again.

"I was blindfolded, but I could see under the bottom a little. I saw a tattoo of a spider crawling over a skull. I could smell the mint and cigarette smoke that came off his breath."

"Did you report it?"

Jensen nodded her head. "They said that forensics found three different DNAs."

"Three people attacked you?" Drill Witcom asked.

Jensen nodded her head again. "I thought I saw him once before. I was going to kill him for what he did, but I actually beat up a man who only looked like him. That's why I'm here."

THE SCHOLARSHIP

"You say a goatee, green eyes and a scar next to his eye?" Sarah asked.

"Yes."

"I see a few dirty tables. I'm going to go clean them up," Sarah said and took the wash bucket out amongst the homeless. She started at the closest table and quickly made her way along the line to where the man with a scruffy beard and green eyes stood patiently.

Sarah finished wiping a nearby table off, collected her bucket and turned, purposely bumping into the man. "Oh. I'm sorry sir. I forgot that you were there."

"Oh. No worries, miss."

"I'm terribly sorry. This is my first time here. I feel a little clumsy and awkward." Sarah said biting her bottom lip to give the impression of a meek little child. She was searching the man's face for a scar next to his left eye.

"Don't worry, pretty lady. As long as you guys cooked a good meal, I'll be perfectly content."

"Are you sure, Mister…?" Sarah paused, raising the tone in her voice to hint at a last name.

"Just call me Bart," he said, giving her a fake smile.

"Hi. I'm Twelve," Sarah said, pointing at the numbers on her generic green sports jersey.

"You do look twelve. Is your mom here, too?" Bart laughed as his hungry green eyes feasted on her young flesh.

"She's here somewhere. I can get her for you if you like."

"Oh, maybe later, my dear. I'm a bit hungry. Will you let me know if there's any leftovers? I'd like to feed my dog a little."

"Aww. What kind of dog do you have?"

"She's a blonde mutt. She's old, maybe sixteen I think, but she still likes to howl with the best of them."

A chill ran up Sarah's back at the possible inference of the "dog's" description. Her new, good girl personality kicked in and prevented her from automatically bashing in his teeth.

****

Sarah had really made a start at being a good person. She liked her classmates and some of the drills. The program was different than any other she had heard her friends speak of. She really liked the dean's speech of building people up and not over-punishing a person for a mistake. She also liked the idea of going to school and belonging to an important piece of society. The morals and values she saw demonstrated in the school were beginning to soak into her soul.

The dean also talked about city crime and poverty as being part of the fabric of life. If a city put all the homeless in a complex, the city would have a larger poverty base because of the extra revenue it would cost the city to do that. The Schultz Business Academy focused on building the person who would in turn build or acquire their own dwelling and not rely on government handouts.

The women had been tricked into building a strong shelter that weathered a storm and the reward for that was confidence and pride. Sarah was beginning to understand the meaning behind the activities that were forced upon them. They were forced to learn the simple tools of life: survival, compassion, empathy, comradery and teamwork.

She was finding a new perspective on what she had previously thought about how life was lived. It took being forced away from her home and living situation before she could step back far enough to see the life she was living and its potential path of self-destruction. Now she could compare her

150

old life to how others lived, treating people with honor and respect.

On one occasion, she and Faireuza listened in as the dean told a grey-haired cleaning lady what a wonderful job she was doing and then invited her to an educational conference the following week. The woman politely declined, saying that she enjoyed the job she had and was happy where she was at.

"Why do you treat her like she's the most important person here? She's just a cleaning lady," Faireuza asked him later, when the cleaning lady wasn't around.

"Regardless of what you might hear to the contrary, businesspeople are always in the business of people. Would you see a cow come up and offer a glass of milk for a dollar?"

"No," Faireuza replied.

"The U.S. has a problem with overcrowded prisons and broken systems that only help a select few. Regardless, you can help someone who doesn't want help just by offering them help. It lets them know that they are worth your time.

"Our system at the Schultz Business Academy seems to work, but we still continue to work to prove the concept and develop it daily. It all starts in the mind. You have to want to change. Like a dog chasing a ball, that dog will do anything for that reward. Our goal is to show you a positive reward that you will wake up seeking every day."

"Wouldn't that make us mindless zombies, bent on getting a fix?"

"Yes, if you didn't add the bison."

"Bison? What's a bison?"

"You might know it as a buffalo." Recognition flashed in Faireuza and she relaxed a little. "Oh. So, what does that have to do with us?"

"There's always two sides to a coin. The bison is opposite of the dog. Bison don't play ball. They do their own thing. What we want you to learn is both sides and the wisdom to know which one to choose."

"So, how does this work when you talked to the cleaning woman?"

"I ask her to clean for me and she asks for money to pay her bills. That is her reward. Just like the dog chasing the ball. Like the bison, she can leave at any time. She does the cleaning in an efficient way so she can get home to her family sooner. We rely on each other to get a job done, therefore we are partners in this business transaction."

"But she's an employee."

"That's just where the company is rewarded a small bit of money to take care of the taxes and insurance for her."

"So, are we partners?" Sarah asked, stepping into the conversation.

"Yes. Think of it as a three-way partnership with society." Both Sarah and Faireuza gave the dean a crusty look, generated by their original perspective of society. "Society puts together rules in this game of life. When you break the rules, you have to pay, whether it's with your time, money or something else. In a way, society said that they don't want you, but we do.

"In turn," Dean Vickery continued, "we'll take you, polish you into gems and present you back to society." In exchange for that service, society buys products from us. We use that money to invest in you.

"That's why you should always treat everyone as an equal, especially in business. A lot of really great deals have been offered our students, just because they were polite to everyone, including the cleaning staff."

THE SCHOLARSHIP

Sarah and Faireuza pondered the different philosophy as they continued with their cleaning chores. "Do you believe all that garbage?" Sarah asked, still pessimistic about the goals of the program.

"I guess it sounds good. I was told it would be like boot camp. I didn't realize it would last longer than my original sentence."

"How long was that?"

"One year if I was good, three if I wasn't." Faireuza lifted the plastic bag out of the garbage can. She put it in their cart and shook out a new one. "What about you?"

"My lawyer didn't explain anything. He said, 'sign these or we'll see you in twenty-five years.'"

"Twenty-five years? Wow. What'd you do?"

"I accidentally hit a cop. They made it sound intentional."

"How'd they do that?"

"Me and my mom got into a fight. She went down, and I continued to hit her. The cop jumped in the middle and I clocked him. He was a bit dazed coming up off the ground. I kept screaming at my mother but somehow the audio and body cams that had the proof of that weren't introduced in my defense. My lawyer offered me this program, so I took it just to get out of Jefferson County." Sarah didn't tell Faireuza the primary reason she took the deal or the primary reason she had developed her distain for societal norms.

****

Sarah now understood what Dean Vickery had meant during their conversation about the cleaning lady and bison a few weeks prior. She could better see and understand the expressions of the homeless that they were serving.

Most of the people had eyes filled with fear, sadness, hopefulness or a mix of all three, but the man she had just bumped into had the eyes of a hunter. She recognized the anger and resentment buried deep inside him because she had stared at those same eyes in the mirror for years.

She made her way to the door where Faith was greeting people and holding a couple of the animals belonging to the homeless while their owners retrieved food for themselves and their pets. Sarah casually walked up and asked her, "See that tall guy with the balding head and the black ripped jacket?"

"Yeah. The one with the chevron patch?" Faith asked.

"Yeah. Eighteen flipped out a minute ago and thought she was hallucinating, seeing the guy who raped her. This guy matches her description, so if shit starts flying, block the door."

Faith nodded her head and smiled warmly at the next person walking through the door. Sarah wandered back through the crowd of homeless citizens and hastily wiped down a table on her way to the serving line. Facing away from the oncoming line and leaning in close to Faireuza, she donned a polite smile. "See the tall guy with a balding head and a black jacket?"

"Yeah, I see him." Faireuza dipped a generous ladle of hearty stew onto the next tray that presented itself. Lisa stood next to her, adding bread to each tray coming through.

"I don't think he's homeless. I think he's here looking for someone. Eighteen described him as the man who raped her. If he has a tattoo of a skull and spider on his chest then that would for sure nail him as her rapist."

"What do we do if he is?" Faireuza asked.

"I don't know. Anything to get him into custody of the police."

"We can't beat him up and we can't hold him."

154

THE SCHOLARSHIP

"I know. We have to think of something," Sarah said, flustered.

"Did Eighteen say anything else about this guy?" Faireuza asked, restraining her desire to use the word 'asshole.'

"She said that he was sensitive about the size of his..." Sarah let the statement hang until Faireuza's eyebrows lifted and she caught the meaning of the statement.

"Okay. I got this. I'll think of something." Faireuza dipped the ladle into the giant pot of stew again and looked at Sarah. "He won't get out of the building..." She dipped another ladle for the next tray. "...unless it's in handcuffs," she said, with a twinkle in her eye.

Sarah gave a smile. The gleam in Lisa's eye told her that she was also on board. They would do anything for their teammate. Sarah returned to clearing off the tables and wiping them down. She hovered in the middle of the room, making sure she had a straight line to the door in case something went awry.

Faireuza dipped the ladle into the stew time after time, politely acknowledging each homeless person while keeping the tall man with the black jacket in her peripheral vision.

"You're welcome, ma'am. I'm happy to see your wonderful smile today." The aging woman in front of her smiled, revealing more wrinkles on her face. Her smile was one of embarrassment, too. She had once been a top executive when her introduction to drugs buy a junior CEO pulled her down from the top and landed her on the streets. She became a throw-a-way employee that the company she worked for used and tossed to the side. Their promise of a large bonus on her sales was ripped out from under her by the fine print of illegal drug use on company property. She thought she had to mix with the bosses, to do what they did in order to make that huge

155

leap up the corporate ladder. She hadn't seen that they were using her talents to boost sales so the stockholders could sell their stocks at a premium until she lost everything.

"What do you think, Fifteen? A dragon wrapped around a sword on my arm or a dragon wrapped around my chest, guarding my heart?" Faireuza asked her teammate.

"I don't know. I definitely like the dragon. I know your heart's been hurt before, but I think the dragon on your arm would suit you best," Lisa answered in the fake conversation.

"I like knowing that someone was guarding my heart," Faireuza continued.

"I know what you're saying, but you'll probably regret it later."

"Why do you say that?"

"As wonderful as you are, you'll probably find some guy who will guard it for you," Lisa said.

"I don't know. Sir, what do you think?" Faireuza said, drawing the tall, balding man into the conversation. "A dragon wrapped around a sword on my arm or one on my chest?"

The tall man looked at Faireuza and devoured her athletic curves before settling his eyes on her breasts as she pointed to a spot just above them where the future tattoo might be.

"I think one to guard your heart would be better," he said as his inward desires worked counter to what he was saying. He envisioned himself trailing a finger around the imaginary tattoo and the ebony skin it would be written on. "You definitely need something to guard that heart."

"Do you have any tattoos?" Lisa asked in a purely naive, innocent tone.

"I do. I have a spider guarding a skull on my chest," the tall man replied.

156

THE SCHOLARSHIP

"Is it a good one?" Faireuza asked. "I don't want to a get a prison tattoo. I was asking if it's good, because if it is, I want to know who did it. Maybe I could ask them to do mine."

The tall man exposed a little of his tattoo. Four legs and a venomous head emerged on his chest. A bleached skull was embedded among other skulls and the image of the decaying rot of hell gave perfect echo to the spirit that emanated from him.

"That is so cool. Wow, look at that detail. Whoever did that is a master of ink," Faireuza said, playing up the innocent novice. The tall man reveled in the admiration of his ink. His ego soared as she complimented the less-than-perfect tattoo.

"Such a tattoo as that needs nourishment. Care for some hearty beef stew?" Faireuza asked, with a hint of seductiveness.

"Well, I am hungry," he said, staring into her eyes.

"Here you go. You've got to feed that appetite." Faireuza went to dribble the stew onto his tray when Lisa jabbed her in the ribs. The ladle jumped and flung the hot stew over the tray and onto the front of his trousers, making a messy streak down to the floor. The chunks of meat and potatoes hit the floor, leaving mostly gravy sliding down the man's pants.

"Oh! I'm terribly sorry," Faireuza said, and rushed around the end of the serving line to help clean up the mess. She grabbed a handful of napkins along the way and used them to blot the man's pants.

The tall man paused at the sudden attention, not knowing whether to enjoy it or be alarmed. "Oh. You're so sma... I mean the stain's so small you can barely notice." Faireuza said, contrary to the large, dark stain that soiled his clean, worn jeans. Faireuza could even detect a hint of Hawaiian fragrance from a popular dryer sheet coming from his clothes.

"No. No. Don't worry about that." The tall man said trying to back away, only to be blocked by the rest of the line waiting to be served.

"It won't be but a minute. Something that small won't take that long." Faireuza continued dabbing at the stranger's pants.

"No, please don't bother." He was now getting a bit irritated from the over-attention and the continuing use of the word "small."

"It's no problem. Wow," she said in amazement. Bart paused, wondering why she would exclaim something like that. "It's a wonder how you could satisfy anyone with something that small." Faireuza said loud enough for those sitting next to the serving line to hear. The man's face turned scarlet as he saw multiple eyes staring at him. He looked at the other servers in the line: one had a knowing grin on her face and clearly had a hairline hold on her laughter.

The hairline broke and the woman in the serving line laughed out loud followed by several others in the crowd. The stranger raised his tray and brought it down hard on Faireuza's head. Laughter turned to gasps and the crowd froze at the sudden turn of events. Faireuza was knocked to the floor in a dazed heap. Drill Witcom, Drill Simpson and Jensen came out the door to observe the commotion in progress. Faireuza lifted her arm to block a second blow from the man.

After realizing so many eyes were on him, he bolted for the door. Sarah watched everything and sprung for the door only to have her feet caught up in the straps of a backpack a young man had left splayed across her path. Sarah landed on the hard tile floor, smacking her hands as she broke her fall.

Faith was busy consoling a dog when she heard the commotion. Looking up, she watched the man as he spun on

THE SCHOLARSHIP

his heels and started for the door. She stood defiantly in the doorway to block anyone from exiting. The large man charged at her. Faith bent forward to receive the blow and shut her eyes.

A scream sounded throughout the soup kitchen and the neighboring street. People all around jumped back at the shrill noise that erupted from Faith. Surprised that she had not been hit yet, Faith silenced her scream and opened her eyes to find three dogs wrestling with the stranger who was continuing his own high-pitched wail. A collie tugged at the sleeve of his coat, a boxer held him by the face and a third mixed breed had teeth buried into the man's crotch. The man was frozen, knowing the teeth were mere millimeters from engaging the flesh of his manhood. His squeal shriveled to a whimpering, breathy panic as he lay still, half-in and half-out of the doorway.

Faith gathered in the scene not knowing what to do. The growls from the dogs stunned her and kept her from doing anything but back away. She tugged on the last remaining leash to pull the dog off the flailing man, but his growl and his insistent hold halted her efforts. She was turning toward the street, looking for anyone to help, when a white Salem cruiser turned the corner with optimum timing. Faith launched herself into the middle of the street to stop the patrol car, her arms waving frantically to get the officer's attention. Red and blue lights flipped on as Faith waved and pointed to where the officer should direct her attention.

The officer hopped out of the vehicle to the chaotic sounds of dogs growling. She drew her gun and pointed it at them as a grizzly old man burst out of the door, waving his arms.

"Don't shoot my dogs!" he hollered. "Don't shoot." The man turned to the sprawled man and commanded in a gruff voice: "Dogs! Here!" The dogs stopped immediately and collected around his feet.

"Oh, thank you, Officer." Bart said as he stood up and straightened his clothes. "Those dogs need to be shot. I come in here to get something to eat and they attacked me."

The officer called on the radio for animal control and for another officer to assist her. "Okay sir. Stand right there." She turned to the grizzly homeless man who now had all three leashes in his hand. "Jimmy, I want you to tie your dogs to that meter over there. Don't leave until after I come and talk to you."

Jimmy nodded and scratched his scruffy beard.

"Officer, those dogs need to be destroyed," the man said, desperately trying to show himself as the victim.

"Sir, no one is going anywhere until I understand what is going on. If the dogs need to be euthanized, then they'll be dealt with humanely," she answered, laying down the ground rules for her investigation.

Sarah and Faireuza walked outside with Drill Smith, Drill Witcom and Faireuza's drill, Drill Hernandez. The blue, crisp uniforms stood out among the crowd and were a surprise to the officer. "Who are you?"

"I am Gloria Witcom, a drill instructor at the Schultz Business Academy. This is Reta Smith and Antonella Hernandez. We bring the students down here to volunteer as part of their course work."

"You need to keep these convicts out of this city. We don't need you," Bart blasted.

"Sir. Be quiet. I will get to you in a minute."

"You would take their side, you little slice," Bart spat at the woman officer.

"What? What did you call me?" Officer Kindelson said.

THE SCHOLARSHIP

"Sorry ma'am. I'm just a little upset. I was bitten by three rabid dogs," Bart apologized.

"What's your name?" Officer Kindelson asked.

"My name is Henry."

"Henry? Do you have a last name?"

"Stotts."

"I thought your name was Bart," Sarah piped up. "Sure, you're not trying to hide something Henry, or Bart, or whoever you are?"

"You stay out of this, you little tramp."

"I would have stayed out of it if you would have stayed out of my friend," Sarah spouted. Faireuza held an arm out to gently nudge Sarah back against the wall.

"What the hell are you talking about? You don't know me."

"No, I don't, but my friend and the DNA forensics team does." Sarah waved a hand for Jensen to come out. Samantha locked an arm through Jensen's and walked with her out onto the street. Jensen's trembling hands shook even more as the terrified woman emerged to look upon her attacker. She stood with two of her teammates, each of them hooking an arm through Jensen's arms in support.

The tall man bolted for the street. He no sooner took two steps when a tree-trunk of an arm uprooted him. A colossal blue uniform fitted with a bulletproof vest and decorated with all the standard uniform fixings towered over him. A large meaty hand flipped him over on his stomach and grabbed both of his hands in one while the other fished out the handcuffs from his belt.

"What did you girls do?" Drill Witcom asked, steamed that they had acted without her knowledge.

"I'd like to know what happened as well." Officer Kindelson stepped closer to listen, not wanting to lose control of her investigation.

Sarah told the story from her grabbing Jensen when she had the knife in her hand to the moment of watching the hulking officer clothesline the man.

The stories from the rest of Sarah's team, as well as the soup kitchen patrons, all made for some solid evidence for a simple battery charge. After stuffing Henry into his cruiser, the mammoth of an officer came up to the group of women.

"Tiny Tim!" Drill Hernandez called out.

The officer spread a grin a mile wide. "Hey, big sis. How are you?" The tree-trunk arms that easily manhandled Jensen's rapist turned soft with affection as he gave Drill Hernandez a quick hug.

"I'm good. How are you doing?" Drill Hernandez asked. "Have you been bumping your head on the clouds or has your wife been disciplining you at home?" She reached up and pulled his colossal head down, so she could look at it more closely. A pale line showed across the top of his forehead.

"It's definitely my wife's fault."

Drill Hernandez eyed him and folded her arms in front of her. "Oh. Now, I know that woman. She would do worse than that if you got on her wrong side. What'd you do?"

"I hit my head on a door jamb," Officer Morales said.

"A door jamb?" Drill Hernandez kept her arms folded across her five-foot three frame and stared at the man. "You gonna tell me the truth or do I gotta beat it out of you? Better yet, I'll just call your wife."

Officer Morales grumbled at having his wife called on something that he was embarrassed to let anyone know. "I hit

THE SCHOLARSHIP

my head on a door jamb after Isabel told me that I'm gonna be a father."

"And that is bad, why? You don't sound enthused," Drill Hernandez observed.

"Oh. He's enthused alright." Officer Kindelson couldn't resist telling the story, since she was the one who was called to go check on him when he hit his head. "He was so excited that he jumped right into the door frame and knocked his ass out. When I got there, he was sitting on the couch with a baseball-sized goose egg on his head."

"You're not supposed to tell that," Officer Morales grumbled again.

"Oh, your reputation is still intact. The only difference is that you have to say that you, yourself, are the only person who can knock you out," Officer Kindelson chided.

"What will happen to the dogs?" Faith asked, worried for her little protectors. Jimmy sat on the curb rubbing his dogs' ears, as they all lay across his lap, soaking in the affection. "Do they have to be put down?"

"Roman, the big boxer there, was a former police dog. His partner was killed last year, and he also suffered a gunshot wound. He recovered but he wouldn't stay with his new family. He kept escaping and coming down here to find Jimmy. So, we let him stay with Jimmy now. It looks like the rest of the pack adopted some of his training."

"But that man said they have rabies," Faith complained for the dogs.

"They don't have rabies. I was with Jimmy a month ago and all three dogs got their shots and a full health checkup. The vet made a deal with us that if we paid for one, he would take care of the other two."

163

"What's going to happen to Bart or Henry or whatever his name is?" Drill Simpson asked. "Will he be released today? Will he have a chance to run or attack again?" The stern look on the drill's face told of the importance of the situation.

"He will be booked on a simple assault and we are already getting the warrant to get his DNA. We want Jensen to come down to the station and do a positive ID and have her give another in-depth statement, and an interview with a sketch artist. If she can accurately describe the tattoo to the artist, that will help her case," Officer Morales said.

"How long will that take?" Jensen asked.

"Probably the rest of the afternoon," Officer Kindelson volunteered. "We may have to have more statements from the rest of you on what transpired here today."

"What about my volunteering here at the kitchen?" Jensen voiced her concern about being held back because of an unfinished task.

"Eighteen," Jensen looked at Faireuza, who had laid a hand gently on the frightened woman's shoulder. "Would you take a tray to the head for me? Would you step up and take a hit to save me from someone?"

"Yes," Jensen said without hesitation.

"Then I think you know what this lesson is all about. I took a tray to the head, so we could catch this guy who did mean things to you, and possibly others. Sarah said he had the eyes of a hunter. He was likely down here looking for his next target. We as a team prevented something horrible from happening to someone else. Because of your detailed description, I'll bet this guy won't see the outside world for the rest of his life. You did good."

THE SCHOLARSHIP

"We all did good." Samantha said. "Don't I get credit for not being in the way?" The women chuckled at Samantha's light-hearted humor.

Chapter XVI

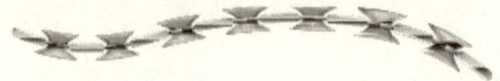

The rest of the week was relatively uneventful aside from the dog bite Faith received after unintentionally scaring the animal. Two stitches and some antibiotic ointment were all that was necessary to mend the incident and Faith continued to soothe the homeless animals at the shelter and promise them that they would have loving homes soon. She was also caught trying to smuggle a kitten out of the shelter to take back to the barracks, but she was reprimanded before she even made it to the door.

After their regular Saturday morning physical training, the teams spent the rest of the day working on building an obstacle course. Those who could handle heights worked in the manlift baskets, stringing ropes under the direction of an expert course-builder. He had also helped to design and build the Tree Umph Adventure Course near Bradenton, Florida, a family-friendly adventure course for exploring and overcoming your fear of heights.

The teams worked tirelessly as the shape of the course started to come together. Excitement grew as the logs were drilled by hand, the rope was cut and burnt, and wrenches were turned on the cable clamps. Every wooden corner was sanded, and every tail of cable was wrapped and clamped into place to prevent someone from getting cut if they happened to slip with the cable still in their hand. Handrails were solidly fastened around the narrow platforms where one could rest without worry of falling off.

For days they tied knots, pulled ropes and tightened turnbuckles until the expert was satisfied with the safety and security of the course. They left off the typical safety cables in favor of a net. The psychological stimulation of actually falling if they failed compounded the result of overcoming their fears and building confidence in themselves. Not to mention the grueling task of starting back at the beginning if they fell mid-course.

Dean Vickery came out to view the nearly-completed course. He smiled at the pride and craftsmanship that the women had taken in the project. Grins were plentiful along with the sweat that dripped off their brows.

Stacey Adams pointed out to her team that one requirement for success in the course was grip strength. Lillie Kirkpatrick agreed and threw a spare chunk of rope over a pole jutting out high above their heads. "Four, I think you should try this."

"Try what?" Helen looked up from tracing a stick in the dirt as they sat on the ground taking a water break.

"Grab ahold of this rope and lift your feet off the ground for as long as you can." Lillie held the rope out to her, offering her the challenge. The rest of the group looked at the woman who had lost nearly forty pounds since she had arrived. Helen stood up and looked at the rope. "You're going to need some upper body strength to get through this course."

Helen took the rope, reached up high and pulled her feet off the ground a couple of inches. "Just hold it there as long as you can." Lillie started counting out the seconds with her fingers. On the eleventh second Helen dropped to the ground. "Four, you're going to have to do better than that."

"I don't know if I can."

"The word is that you can't graduate until you've completed everything, including this course. That's what the dean meant by paying all your debts. He wants us to hold ourselves accountable for our actions whether anyone is watching or not." Lillie gave the rope a tug and held her feet off the ground for forty seconds. "If anyone else has doubts on their strength step up and see. For those who can't make thirty seconds, we need to figure something out."

"They want us to graduate as a team, so we have to work as one. Everyone needs to go across. If you fall you have to start back at the beginning," Heather added. "I didn't see any ladders part way through the course."

"I think everyone should test their grip strength," Faireuza said. "Whoever is weak, we'll figure out how to get you across."

The group of women smiled at the gesture. A whistle blew signaling that they had sat around long enough. Dusting the grass off their backs, the teams split up to their assigned tasks. Excited to have a challenge that would signal the last of the seven values and closer to finishing boot camp, they worked feverishly to complete the course.

Periodically, women wandered over to the beam and threw a rope over it and counted the seconds of how long they could hold on. Some hung there for a long time while others lasted only a few seconds.

THE SCHOLARSHIP

****

Group counseling was reserved for late afternoon and had become a more cheerful event where each student looked forward to what they would soon accomplish. For the most part they had put their pasts behind them. Sarah was all smiles too. She was excited about moving on with her team and seeing what lay beyond the walls and fences of this trial. Her mind and body had been pushed to the limit and she had survived. Now she was ready to move forward.

Sitting in the counseling circle with her team, Sarah listened and participated in the session. Faireuza had taken the lead by introducing meditation into their routine. Each student sat cross-legged on a mat, wrists placed on their knees, as she instructed her team through the breathing and calming exercises. Sarah rolled her eyes at first but eventually joined in, just to appease the counselor and her classmates. It wasn't bad and she didn't feel as embarrassed as she thought she would. Her idea was to just go along with the program and get it done. She wouldn't have to meditate after that. However, during the several days they spent building a shelter and seeking clean water, she had gotten off the regular meditation schedule and noticed that she missed it. For some reason she was drawn to it and welcomed it back with open arms. It was one of the small simple things that brought her peace and stability.

She liked the peaceful quiet she had trained her brain to crave and acquire. For a few minutes a day she learned to center her spirit and calm herself down. She found herself able to understand and communicate better with people. Her mind felt clear and not a jumbled mess of thoughts. She understood her feelings and was able to stop herself from making a rash decision on several occasions.

Today, after the meditation ended and the others began the discussion, she focused on her future. She wanted to see into the future instead of just the confines of their current facility. She didn't know much about the outside world. She had blocked everything from her past and focused on the present. Her future was marred by lack of knowledge and the uncertainty of what she wanted to do. She thought about Drill Hernandez and her desire to be a police officer. She thought about being a camp counselor for children, like Lisa had mentioned, but she reasoned that she wouldn't be able to get the background clearance required to oversee youth activities. Sarah couldn't think of anything she wanted to do with her life. Dredging up any occupation from her past sent her mind spinning.

"I don't know what I want to do!" Sarah blurted out. The group stopped mid-discussion on the anger issues that Galaxy was discussing and turned their eyes to Sarah.

"Sorry. I didn't mean to speak out of turn," she immediately apologized.

"Twelve. What prompted you to speak out like that?" Gearda adjusted the clipboard on her lap and she turned to face the interrupting student.

"Sorry, Twenty-one. Sorry, team. It wasn't my place to speak. I'm sorry." Sarah slouched in her chair, trying to make herself small.

"Twelve. Will you please share with us the subject so we may come back to it when Twenty-one is finished explaining her frustrations?" Gearda pried.

"It's nothing. Sorry. Please go back to Twenty-one. Her issues and frustrations are important. Please. I'm sorry." Sarah lifted a foot up on the chair in an attempt to hide behind her knee.

"Twelve, I feel I have a good grasp on my anger. We don't have to continue. We can come back to it," Galaxy reassured her teammate. "Something was important to you to blurt it out like that. We're here to help you as much as you're here to help us."

"You said something about not knowing what you're going to do." Faireuza leaned forward in her chair a little. Since the teams had been developed, Faireuza had stepped up more and more as a leader. She dealt with all the minor issues flawlessly and took half a step back when the drills stepped in to handle anything else.

Sarah looked at the stares from the other women, expecting them to be condescending, but they weren't. They were inviting and comfortable. "I don't know what I want to do," she finally said.

"How do you mean?" Gearda asked.

Sarah looked at her teammates, then at the counselor. "Three has talked about designing her own exercise equipment for women. Twenty-one has mentioned designing video games. Nineteen, I am sure will do something with animals." Sarah caught her tone as being a little sharp, took a deep breath and continued. "They like you for some reason." Sarah smiled at her teammate. "They just melt into your hands like butter in a skillet." The grouped laughed and nodded recalling the incident in Salem and how the dogs jumped to Faith's defense from the charging man. "What I'm saying is, everyone here seems to have a direction in life that they want to pursue. I don't know what I want to do. I don't have any family. No one on the outside. Not anymore."

"Why do you feel that you don't have family?" Gearda asked, knowing only that Sarah didn't want anything to do with her parents as she guided the conversation for the rest of the group.

Sarah sat back in the chair and pulled both knees up to hide her face. She was regretting having said anything at all. She ducked her head behind her knees. "My mom's a drunk and my father kicked us out. I don't have any siblings," she said with a conclusive tone.

"Twelve," Faith said, waiting for Sarah to look up. "We're your family now. We're your siblings. We're not allowed to argue here, but later I'm sure we can argue like sisters, be mad at each other for a while and forgive each other a day later. My mom would be ecstatic to have all of you over for the holidays. She loves cooking and making sure that you're so full you roll out the door when you leave."

Sarah looked over her knees at the group. Their pleading puppy-dog eyes drilled into her, causing her unrest and a desire to respond to their invitation, yet she remained motionless.

"Why do you hesitate?" Gearda asked.

"I don't want my past to drag them down," Sarah said, confident that it was a good enough reason to settle their curiosity.

"How is your past connected to your future?" Faireuza asked. "You were upset about one thing and not knowing what your future holds, then suddenly you switched to worrying about your past."

Sarah pulled her feet tighter into the chair but remained silent. Jensen sat up in her chair fidgeting with her fingernails. "Sarah, I want to thank you for what you did for me. I want to thank all of you for what you did. Being able to see justice served on someone who hurt me was satisfying, but I still feel empty. Maybe like you feel, Twelve. I don't know what I'm going to do either, but I have to believe that it will find me. Just like you guys found me and helped me bring closure to a really bad thing. So, Twelve, you don't have to know all the answers right now. I sure don't. I don't expect to, not now anyway. I'm just trying to survive this course."

Sarah loosened her hold on her feet. Jensen was right. She didn't have to have the answers right now. She had to survive the course first. Tension eased inside her mind and her body relaxed a bit.

"We don't know what is beyond these fences or if the next part is better or worse than this. We are running on blind faith that what we find on the other side will be good and wonderful. I believe that must be true, otherwise there wouldn't be so much praise for this program. Not every program is right for you, but this one is. The dean said it himself that he wanted all of us to succeed. That's why they put that team exercise together, so we all had to work together to succeed."

"And we did!" Faireuza said. "We succeeded then, and we'll continue to succeed."

"I'm an only child, too." Galaxy said. "I would be honored if you were my sister, Twelve. All of you. I would love to call all of you my sisters. I want to know what simple bickering is about, and I want to stand with all of you when shhh…stuff hits the fan."

"Nice save," Samantha said.

"We all have had that moment when something got under our skin and tripped our freak-out button." Faireuza shifted in her seat before continuing. "It still may happen after we get out of here, but with the help of the program and the wonderful Miss Gearda, our triggers will be harder to trip. We now have a better understanding of who we are, and we can take the time to process what angers us and deal with it better. And yes, number twenty-one, simple squabbles are funny when you look back on them. Nineteen, I would love to help your mom in the kitchen. A big home-cooked meal sounds wonderful."

"Twelve, how do you feel about this now?" Gearda asked, steering the conversation back to the initial interruption.

"Better." Sarah smiled and accepted a hand from Samantha sitting on her left and Lisa on her right. She squeezed their hands in thanks, and they squeezed back in reassurance.

After the gesture of friendship had completed its message Gearda turned back to Galaxy. "Back to you, Twenty-one. We were talking about how to recognize when you reach that point of going off."

"No. I'm good. Everyone was a little quiet this morning, so I thought I would ask something that would help everyone," Galaxy rambled.

Sarah laughed out loud, along with most of the group. Faireuza grinned. "Who would've thought that the youngest one in the group could turn out to be our big sister?"

Chapter XVII

The sun was warm on their backs as the students sat on the ground receiving instruction on safety. The first safety tip they practiced was passing around a bottle of sunblock to use on their exposed skin. The expert rope course designer commended them on a job well done in rigging all the ropes, cables and wires. Many of the students were apprehensive about the task ahead, while others were enthusiastic. The safety talk included instructions on how to fall and land in the net, which meant that they would have to start over from the beginning as that was the only way to get back up to where they fell from.

As practice, each student took turns falling off a lower platform. They were instructed to turn onto their back to land in the net, then roll out of it and plant their feet safely on the ground. The obstacle course was the last lesson on personal courage, though many thought it was play time.

"Class. Attention," Master Drill Ietel said, bringing the focus on himself. He pivoted and saluted the dean before turning and leaving the head of the formation. One drill headed up each team as they prepared to take on the obstacle course.

"Class, at ease." Dean Vickery's face spread in a joyous grin as he gazed out over his transformed students. "It brings me great happiness to see how far you've come in such a short amount of time. This class has done some amazing things, some of which we have never experienced here before. Some we would like to forget or wish never happened, but that is what learning is about. You see, our primary goal isn't just to make you good citizens with honor and integrity. Our goal is also to offer you a chance to be a kid again."

Some students laughed while others tilted their heads in confusion. "That's why we give you a number. It is not meant to be demeaning in any way, so don't look at it like that. Think about the time before you were born. I know you can't remember that time but imagine it anyway. Your parents may or may not have had names for you. You may have been baby number one or number five. Your parents didn't know who you were going to be. They didn't know if you were going to be a boy or a girl. So, there was this great mystery of who you would grow up to be.

"Some of you may be named after a movie star, or maybe your great-grandmother, but that is all in your past. Soon, you will be born again into this world. You will have the opportunity to make the same mistakes that you did in the past or forge ahead to make new mistakes, growing from your experiences and helping teach others by way of example or failure. There will be failures; I am sure today that many of you will fail. In fact, I expect there to be failures, but don't you ever think that failing is a bad thing.

"In business, and in life, you will fail. I don't want that hard landing to stop you from learning. If you're in here, you've had a hard landing or two… or three." Some of the students chuckled knowingly at the mention of multiple hard landings. "We want you to fall going forward not backward." Dean Vickery looked at the safety instructors, who gave him a concerned look in return. "Except for in this course," he corrected. "We want you to fall backward on this course today. We don't want anyone going to the hospital. No matter how you fall, the important thing is to get up, dust yourself off and climb back up. Finish what you started."

Nods of approval circulated throughout the class. "Speaking of hospitals," the dean looked to the ground. "they are short one resident now." A worried look grew among the class as there was only one person that they knew in the hospital. "I'm sorry to say that she won't be participating with you today."

Sarah's hopes were crushed. She had prayed multiple nights for her friend to recover and be here and now that wouldn't happen. Just like all her other hopes that had been dashed starting from so many years ago. All of her hurt from her youth began to well up inside her. She would never be able to live the childhood that so many had had the luxury of living, and now today was ruined as well.

"She won't be participating, ... but she will be cheering you on. Turn around and give a warm welcome home to number eight." Dean Vickery grinned from ear to ear as the students spun in their tracks to find Anna McKieel pushing a wheelchair across the field. Harley was sitting in the seat with a blanket draped over her legs. The P.A. pushed her up to the yellow team.

Sarah was the first to break ranks and descend on the recovering student. A split-second later the rest of the formation broke to gather around their very own hero. The drills didn't move, although they did applaud the student who was returning to watch her team go through the obstacle course that they had started to build so many weeks ago. Sarah knelt next to the tiny woman and embraced her, tears flowing from her eyes as she clung to the miracle of life.

Dean Vickery gave the women a few moments together before calling them back to formation. "Like I said before, we are not building soldiers. We are building strong women who have balance in life. Women who can balance their emotions, their checkbooks and their bodies. This will be the last major obstacle in this part of your training. I want you to learn what strength you have inside and learn to overcome these obstacles just like you will have to do in the future. Most importantly, I want you to have fun while you're learning. I'll see you all at the finish." Dean Vickery returned to the center of the formation. "Class. Attention."

Master Drill Ietel resumed the control of the class. "On the word 'move' I want the green team to show the rest of the class how to tame this beast. Everyone else will sit in their spots and watch. Try and learn from their mistakes and push on to the end. The blue team will follow, then the red team, then the yellow. Are there any questions?"

"No, Master Drill Ietel!" the class sounded, in unison.

"Are you going to fail?"

"No, Master Drill Ietel!" the class sounded again.

"Move!" Master Drill Ietel ordered. The green team bolted for the first obstacle, the cargo net that would take them to the first elevation. Climbing it was a breeze for Sarah and most of her crew. Samantha was a bit hesitant because of her fear of heights. She placed her feet securely on each rung of the rope and slowly made her way up, receiving a helping hand from her team who hoisted her the rest of the way up.

"Okay. Good job Twenty-two. Are you ready?" Faireuza asked.

THE SCHOLARSHIP

"No! I'm not ready!" Samantha cried.

"We talked about this. It's best to get it over with now than to have to traverse the whole thing again."

"I'm scared."

"I know sister, but it is part of reaching beyond your boundaries," Faireuza coached. "We can do this."

"Okay. Okay. I know. I know," Samantha stammered.

"Turn around and back slowly up to the edge. The net is below you. You've seen our classmates crawl all over it when we set it up. The experts have double-checked every knot and bolt. It will not fail you."

"Okay. Okay. Okay."

"You can do this, double-dos!" Galaxy called out.

"Cross your arms in front of you and fall backward like you are falling on your bed."

"I can't. I can't," Samantha complained.

"Twenty-two you got this. It's just like the practice net," Sarah said.

"It's not. It's higher than the practice net."

"You promised that you would," Faireuza said.

"I know, but I can't." Samantha continued to resist their pleading. "You promised that you wouldn't push me."

"That we did, and we won't push you," Sarah said.

"Hey, guys! Guys, back up a step," Faith interjected. "Don't say anything." While her teammates backed up, she whispered in Samantha's ear. Then Faith backed to the opposite edge and waited.

Samantha stood on the edge of the platform for a moment before teetering and falling backwards over the edge. She screamed all the way to the net. The team rushed forward to stare over the edge. Samantha lay in the net with the biggest grin she had ever produced. "I didn't pee myself!" she yelled and raised a fist up.

"What'd you tell her?" Faireuza asked.

"I told her to imagine the best orgasm she could think of and play it out in her mind. When she came... she went." Faith looked down at their teammate, whose face was a little red and a lot of teeth.

"She's a screamer," Sarah said.

"'Guess we'll have to buy her future husband a set of earplugs for their honeymoon." Faireuza grinned down at their teammate.

"Okay. Just don't say anything else or she'll be falling off this obstacle all damn afternoon," Faith added, still staring down at her teammate. "That must have been one hell of an orgasm."

****

The green team completed the course with only two team members falling. They had to wait for Faireuza and Jensen to re-navigate the course to catch up to the rest of their team. According to the rules the group could only be spaced between two sections if someone were to fall. The fallers had to catch back up to the team before the whole team could move on.

Sarah sat back on the ground in her team's spot while the blue team made their rounds. Being a little taller than the rest, Sarah sat in the rear of the two-column team formation. She took a pull on the water bottle and watched the blue team navigate the course, cheering them when they completed a more difficult part.

"Twelve." Sarah continued to watch her classmates climb single file across the cargo nets strung solidly from pole to

THE SCHOLARSHIP

pole. "Twelve." Sarah jumped this time, and turned to see Harley roll her wheelchair up next to the green formation.

"Hey. What are you doing?" Sarah said, with a grin.

"I want to thank you for saving my life," Harley said, "and say I'm sorry for knocking you out."

Sarah looked at the fragile-looking woman and patted her hand. "I am the one who should be sorry. My eyes were full of greed and I didn't see the big picture. I deserved the ass-whooping and you don't have to apologize to me. I know you'd do the same for me."

"No, I wouldn't have." Sarah's eyes widened at the admission.

"I'm a germaphobe. You'd be dead to the world unless someone else jumped in," Harley admitted.

Sarah was a little taken aback by the statement. She hadn't thought that some people have their own tendencies that guide them in their everyday life. She looked into Harley's eyes for something that would indicate that she was kidding. There was nothing.

"I am getting past the germaphobia. The counselor is helping me, and I'm making progress. I need something from you and wonder if you would help me."

"Help you? To do what?" Sarah was eager to help her injured classmate even though Harley had once knocked her out with a single swift kick.

"I need your right shoe," Harley said.

"Why?"

"The lightning blew off three of my toes and a small piece of my foot. They won't let me do what I know I can do in therapy. They want me to take it slow." Sarah looked at her classmate. Her pleading eyes begged Sarah. "I have to finish with my class. I have to show what I'm made of, both to myself

181

and to the world. I am an athlete to the core. This injury will not define me." Sarah mulled it over in her head. Building the course was a test and completing it was another test. It didn't have a letter grade, only a pass-fail. "I'd do it for you."

Sarah looked up into her classmate's eyes and saw the conviction. She grinned and slipped her foot out of the hiking boot. Sarah's oversize shoe was a snug fit for the small girl when taking into account the layers of bandages that kept her healing foot intact. She slipped it on, then took if off again. "Give me your sock."

"Why?"

"I have to put something where my toes used to be," Harley said in a hushed tone.

Sarah ripped the sock off her foot and handed it to Harley. Harley quickly stuffed it in the toe of Sarah's boot, then slipped the boot on her foot and covered it with a blanket to keep it out of view of the rest of the crowd. Sarah also tucked her bleached-white foot out of sight to keep from having to explain her missing boot.

"Give it hell, girl," Sarah whispered.

"Thanks." Harley whispered back. She rolled herself back to her team and waited for her chance to move. The event was entertaining, as many times the women would fall and have to restart from the beginning. The height was a staggering thirty feet in the air for most of the course. Students fell the most often on the trapeze and the rings, where good upper body strength was vital.

"Yellow team. Go." Master Drill Ietel gave the order for the final team to start the course. Helen carried two lengths of rope that she had been practicing with to give her additional support on the trapeze section. They had watched very carefully the things that the other teams messed up on and

182

moved slowly and with precision. Three sections before the zip line they came to the trapeze bars. Two teammates had made it across and were instructing Helen on how to wrap the rope around the swinging bar and stuff her foot into the loop at the end. Doing as instructed, Helen made it onto the first trapeze.

Though Helen was strong in many ways, her grip strength was not enough to support her weight across the three trapezes. They had devised the plan with the ropes to be able to give her a chance to use her feet as well on the overhead bars and rings. Helen made it securely onto the first trapeze. Cheers went up from all around and the teams on the ground wished they could be up above assisting their classmate.

Stacey Adams pushed the first trapeze close to the second so Helen could wrap a rope around it. Twisting it twice around the bar then a wrap back around itself, she transferred her weight to her right foot. Releasing the rope in her left hand, she moved to transfer it to the next bar. A small slip from the rope on the right sent the left-hand rope out into space as she clung to the trapeze. The rope slipped off the end of her foot and plummeted through the net to the ground.

Harley bolted from her chair. She had snuck in an extra pain pill when the yellow team had started climbing the net and was well ready for the course. Her athletic training in high school and the martial arts classes she had taken since she was five, had developed her into a top athlete. She had the balance and agility of a cat.

Sprinting under the net she scooped up Helen's rope on the fly. Taking the cargo net two rungs at a time, she ran up the first part of the net with her hands pumping at her side, as if she were running up a steep hill. Only at the top third of the net did she use her hands to grasp the heavy ropes and pull herself up.

Master Drill Ietel leaned close to Drill Walker. "I want a release form here in two minutes. Send them a video if you have to." Drill Walker ripped her cell phone out from her pocket and ignited the video recorder as Harley ripped across the horizontal ladder. Without slowing she banked a right-hand turn across a two-by-twelve beam. She sprinted across it without the aid of the overhead cable. Three bars of walking trapeze slowed her down only slightly. Sarah's oversize shoe fit well but the unexpected bulk of it added more to Harley's mental concentration.

After crossing the tightrope in four bounds, she made a left, throwing Helen's rope over the overhead grab line. Stretching her arms far to the side, she trotted across the slack line. Reaching the next platform Harley bolted into a sprint leaping as if to jump past the vertical cargo net. At the last moment she reached out and grabbed a handful of it.

"Damn!" Galaxy exclaimed. "Look at that flying squirrel." A roar went up from the rest of the classmates as they watched their friend defy gravity and sail through the course in record time. The next obstacle was the rope swing. Harley only paused a moment as she sprinted past the tagline rope and leaped.

Time stood still for Sarah. Her battle adversary hung in the air like a floating spirit, her arms stretched out reaching for the net on the other side of the void. Traditionally, one would swing on the rope provided and land against the net where they would climb up to the next platform. Harley leaped like she was launching for the moon. Gravity pulled at her with undying effort, but her momentum carried her across. With the salvaged rope slung around her neck and her different sized shoes trailing through the air, Harley landed against the bottom part of the net. One hand slipped but the other held fast to the net.

Gasps radiated through the small crowd that watched. Drill Walker carefully walked forward videotaping the acrobatics of the recently released patient who was obviously going against the doctor's orders of staying off her foot.

From the vertical net, she raced across a pair of cabled boards and a pivoting, horizontal ladder like the common, amusement park ladder game. She kept her momentum going and placed her feet in the bee-line center of the obstacle. A slight wobble sent her off course but not before her momentum could carry her to the solid wooden platform at the end. She turned right, using centrifugal force to mash her feet against the vertical wall which propelled her most of the way across the two-by-four blocks screwed to the solid wooden wall. She grabbed one with her hand, which was enough to make one last step, pushing her onto the platform where half of her teammates stood, still looking for a way to help Helen complete the obstacle.

"Eight!" Maralah White Eagle reached an arm out to grab the flying squirrel as she slapped a foot on the platform and nearly careened off the edge. If she fell onto the net, she would have to start all over and try to make a leap she knew she wouldn't be able to complete again. Harley clambered up and into the arms of her teammates.

"The hell." Stacey Adams pulled Harley into a hug. "What are you doing?"

Out of breath, Harley stammered, "y...you dropped something."

"And you're the angel who flew it back up to us." Stacey passed the rope off to the rest of the team. Maralah draped the rope around her neck and grabbed the first trapeze. She hoisted her lithe body on top of the rung. Stacey steadied Maralah's feet as she reached out to grab the trapeze that Helen had been hanging from. Helen had been stuck on that second rope, unable to advance to the third trapeze and on to the safety of the next platform.

Maralah scrambled across the tops of the trapezes and wrapped the rope around the third trapeze. She tied a knot this time and held the rope steady for Helen to place her foot in the stirrup. Two teammates stood ready to catch Helen when she swung across. Helen stepped into the stirrup and grabbed the rope. Swinging the last leg of the section, Helen grabbed for her teammates and got part of her right foot on the platform. They pulled the collapsing Helen onto the wooden planks and away from the certain drop she faced.

Cheers went up from all around as the team paused to catch their breath. "Eight. What are you doing up here?" Helen huffed.

"I'll be danged if I'll let you graduate without me." Harley grinned and easily swung across the trapezes as if she were born to them.

"You might catch hell from the drills," Stacey said.

"True, but not before we complete this course," Harley said. "On the rings, we're going to tie one rope to the second ring and one to the fourth. Helen, we'll hand you the rope and you put your foot in it."

"I don't know," Stacey said. "What if we put it on the third or fourth ring and do it all in one swing. We can use the second rope to pull her over to the platform."

"Four, what do you think?" Maralah asked.

"I like the single-one-time shot," she said, still trying to catch her breath.

THE SCHOLARSHIP

"Okay. That's what we'll do." Stacey stood up and surveyed the rings. "Which one?"

"The one on the far side. Then we just have to help her climb up." Maralah said.

"No. She'll hit the platform hard and might lose her grip and fall," Harley mentioned.

"Okay the fourth one. The happy medium. Four, are you alright with that?"

Helen looked at the rings and the distance across to the other side. "Yeah. I think I can hang on for that."

"Alright. That's what we'll do." Stacey confirmed their plan.

The yellow team assembled the rope swing and positioned three members on the far side, leaving Harley and Maralah to send Helen across the chasm. With a bit more confidence from the previous pitfall, Helen swung to the far side where her team pulled her to safety on the platform. They made it up the last obstacle, a spiral staircase to the top level, made up of a series of poles jutting out of a large timber. After that, it was the easy zip line all the way back to the ground.

Chapter XVIII

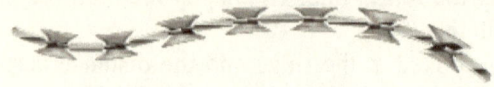

"Gloria, is there a reason that you won't sign off on Sarah's paperwork?" The head counselor, Mika Glenrock, tapped her pen on the table, slightly irritated with the single yellow flag that Gloria was continually throwing on their play. "She has exceeded all the standards that we've set forth. Her attitude is excellent. She is a leader among her peers. What more is there?"

"There's something that she's not telling us," Gloria said.

"What is it?" Dean Vickery asked.

"I don't know. She's young, so it must be something from her youth," Gloria said.

"Has someone been able to talk to her parents?" Gearda asked.

"No. Her mother is drunk most of the time and won't acknowledge that she has a daughter. Her father flat out refuses to talk with us," Mika said.

"Has she spoken to any of the other students about her past?" Dean Vickery asked Gloria.

THE SCHOLARSHIP

"Not that we can tell." Gloria said. "She's mentioned a bit of a rough childhood much like some of the other students, but nothing stands out."

"Was there any abuse in the house?" Mika asked.

"Yes, there was, but nothing outstanding or different than the rest of her classmates." Gearda replied. "But, with her parents not wanting to cooperate it's hard to tell. With her attitude like it is, I don't believe that she'll be a recurring offender."

"There's not that much more time before we have to graduate them or send them back. I don't want Sarah to be the first student that we send back," Dean Vickery voiced his concern.

"I'm not going to sign off on her papers until I know what has been eating her. There has to be something that would trigger the kind of anger that she's exhibited in the past." Gloria defended her position to keep Sarah from graduating. She knew that something within Sarah was tearing her up and she wanted to do everything that she could to dig it out. She didn't know if it would make it better or worse, but she suspected that at some point in time Sarah could very well blow up again and injure somebody else. The way the incident was described on the police report suggested that something her parents did caused her to act out in that way. Her anger was targeted, not random.

"We start graduating teams tomorrow, one each day. After nine days, if Sarah still hasn't come forth with the information that you seek, we will have to graduate her class without her and send her back to prison. I know that it will be a first, but we can't hold out forever just for one student. I really hate to do it, especially after seeing her come all this way. There's a limited amount of time before we have to make that decision," Dean Vickery stated.

"I understand sir." Gloria closed the folder to her notes.

****

"I'm glad that we don't have to haul boulders today," Faith said, as she and her teammates mowed the front lawn. Each of the four teams had been sent to different parts of the campus to tidy up the complex before the next class of students arrived to begin their own scholarship. The yellow team was selected to haul boulders. Up and down the mountain they grumbled as they stuck together working as a team. Soon they could be heard singing and laughing as they hauled boulder after boulder up the hill. Disney songs were common as they packed the heavy rocks to the top, only to send them sliding down to the bottom. The rock hauling had become viewed as a demeaning task and not cherished by any student.

Sarah forced the push mower through the tall grass. After several encounters with the medieval device, she realized that it would be easier to care for the front lawn if they could mow it a few times a week instead of just once a week. The thick grass jammed up the blade reel and she was forced to back it up and push it forward over and over. They had all become used to manual labor as no sort of power tools were allowed, except for the two rented manlift baskets for assembling the obstacle course. Rakes, shovels, hedge trimmers and a wheel barrel rounded out the rest of their tools.

"Any thoughts as to what you want to do with your life, Twelve?" Jensen asked.

"No, Eighteen. I thought I would try your strategy. Let it find me."

190

THE SCHOLARSHIP

"What ya going to do until then?" Faireuza asked, as she took a break from trimming the grass around the edge of the brick retaining wall.

"I don't know. Probably flip burgers or make popcorn at the movie theater."

"If you work at the movies, you'll probably get to see a bunch of those for free," Galaxy interjected. Sarah thought that she sounded a little too enthusiastic to let Sarah have the job to herself.

"Why would I want to watch someone have a happy ending when I won't have one?" she grumbled to herself.

"Twelve," Drill Zefon called to Sarah.

Sarah snapped to attention. "Yes, Drill Zefon."

"I'm to escort you to Drill Witcom in room one-fourteen. Come on. Double time."

****

Sarah sat on the hard-plastic chair, waiting for her personal drill to come in for what she considered an interrogation. She hated the one-on-one sessions, because the discussions always returned to her childhood and the problems that triggered the boiling cauldron of anger held deep inside her. She had pushed her anger back into a vault where she hoped it would remain hidden and forgotten and didn't want to take a chance on bringing it back to life.

Drill Witcom came in the door and closed it behind her. She sat in the chair on the opposite side of the round table. She set her drill hat to the side and stared at Sarah. "I want to tell you a story," she finally said after a long silence. "It's a story that I tell few people."

"Are you going to tell me how you got in trouble and ended up a student here?"

"How do you know that?"

"It's not hard. There's one drill for every student. If you were a professional, you would be watching twenty people. It's almost as if I'm your child and you're trying to mold me into your image," Sarah ridiculed her drill.

"Like it or not, yes. In a way, I am. 'Cause you see, I only know how to be me. I can tell you how to be me until I'm blue in the face. That won't work for you. It won't be near good enough for you. You will never accept what I have to say. Because something deep inside you won't let you be free. I don't know what has made you so angry inside, but it is holding you back."

"I'm not angry. I know what I did was wrong. I know I can't do it again. Why are you hounding me so much? None of the other students have gotten hounded like this. Why me?"

"Twelve…"

"I have a name. It's Sarah. Don't I deserve to at least have a name?"

"Yes, you do, but I want to know what's bothering you. We can discuss the use of your name later."

"That's just it. You don't even give us the dignity of a name. We get crappy clothes, generic shampoo and conditioner, single-flipping-blade razors."

"Come on. That's not what's bothering you. I know it's not."

"You treat us like animals. How are we supposed to act when you lock us up in a cage? No one to talk to. No family to call. No one to receive a letter from. No one to send a letter to. Just how am I supposed to act when no one wants me?"

THE SCHOLARSHIP

Gloria felt for the young woman. She didn't know what it was like not to get a letter. She received at least three a week, one from each of her boys. In the first boot camp phase of the program, they were not allowed to receive any mail unless it was court-related or a death in the immediate family. After that, everyone could receive and send mail.

She knew she was a good mom. She just made one serious mistake. A decision made for all the right reasons that backfired and cost her more than what she had gambled on.

"Your teammates want you."

"That's here and now. We're forced to be together. What happens when we're no longer forced to be together? Who's going to be there? Who's going to send more than a Christmas card every year, if even that?"

Gloria leaned back in her chair, surveying her charge. "With that kind of attitude, who would want to?" Sarah fell silent. She realized she had just backed herself into a corner. She lost the argument. "Twelve."

"My name is Sarah."

"Why is a name so relevant now and not before?"

Sarah glowered at her interrogator. She had stepped over an invisible line. One that confirmed to Gloria that Sarah was withholding something.

Sarah sat back in her chair, folded her arms and tuned Gloria out. She knew that she had said too much because the pain had resurfaced in her heart. This was the pain that she had successfully locked away until now. She tried to force it back down into the depths of her forgotten soul, but it was now there staring her in the face. The secret she had been hiding from herself had resurfaced and Gloria was licking her chops to hear it.

ALEX R PRICE

****

Three teams in three days disappeared at the top of the mountain. Each team hauled boulders continuously until suddenly their singing stopped and they never returned to the barracks. A cloak of trees concealed the top ridge of the hill, which had prevented them from an early detection of the reward that lay beyond. When they graduated from the boot camp into the second phase, which was rumored to be textbooks and lectures, they passed through that cloak of trees to the main campus area. They no longer had to haul boulders.

The next day the green team was sure that they would get to follow their peers through that glorious gate to the other side of the mountain. They hauled boulder after boulder all afternoon but there wasn't a drill to unlock the gate at the top. Sarah suspected that it had something to do with her. At the end of the second day of boulder-hauling, she was sure that she was the one holding up their graduation. The gate at the top remained locked and not a drill in sight to offer a key.

Their voices sang out loud and happy when their achievement felt certain. The second day was still hopeful, the songs were joyous, yet fizzled to a whispering grumble as the day drew to a close.

"Why haven't we graduated?" Faith spoke what the rest of her team wanted to know. "We have turned our lives around. I mean we've changed, grown to be better people. We've learned all kinds of ways to argue properly. We've learned how to take criticism, how to use it or toss it out the window. We've mastered the art of counting to ten and we've learned how to identify our triggers. What else do they want from us?"

Faireuza dipped the mop in the bucket then squeezed out the excess in the wringer before setting it back on the floor.

194

THE SCHOLARSHIP

Their chores had varied around the campus, but the kitchen was a daily task that needed to be maintained. The other teams had left behind extra burdens for the green team, but the drills filled in to assist when personnel ran short for the job. Instead of a full-course breakfast, trays were made and sent over from the main facility. With the reduced workload, it only took a fraction of the time to clean the kitchen, now that the cooks had departed for the main facility.

"There's probably just one or two people holding us back." Faireuza paused in her task of eradicating the germs on the floor.

"How do we tell who's holding us up?" Faith asked.

"Pure integrity," Faireuza said. "I don't think there is any other way."

Galaxy raised her hand, drawing everyone's attention. "I kinda got into an argument with Drill Mackleson."

"Twenty-one, what'd you do that for?" Samantha asked.

"She was pushing my buttons. I blew up on her. When she told me that she was doing it intentionally and explained her objective, I settled down and listened. She made me watch the video over and over, making me identify things she said and how I could have responded differently. I didn't know I could act like such a bit... female dog."

"Nice save, Twenty-one," Faireuza called.

"Thank you," Galaxy acknowledged.

"That might be it." Faireuza said. "Or, it may be something else. Anyone have any ideas?"

The rest of the team shook their heads. Sarah stood in silence, stewing over the fact that it could be her. She didn't want to admit that it, or reveal that empty, black thing that she felt like a weight around her neck. At times, she hoped it would choke her into the deepest part of hell, to suffer for all eternity.

Drill Witcom continued to hound her every day, prying at her past, trying to get to the one thing that she dared not admit to even herself. She knew that it had resurfaced after years of suppression. She turned her thoughts inward and blocked out everything that Gloria was saying, desperate to send that disgrace back into the blackness where she had buried it.

Gloria read aloud from the bible for the remainder of the ninety-minute session. The verses she chose centered on adversity from within. "If thou faint in the day of adversity, thy strength is small. And though the Lord give you the bread of adversity, and the water of affliction, yet shall not thy teachers be removed into a corner any more, but thine eyes shall see thy teachers."

****

Sarah leaned against the corner of the building staring at the fence. She felt the stress levels rising within her and the rest of the team. Everyone could see the light at the end of the tunnel, but just couldn't grasp it. It was as if there was a hidden key that no one could find, to a lock that kept them away from the next step in their lives.

"Thinking about running for it?" Sarah turned at the familiar voice. Drill Hawkins walked up to her side and looked out at the lush grass, the fence, and the mature corn field beyond.

"No. Just wishing I knew then what I know now." Sarah faked a half-truth.

"I see. I can't turn back the clock for you."

"I know."

"But there's something that I can tell you. Maybe it will help."

THE SCHOLARSHIP

"What's that?"

"Think about the knowledge you'll have tomorrow because of the lesson you learned yesterday."

Sarah mulled the thought over. It did make sense. Much of what they taught focused on moving forward. She felt like she was stuck in limbo. If she could go back, she would fix so many things. Then life would be perfect. Her mom wouldn't drink; her parents would still be together. She would have a normal childhood and do normal things that children did. "Whatever that is?" Sarah mumbled to herself.

"Drill Hawkins," Drill Abernathy called from the doorway to the barracks. Drill Hawkins turned her attention to her sister drill. "Dean Vickery wants to see you in his office."

"Thank you, Drill Abernathy. Tell him I'll be right there."

"Drill Hawkins, I would have the knowledge today for the lesson learned yesterday," Sarah said.

"No. It doesn't work that way." Drill Hawkins turned to leave.

"Why?"

"Because you need time to process the lesson into the knowledge."

"Drill Hawkins," Sarah waited for her to pause. "I'd... like to make a run for it. I'd like it if you joined me too."

Drill Hawkins paused a moment, evaluating the sincerity and meaning of the request. "Alright. I'll see you after dinner." She gave a slight grin before turning and disappearing into the barracks.

Chapter XIX

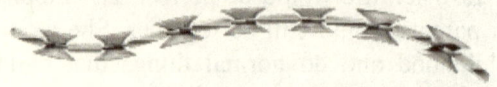

Sarah laced up her running shoes, straightened her sweats and walked out the door of the barracks. The sun had just set. Drill Hooks and Drill Smith were lowering the flag in the center of the barracks courtyard.

"What are you doing out here? You're supposed to have someone with you at all times."

Sarah snapped to attention. "Sorry. Drill Hooks. I asked Drill Hawkins to run with me. I thought she might be out here already."

"She's not. So, you better wait for her inside."

"Yes, Drill Hooks."

"I'm here now." Drill Hawkins walked around the corner of the building.

"Are you two going to be out here for a while?" Drill Smith asked.

"Yes. Twelve has some issues that she wanted to work out. She asked if I would supervise."

"Okay. You'll bring the flag down when you're done?"

"Yes, ma'am, we will." Drill Hawkins reassured her colleague.

THE SCHOLARSHIP

"I'll turn the lights on for you."

"Thanks, Drill Hooks."

Drill Smith retied the rope on the flagpole and walked with Drill Hooks back to the barracks.

"We'll do a couple of warm-up laps, then stretch," Drill Hawkins said, pointing to the track. The warm-up and stretching held no words other than the quiet commands Drill Hawkins used to switch to the next stretch. The night was crisp and fresh with a half-moon adding its light to the lights on the field.

The pace was rigorous, but not torturous like the first time they ran together. Drill Hawkins let Sarah set the pace, and then urged her a little more by staying a slight bit ahead of her. She held that pace for the better part of thirty minutes. Not a word was said, only the pounding of feet against the earth and the steady rhythmic breathing from their lungs.

The two miles around the track had been beaten into the earth from ten years of students learning how to be productive citizens. It felt good to Sarah. For a brief time, she was able to let go of the tedious annoyances that plagued her brain. She could focus on putting one foot in front of the other. In the cool night air, she could just run and let her mind go blank. She could feel the ground underfoot, the air in her lungs and her heart drumming to a steady rhythm.

Rounding the corner at the base of the hill they turned back to the barracks. From the tall pole holding the zipline, an owl spread its wings and leaped into the air. Silently he fell from the sky landing on a patch of thick grass. As the two women approached, it launched from the field, carrying a mouse in its claws. Its powerful wings carried it into the air where it circled back to the tree line.

Sarah paused on the track to watch the owl silhouetted against the night sky. "Wow," she said, in between puffs of breath. "I've never seen anything like that. Not in person anyway."

"Just watching nature in all its raw beauty can be a reward in and of itself." Drill Hawkins paced the ground around Sarah, not wanting to stop.

"Drill Hawkins, what are you going to do when you leave here?" Sarah asked, picking up a slower jog to allow them to talk a bit. "I know that you were once a student here along with the rest of the drills."

They ran on in silence. Sarah wondered if Drill Hawkins would ever answer. They had completed another lap and then some before she answered. "I don't know. I like it here. The question has been in the back of my mind though. I keep shoving it back there because I'm too afraid of what the future might hold for me."

"What about finding a husband and starting a family?" Sarah asked.

An icy chill filled the air. Sarah shivered as goosebumps raced across her body. She drew her next breath of cool, night air and she realized she had over-stepped an invisible boundary. Recognizing her mistake, she strode out ahead to gain some distance and not be in the uncomfortable bubble that now surrounded her running partner. Continuing at their earlier fast pace, Sarah made another lap around the extended mile-long track, letting her mind drift back to her own problems. Her teammates were going to fail because of her. They were not going to graduate because Drill Witcom wanted to hear something from her that she couldn't say even if she wanted to.

THE SCHOLARSHIP

The obstacle course loomed like a giant ocean monster waiting for unsuspecting prey to fall into its rope-like tentacles and become its next meal. Sarah passed it twice, then stopped suddenly, turned and looked at the towering poles interlaced with cables and rope. Drill Hawkins caught up to her and stepped in place to keep her limbs moving so that they wouldn't cramp up. Sarah walked in small circles waiting to catch her breath so she could express her thoughts in one fluid spill.

"I want to talk to the dean about our team graduating individually," Sarah huffed, as she regained her breath.

"Why do you want to do it that way?" Drill Hawkins continued to jog in place.

Sarah turned and continued on the path, but at a conversational pace. Drill Hawkins jogged beside her. "I know I'm the one holding our class back from graduating, and I know that my teammates will stick with me to the end. I think that they are that loyal. I don't want them to fail because of me. I don't know what it is that I am doing to hold everybody back. If I can't figure it out, I don't want my teammates to suffer because of it."

"Why do you think that you are the one holding your team back?" Drill Hawkins said, trying to draw out any information she could to help Drill Witcom.

"I don't know." Sarah told a half-truth. "Drill Witcom keeps asking me about my past, trying to dig out something that will supposedly make my future better. My mom was a drunk and my dad kicked us out."

"Why did he kick you out?" Drill Hawkins asked, keeping the conversation going.

"He brought home a younger, sportier model," Sarah confided.

"How old were you?"

"Fourteen."

"Why didn't your dad let you stay with him?"

Sarah didn't answer. It was Drill Hawkins' turn to feel the awkward silence of stepping over a hidden boundary. She didn't shy away but instead kept pace with Sarah and let her know that she wasn't alone. They both had troubling issues from the past that they didn't want to talk about, so they ran on in silence.

Chapter XX

Rain hammered down on the complex. Gloria struggled to contain her last nerve staring down on Sarah. This was the nerve that, if Gloria severed it, would send her away for the next ten years. She had feared it would come down to this and had tried everything else to bring Sarah out of her shell. Gloria knew that there was something in Sarah's past that she was so ashamed of that she dared not let anyone know. Drill Hawkins informed Gloria of their conversation about Sarah's father during their run and how she had then clammed up and refused to talk any more.

Ever since Sarah's early attempt at escaping the compound, Gloria knew that she had her work cut out for her. She had been lulled into a false sense of accomplishment during the second week of boot camp when Sarah put forth remarkable effort. She smiled and encouraged the other students, helping them with their chores, while following the rule to only assist and not take over. Gloria thought everything was going well until Sarah made that run for the fence. Since then, she guarded the idea that something was amiss. She tried counseling Sarah from all the different angles suggested by the staff, but nothing made her even wink a hint as to what she was hiding.

The rain made a steady dribble off the rim of her drill hat. Her mind raced for any other options. She had been cordial, polite, and strict, doing everything that the therapists had recommended. In her gut, she knew what was needed, but if she followed through with her intuition, she wouldn't see her boys until they were men. Still, she had made a promise to Sarah, and herself, that she would never give up. She wanted this young woman to have the best life possible and if that meant ten years behind bars for herself, then so be it.

Sarah stood her ground, refusing to haul another boulder up the hill. Rain had soaked through her scalp and most of her clothes despite the waterproof gear that she wore. Her anger had grown each day that one of her teammates disappeared at the top of the hill and she did not. Though she knew what the drills wanted, she was determined to take that information to her grave. She had done everything else that they asked. She had been a leader and a counselor to her classmates. She had given it her all starting the day after her confrontation with Fern. She wondered why they couldn't let her leave this one private moment in time alone and forgotten. Why did they insist on knowing everything in her past? It was just one event that was better left buried. No one needed to know how badly she had failed in the past. She knew that that failure would cost her more than time behind bars. It would cost her a lifetime of humiliation.

It had been four days since the last of her teammates disappeared at the top of the hill. She was happy for them, but sad, angry and depressed at her situation. She knew it was a matter of time before they would just send her back to prison to serve out her sentence. She didn't want that, nor did she want to buckle to their demands.

The weeks of morning to night physical activity had built her into a strong woman. Her baby fat was gone, replaced by lean and toned muscle. She had hauled countless boulders to the top of the hill only to have then slide back down the zip-line. If the rock fell out of the sling that she tied around it, she would have to haul it back to the top. There weren't any shortcuts and a rock that fell out prematurely was cause for a re-do. She learned to tie the rope around the boulder well to prevent it from falling to the ground during its descent.

She now hated the drills. From day one she disliked them, though at times she held respect for Drill Hawkins. Now she was appalled by them. Their demeanor made her skin crawl, always in her face forcing her on to the next task. Drill Witcom had tried to get inside her head and she knew it. Sarah blocked her at every roll of the dice. She forged her mind against the battle of wits. She wouldn't let herself be beaten. There wasn't anything that this drill could do to break her. She was a master at shutting her feelings off. That's what this was about: making her sway to the beat of their drum, not her own.

She had heard it whispered that Gloria had children. She remembered seeing the scribbled note about an emergency appendix surgery and the prayer scratched over and over on her clipboard. Sarah didn't care. Gloria's children had no bearing on her life.

"Go to hell," Sarah huffed through the drizzle, "and take your bastard children with you."

A sting to her face, followed by ringing in her head and a throbbing skull supercharged Sarah's adrenaline. She flashed a wicked grin and stared at her supposed teacher. "Is that all you got; you piece of…"

Gloria swung her fist again. The lightning-fast cannon caught Sarah square in the jaw, and she rolled with it like she had done so many times before. So many boyfriends had hit her in the past that she expected it. She had learned to turn with the punch and come back with one of her own.

Gloria found herself face down in the mud. She hadn't expected retaliation, or a solid connection from Sarah's right fist. She shook her head to clear her mind.

"You want some more, momma?" Sarah taunted.

Gloria's blood boiled at the insult to her children. Other drills began to pick her up, but she shook off the assistance. She picked herself up and turned to Sarah.

"You want some of this?" Sarah egged again.

Gloria feigned a kick to the mid-section. Sarah pulled her gut back but allowed her face to go forward, right into a left jab from Gloria's fist. Bone crunched, and blood streamed down Sarah's face. The wicked grin remained on her face, giving Gloria pause. Her face was suddenly turned monstrous from the intent eyes, the crimson red and the rain dragging the blood down to stain her teeth.

Blood pouring from her face was not new to Sarah. Just about every boyfriend she had in the past few years had hit her. She expected it. Now she craved it. This was her world now. She drew Gloria into the surroundings that she was accustomed to, a world of pain and suffering. She relished the old feelings of physical violence. The new comradery that was introduced to her was great, but it didn't have the physical connection that had been so prevalent in her life. The academy did not encourage physical contact of any kind, hateful or pleasant. That was one element that Sarah needed, though she had said that she didn't.

THE SCHOLARSHIP

Gloria recognized the signs of anger she had seen in Sarah from when her oldest boy had become defiant in his early teens. He had lashed out, trying to set his own boundaries for his emergence into manhood. She had barely overcome that obstacle when her sister called her for a ride. From that one ride everything changed for Gloria.

Gloria set her mind to what had to be done. She knew it was against the rules and that it would cost her dearly, but she made this promise to only three other people in the world. She promised to never give up on her children. She looked at the evil grin on the rain and blood-soaked face. It gave her pause but didn't send her running for the hills. She stepped forward ready to take on the challenge of what she started a few months before when she selected the file from the bottom of the stack.

Punches flew as both women tore at each other in an increasing rage. Drill Hanks moved to step in between the two but was stopped short by Drill Hawkins. Several other drills stood and watched, also ready to step in if needed. They all knew that a physical altercation had been coming between Witcom and Menendez, and most knew that if anything could change Sarah's attitude, it would be a sound beat down.

Gloria didn't have a mean bone in her body when she joined the academy, and she still didn't. In her self-defense training she had learned to tap into the energy derived from anger, and leave the actual anger locked away where it would collect dust forever.

Gloria swept Sarah's legs out from under her. The orange sweats collapsed in a heap. Sarah rolled and captured Gloria's legs to bring her down in the mud as well. Gloria grabbed a fistful of hair and popped three solid punches into Sarah's eye.

Sarah shoved, then kicked Gloria away. She jumped to her feet ready to take on a bear and Gloria came at her like a lion. She body-tackled Sarah back into the mud, sliding several feet down the hill. Sarah used the momentum to lift her bottom and buck Gloria over her head sending her even farther down the hill.

Each jumped to their feet and came at the other. Punch for punch and kick for kick they battled to show who was more stubborn. Gloria swung. Sarah dodged out of the way. Off balance, Gloria slipped and landed on the boulder that Sarah had refused to carry up the hill. Her left arm bent awkwardly underneath her, snapping between her weight and the boulder.

Pain shot to her brain to warn her of the impending danger. Gloria was having none of it. She had a lesson to teach and bulled her mind back into the fight. She rolled and booted Sarah in the gut, knocking the air from her lungs. Jumping back out of the mud, Gloria swung a hard right, knocking Sarah face-first to the ground.

She jumped on Sarah's back, grabbed an arm and twisted it behind her. Gloria used her left knee to pin her student's arm and body in place as she picked up a stick and began beating it across Sarah's butt.

Gloria continued paddling Sarah in the downpour. "Tell me what you're afraid of."

"Get off me," Sarah screamed.

"What are you afraid of?"

Sarah gritted her teeth, determined not to appease her drill.

"Answer me." Gloria continued to spank her student with all the force she could muster.

"I hate you."

"Wrong answer." Gloria continued to beat Sarah's back side.

"I hate you."

208

THE SCHOLARSHIP

"What?"

"I hate you."

"Wrong answer!" Gloria screamed at the woman pinned beneath her. Sarah refused to talk. She planted her face in the mud with the intention of drowning herself in the puddle beneath her. Gloria dropped the stick and grabbed a handful of hair to keep Sarah's face out of the puddle. "Who do you hate?" Gloria surmised that someone had wronged Sarah in the past and was the key to unraveling and repairing the broken woman.

"I hate him."

Gloria kept her knee firmly in place to prevent Sarah from trying to move. "Who?"

"I hate him."

"Who?"

"My father." Sarah caved to the release. Her muscles softened as the secret was breeched. Her face was inches from being buried in the puddle she was sobbing into. . She craved the puddle. She wanted to end her life right then and there. Her mind begged to be let go, to drown in the puddle and end the torture that her heart was filled with.

"Why?" Gloria asked with concern in her voice.

Sarah didn't answer.

"Why do you hate him?" Gloria growled in her ear.

"He raped me."

Gloria knew that this was the element that was preventing Sarah from graduating, from moving on to the next phase of the academy, from freeing herself from the burden. She rolled Sarah over and pulled her up into an embrace.

Sarah beat at Gloria in a half-hearted attempt to shove her away, but Gloria held the grieving woman firm and did her best to soak the pain out of her soul. "He raped me," Sarah sobbed.

"When?" Gloria pulled her face around so she could look into Sarah's eyes.

"I was ten and he forced himself into my room. He was drunk. I could smell the alcohol. My mom held my arms and let him rape me. He raped me nearly every night until he kicked us out of the house."

Gloria held her tight and stroked her hair, doing her best to comfort her. The rest of the drills stood there in various stages of shock and concern.

"He raped me until I was almost fourteen. I hid my face under the pillow until it was over, and he stumbled out to sleep on the couch."

"Did you tell the police?" Gloria smoothed the back of her head.

Sarah shook her head.

"Why not?" Gloria continued to stroke her head to soothe her.

"He was the police."

Gloria sighed at the last piece of the puzzle. She understood now why she had been so resilient. If in the same shoes, Gloria guessed she would also have some animosity toward anyone with authority.

"I ate to gain weight so that he might think that I was ugly, and he wouldn't bother me anymore, but he kept coming into my room every night. He told me that I was his girl and that I would go to jail if I told anyone. He told me that it was my fault and if I had been a better student, things like that wouldn't happen to me. He told me that jail was a place for those who told on their families." Sarah slumped into the mud, held up only by Gloria. Her tears rivaled the downpour that hammered down on them.

THE SCHOLARSHIP

"I got pregnant. I was so scared. My mother was always drunk. I didn't know who to turn to. He continued to rape me through the first part of the pregnancy." Sarah sat in the mud waiting for God to strike her down now that he knew the truth that she had been hiding. Gloria held her up and listened. She listened like a mother who cared, like someone Sarah had secretly been begging for most of her life. Sarah was reduced to a young girl clinging to a mother and begging her to take the pain away.

"He left for a couple of months and my mom was only in the house long enough to change clothes before she would leave again. I got sick and the baby stopped moving."

Sarah sobbed like the rain that pounded down upon their heads. She trembled from the emotion that poured forth.

"I gave birth to my baby in the bathtub. I knew she was too small and that the baby had been…"

"Shh. Shh. Shh." Gloria rocked her gently, holding her tight while comforting her.

"I buried her outside the back door. I wrapped her in a garbage bag and buried her. I placed a small stuffed bear in with her so she would have a friend to talk to and I buried her. I'm sorry. I'm so sorry. I didn't want to. I knew I would get in trouble, so I didn't say anything."

Gloria continued to hold her and let her spill all the pain that had been bottled up for so long.

"When dad came home, he brought a new girlfriend and kicked me and mom out. I went back a few weeks later to say goodbye to my baby. There was a fresh concrete slab poured. The cement was still wet, so I drew a heart above where I buried her."

Gloria pulled Sarah tight against her in a hug that only a mother knows how to give to a grieving child. She clung to

211

the child, trying to soak away all her heartache. She desperately wished she could turn back the clock to change something, anything that would prevent the child that Sarah was from having to go through such an ordeal.

With the smallest of voices, Sarah whispered. "I love you, mom."

Gloria's heart dissolved. She had no words. She clung to the child fearing that if she let go, she would not see her again.

Chapter XXI

Sarah woke to an oddly peaceful morning. The scrapes and bruises from the day before caused her to move gingerly. A bright sun lit the sky. She had overslept, yet Gloria had not come to wake her.

She rose out of her bunk and walked into the latrine. The mirror in front of her illuminated the purple ribbons from the day before. Her eye was swollen. Minor cuts and scrapes covered her face, hands and arms. She noticed a bit of mud that was still caked in her hair. The shower had not gotten everything out.

She hobbled back out to the main barracks area. One of the nurses stood with the door open.

"Come on Twelve. Let's take a look and see if you need anything patched up."

Sarah nodded her head and followed the nurse. Several bandages and a couple of Tylenol later she changed into some clean sweats and walked over to see the dean as she had been instructed.

He was in another meeting and it stretched into overtime. Thirty minutes ticked by as she waited wondering what her fate may be. Finally, she was ushered in to stand before the dean. Waiting quietly, she watched as he shuffled through a couple of remaining memos followed by a signature at the bottom of a contract. It was a contract with nearby Fort Lenard Wood to hire a few of their drill sergeants to come to Schultz Business Academy and help train new drills for future classes. They had to teach the next class of drills to perform the monumental task of preparing the incoming new students for the beginning of their new lives.

Dean Vickery looked up at Sarah, who was standing at parade rest waiting for him to address her. She stared at the Army Core Values that were listed on the wall behind him.

Loyalty, Duty, Respect, Selfless Service, Honor, Integrity and Personal Courage stared back at her as if taunting her, daring her to live up to them.

"Sarah, I am afraid you have failed this course."

"Sir?"

"Drill Witcom is gone. She broke the rules and has failed her part of the course."

"Sir, I don't understand."

"This is something that we don't tell incoming students. The drills were where you are. They came through the doors the same as you. They struggled and tested the drills before them, pushing to prove their worth.

"Drill Witcom came here on a deferment to an extended prison sentence. She was charged with a serious crime. Before they can leave here, they must confess to everything that they have done wrong and the reasons they did it. You would have had to do the same."

"Sir? Had to do the same?" Sarah asked unsure of what was happening.

214

THE SCHOLARSHIP

"Yes. Since Drill Witcom hit you, she'll return to prison and won't be allowed to graduate."

"Prison?" Sarah panicked. Her head spun from the knowledge. She had just found the one person who would not give up on her and now she was gone.

"Giving back is something that we require in this program. One way to give back is to mentor another student coming in. Gloria was the first to graduate in her class and she was the first to pick from a stack of thirty files."

"But there are only twenty-five spots available in the class." Sarah countered.

"Yes. We have a few extra files. When it is time, the first graduate gets first choice. The files are ranked by a series of doctors and psychologists from most likely to succeed to least likely to succeed."

"What does that have to do with me?"

"Your file was at the bottom."

Sarah's heart hit her stomach. She felt lower than dirt. She had her very own angel and she had banished that poor saint to hell.

"She didn't even look through your file. She simply grabbed it and told me that even those at the bottom deserve a shot."

Sarah had screwed up Gloria's chance at going back to her family. She looked back at all that Gloria had done and saw that every ounce of it was for her. She was treated like a child, Gloria's child, and Gloria was her mother. Every scolding that Gloria dished out was meant to build her into a good person. She didn't know if it had worked, but it was too late now, and she would be going back to prison just like Gloria. She had sealed both their fates.

"What happens now?"

"You've failed to graduate. We will make arrangements for a transport to take you back to the corrections facility. Is what you told Drill Witcom true? About your father, that is."

Sarah lowered her head. She tried to hide from the long-ago, hurtful memories. It was one of the reasons she shielded herself with anger for so long. Being angry was easier than feeling lost and alone. If she was lost, sad and alone, she would not have survived for as long as she had.

Drill Witcom made her face the secret that had been eating away at her from the inside. The secret had been her burden, her mistake, her personal hell until last night. When she confessed, she broke the chain that kept that dark secret to herself. Gloria pulled all the hurt that she could away from Sarah. She held her and comforted her trying to soak as much hurt as she could away from Sarah. Gloria was a real mom. One who cared and put all her effort into her children. Sarah understood that now and was deeply ashamed of her behavior.

Sarah looked at the Army core values listed behind the dean. Selfless Service stood out among all the rest. Gloria sacrificed her freedom for Sarah. She looked back at the dean.

"Yes, sir. It is true. I have never told anyone until last night." Sarah lowered her head in shame. She was ashamed to be standing in front of a sign that was opposite of what she was. She did deserve to go back to prison, not for hitting the woman who gave birth to her but for failing the only woman who acted like a mother to her, the only woman who didn't give up, the only woman who made her face her demons and made her realize that the real demon was herself.

"This is a crime and it needs to be looked into."

"Yes, sir. Is that all, sir?" Sarah said eager to be anywhere but where she stood.

THE SCHOLARSHIP

"I will have an officer and a therapist come visit with you about what happened to make an official statement on the matter."

"Yes, sir."

Dean Vickery looked up at Sarah. Sadness filled his eyes. "I am sorry to see you leave. We all try our best to make this program as successful as possible. We have had a one hundred percent success rate until this class. Maybe our heads have gotten a little big and we've become complacent in the light of that success. Like you, we are still learning and doing everything we can to make improvements. I believe in this program, as does everyone else here. We ask people who want to work here if they would continue to work if there was a budget cut and they had to go without pay for one to two months. Everyone we have hired checked the box that said "yes." That is one measure that we take to let the students know that we won't give up on them, even if they give up on us.

"We will see that you are well represented by a competent attorney in the matter between you and your parents. I know you had a hard start in life, and I wish there was a magic wand that could erase all of that, but we are grounded in reality here and forced to do the best we can with what we have.

"You will have to be fitted with an ankle monitor until you are transferred into the sheriff's custody. Drill Stotsman will see you to the therapist."

"Yes, sir. I'm sorry that I failed the academy," Sarah said quietly, as she turned to leave.

Chapter XXII

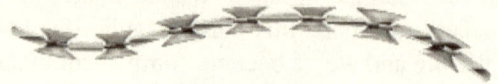

A sliver of a moon bled just enough light to see the larger objects that stood between her and freedom. She had slipped the ankle monitor off her foot and left it under her pillow-stuffed bedroll. By the time anyone noticed, she would be long gone. The weeks of planning her escape came back fresh into her mind.

Dodging from building to building she made her way to the edge of the common area an expanse clear of any obstacles. In the distance she could see the perimeter fence topped with several rolls of razor wire.

The bumps and scratches from the day before had loosened up and now allowed her to run for the fence. She kept to the darkest corner of the field. In the backpack she carried were a couple of blankets to drape over the razor wire and help her escape into the vast farm fields. The corn was head high now and would make easy cover to help her get further away.

Reaching the fence, she glanced back. All the usual lights were on to illuminate the walkways and parts of the field surrounding the academy. The air was still. Sounds of the distant highway echoed off the hills in a barely audible rumble.

THE SCHOLARSHIP

Crickets chirped around her and lightning bugs lit up the night with their unique bodies.

Scaling the eight-foot fence, Sarah flung the blankets over the razor wire and scrambled over the top. Dropping to the ground on the other side, she stared at the long rows of corn that stretched into the distance. Five steps and she would be gone.

Her foot hesitated in midair. She looked at the field again, at the freedom that she had just acquired and at the image of Gloria in her mind. She turned and looked at the academy. She was free. She could leave. Yet, she stood there. Kicking at the ground, she expressed her frustration at the choice she was on the verge of making.

On day one, when Gloria came face-to-face with her for the first time, she remembered seeing a stern woman who was bent on dealing out punishment. Sarah also saw a hint of something else she didn't understand until just now. What she saw was love, a genuine love and caring for her, the student who had been pulled from the bottom of the pile. A young woman she didn't know except that she was ranked most likely *not* to succeed. Gloria cared deeply for her from day one. Sarah now understood all the pain that woman had gone through trying to get her to come out of her shell. Gloria had read Sarah like an open book. She knew that there was something more and she dug at it until Sarah broke.

Sarah beat her head against the tall post and stamped her foot into the ground. The word honor popped into her head. She had to honor Drill Witcom. She had to do something to make it right. Gloria had broken the rules in order to help Sarah. She had needed her ass handed to her to make her see how selfish a person she had become. Sarah had needed that discipline, that loving discipline. She grumbled at the choice

219

she was fighting against. She knew that her choice would have her honoring Drill Witcom for the next twenty-five years from behind bars. The lesson on integrity hit her. "Do what's right no matter what happens." Sarah mumbled to herself. She slammed her head against the post and clenched her eyes shut.

"Maybe," Sarah said to herself, "I have to ask." With a sigh and a grunt of effort she climbed back over the fence.

****

Sarah sat facing her food in the chow hall. It was quiet save for the occasional clang of a dish from the other side of a thin wall, where the drills ate their food. Muffled excitement filtered through the walls as Sarah toyed with her food. Her appetite dwindled to that of a mouse. Her anxiety grew as the time drew closer to ask to see the dean again.

Jerked from her thoughts, she looked up to see Drill Hawkins and Drill Dawson standing opposite her table. Each wore a poker face with a hint of malice. Drill Hawkins sat down opposite Sarah.

"I'm curious as to what is going on inside your brain," Drill Hawkins said.

Sarah stared back at her with a puzzled look.

"I don't care that you say anything. In fact, I really don't want to hear it, because actions speak louder than words. You know, everyone screws up in life. Sometimes it's from ignorance, sometimes from arrogance, sometimes it's from being a damn stick in the mud. It's what they do after the mistake that shows what is really in their soul."

Drill Hawkins pulled from her pocket the ankle monitor that Sarah had slipped off her foot and left in her bed the night before. When she climbed back over the fence and sneaked

THE SCHOLARSHIP

back into her bunk, she had forgotten about it and drifted off to sleep.

"This must have slipped off in the shower. Drill Hollister has the key. She can help you get it back on."

Drill Hawkins stood up from the cafeteria bench. She straightened her uniform and looked down on Sarah. "Drill Witcom is a great friend. Now I won't be able to see her for a decade."

"C'mon, Drill. We need to investigate the perimeter fence. It seems that someone broke into the academy last night," Drill Dawson said, as they turned to leave.

"Broke into the academy? Why would someone want to do that?"

"I d'nno. Maybe it's the food?"

Sarah stared at her plate. Her appetite had now disintegrated to nothing. They had been watching her the whole time. She knew now that she wouldn't have gotten away. They were testing her, waiting to see what she did. *'It's what they do after the mistake that shows what is really in their soul.'* The words drew on Sarah, she knew what she had to do. She had to go talk to the dean.

Butterflies raged war inside her stomach as she stood outside the dean's office. She didn't want to go to prison, but more than anything she didn't want Drill Witcom to be viewed as a failure. She wasn't. Gloria had succeeded the moment she pulled all the hatred out of Sarah. It took a beat down to get her to come around and Sarah was reluctantly relieved to be rid of some of that burden. The feeling of relief was foreign to her, something that she wasn't sure how to handle. She felt differently about the situation that had happened so many years ago. The motherly embrace that Gloria used to comfort her melted years of built-up anger. She knew that she would need

221

more counseling. She would seek a counselor to help her sort out her feelings when she got to where she was going, but that would have to wait. Right now, she needed to talk to the dean.

Sarah knocked on the door to the dean's office as Drill Hollister stood just a step behind her. "Come in," the dean's voice invited. Sarah opened the door, then took two steps and placed her toes on the blue tape stuck to the floor. Her hands snapped to parade rest, tight and snug against the small of her back.

"Yes, Sarah. What can I help you with?"

"I want to finish, Sir."

"You are finished. You have failed."

"Yes. I know that, Sir. I want to finish for Drill Witcom."

Dean Vickery sat back in his chair and studied Sarah for a moment. "Why?"

"Sir, I failed her. I failed the system. I didn't see what you were trying to do because of a deep hatred I had for any authority figure. I wish I had Gloria for a mother, because I know she would have beaten some sense into me long before I would have come here."

"So, what are you asking?"

"I want to finish for her. I can't let her name be a failure on these walls. I will happily go to prison if I get a chance to finish what she started."

"You were already given a chance."

"Yes, sir. That chance was for me. I know that I've messed that up already. I want this chance for Drill Witcom. She went beyond what was required to save me from the destructive path I was heading down." Sarah stared at the Army's 'Selfless Service' printed on the wall behind the dean. "It was her selfless service of sacrificing her freedom that saved me."

THE SCHOLARSHIP

Sarah choked back the lump in her throat. "She doesn't deserve to go out like this. She is too good of a person to be listed as a failure here."

"Do you know what the drills go through when their student doesn't graduate on time?"

"I've heard that there is some kind of punishment, sir."

"For every day that their student doesn't graduate they have to haul a boulder to the top of the hill. The first day past the deadline is one boulder, the second is two. Each day the amount doubles. If they don't finish by six AM, then it is doubled again."

Sarah choked at the thought of so many trips up and down the mountain. It couldn't be humanly possible.

"They have to pay the old debts first." Dean Vickery continued. "You can't pay today's debt without paying yesterday's first. This is the lesson that they learn. It is vital that the students understand the debt that they take on in their lives. Everything we do here is in some way a lesson. Gloria learned that the only way to get through to you was to sacrifice herself. She could have let you fail. You were days away from the deadline. She would have gone home, and you would go back to prison. We have structured the program in a way that puts heavy emphasis on the need to be in control of yourself and the life around you.

"The national debt will soon be so large that we, as a society, won't be able to pay for the interest. So, the interest will either have to go to zero or we, as a nation, will have to declare bankruptcy. Whether you work at a job, operate a small business, run a large business, or a nonprofit charity, you have to have the mindset of a businessperson in order to be successful."

"What do you mean by interest going to zero?" Sarah asked.

"What that means is that the Federal Reserve, who loans money to the United States, will charge zero interest. This means that everything you pay will go to reducing your overall debt. You see, they are a company. If the U.S. declares bankruptcy, the Federal Reserve loses massive amounts of money, but if they charge zero interest for a while, they can maintain that money they have invested.

"So, when there are more boulders to carry than there is time to carry them, you become bankrupt and the consequences are steep. Does that make sense?" Dean Vickery asked.

"I think so." Sarah said still trying to digest the information.

"Gloria is a great friend to many of the drills here. She earned their respect by taking on a difficult task. Because you failed, there are a lot of people here who don't like you very much. In this program she has incurred a lot of debt because she couldn't get you to come forth with what she felt needed to be done. It cost her a lot of time here and now, since she has failed the program set before her, it has cost her the maximum sentence of her original crime. To be honest, I really don't see how you can succeed."

"I understand, sir."

"You've changed. That's a good thing. Hold on to that."

"Yes, sir."

"I'll give some thought to what you've asked. I don't think it will happen for you, but in the future, it may benefit someone."

"Thank you for your time, sir."

THE SCHOLARSHIP

Dean Vickery nodded his head. Sarah turned and walked back to the main barracks. She looked at her neatly made bed. It called for her to sleep and wait for the transport. The idea of sleep turned her stomach like the food did that morning. Walking outside, she found herself automatically moving toward square number twelve. She placed her feet into the yellow outlines and stared at the hill. She had been up that hill hundreds of times. At first, she thought it was for punishment. It took her until just now to realize that it was a representative of all the meaningless tasks that had to be done every day of her life. It wasn't necessarily character building as it was the dull task of wiping the counter off or taking out the trash. It just plain had to be done. There was no award, no recognition. It was just part of life.

It was like brushing your teeth every day. The reward was never meant to be immediate; the reward was far down the road when you still had your own teeth and others of your age where whistling though their dentures. It was being cautions enough to avoid blunders and the emergency room visits. It was watching the bottom line and avoiding paying excess money out to creditors.

She had been up that mountain countless times and hated every minute of it. Gloria's words were coming back to haunt her. *"When I get through with you, you're going to love this hill."* She stared at the pile of boulders at the base. Boulders of many different sizes and shapes beckoned to her. She didn't know what started her moving forward but she knew that it felt good to move. She felt as light as a feather, as if all the burdens of the world had dropped away and allowed her to float weightless. At her feet lay one of the many stones that she had carted up the hill. A rope tied to a pulley lay close by.

"For you, mom," she said and picked up the rope. Lashing the opposite end around the rock, she pulled the stone high on her back and slung the rope over her shoulder. She fell into a numb trance and put one foot in front of the other. At the top she didn't even stop to look down. She simply put the pulley on the cable and sent it to the bottom. She focused only on where her next step would be.

Down the hill she walked back to the pile of boulders. Picking up the one she had just sent down the mountain, she pulled it over her shoulder and marched back up the hill again. This time the determination grew within her to keep going faster. She had a new purpose. She had to clear Gloria's debt. At the moment she didn't know how many trips she would have to make before her debt was paid off. It didn't matter to her now. She was relieved that she could do something about it before they came to haul her away.

She ran across the flat parts of the trail and made a steady climb up the steep sections. A new liberating energy filled her soul as she made trip after trip hauling one boulder at a time up to the top only to send it back to the bottom. The sun stretched high into the sky and began its descent back toward the horizon. For the first time in hours she stopped to rest on a rock shelf jutting out from the side of the hill. Looking out across the academy she saw two drills standing together watching her and two more walking up the trail to where she was sitting.

Her stomach grumbled, and her mouth was dry. She hadn't noticed hunger or thirst due to the feel-good energy that had carried her until now. She wished she would have eaten something that morning, but she knew that her nervousness would have made her throw anything she ate back up anyway.

Drill Dawson and Drill Hawkins walked up to sit on either side of her.

226

THE SCHOLARSHIP

"It's a pretty good view from up here when you're not hauling boulders," Drill Dawson said, as she rested on the rock shelf. She handed a water bottle to Sarah. Sarah accepted it and took a long pull from the chilled bottle.

"You know our secret, too." Drill Hawkins said.

"Secret, Drill Hawkins?" Sarah asked.

"Yes. You now know that we get punished when you don't graduate on time."

"I suspected that there was a penalty but didn't think it was as severe as hauling boulders to the top of the hill, Drill Hawkins."

"Here." Drill Hawkins handed her a protein bar. "Best keep your strength up."

"Have they come for me yet, Drill Hawkins?"

"They've come and gone. They took Gloria back to be processed into prison."

Pain shot through Sarah's heart. "It's not right. She did those things out of love for me, to keep me from going back to prison."

"Doesn't matter, rules are rules. It doesn't matter how unjust they may be. Do you know how she got into trouble in the first place?"

"No, Drill Hawkins."

"She pled guilty for the drugs that her sister was transporting, just to keep her new niece from being born in prison. She wanted that baby to live its entire life outside of the prison walls. It didn't do her any good. Her sister got caught with drugs two weeks later and is now serving her own sentence."

"I didn't know."

"Drill Witcom is a saint. No one who has passed through those doors has been able to achieve what she has. Everyone knew that she would be the first to graduate. Her love for not leaving someone behind is what sent her back to prison."

Sarah hung her head with a mountain of guilt on top of it. Drill Dawson turned toward Sarah and nudged her with another bottle of water. "Do you remember what Drill Hawkins said this morning?"

Sarah shook her head.

"She said that everyone makes a mistake, it is what you do afterward that determines who you are. So, who are you?" Drill Dawson asked poking Sarah with the bottle of water.

Sarah looked up into Drill Dawson's eyes. Hair stood on the back of her neck as she finally understood what the drills were looking for in order to graduate someone and move them on to the next stage. She nodded her head and stood. She accepted the bottled water and the energy bar from her superiors.

"We can't tell you how many trips you need to finish what you started, but you have three days to complete it, counting today," Drill Hawkins offered.

"All the drills are furious that their friend was sent away. They also understand what you have gone through. That's why we've agreed to leave you to your work until inspection tomorrow at zero-six hundred," Drill Dawson said, "and you better be ready."

Sarah nodded her head. "Yes, Drill Dawson. How will I know when I've completed everything?"

"We'll tell you." Drill Hawkins said as she rose to her feet. "Remember, I don't like you either. You are pigheaded and disrespectful." Drill Hawkins turned to walk back down the hill.

"Drill Hawkins?"

The drill stopped and turned to Sarah.

THE SCHOLARSHIP

"I'm sorry for mean mugging you on the first day. I didn't realize how much you all cared about us." Hawkins turned to leave again.

"And, Drill Hawkins. I think you would make an excellent master drill."

Drill Hawkins only paused a moment at the compliment, then continued down the hill with Drill Dawson while Sarah turned up the hill.

Chapter XXIII

Sarah tried to keep track of how many times she climbed the hill in the two days that she forced herself to push on, round after round. The drills were stationed all along the trail up the hill, insulting her and hindering her at every moment. The only time she had any privacy was in the toilet. As soon as she emerged there would be two drills screaming: one telling her to move while the other told her that she wouldn't amount to anything, encouraging her to give up. The previous forty-eight hours had become a blur. She slept three hours two nights before and nothing the previous night. She stopped hauling boulders forty minutes before the six A.M. inspection and saluting the flag. It was enough time to shower, change clothes and stand at attention for Drill Hawkins to inspect her quarters. Zero-six hundred was an earmark of a new day. The academy's day used this as its base line mimicking the military in many ways.

Each day was a new opportunity for each student to build their own castle. In their boot camp phase, they laid the foundation of solid moral values. With a solid foundation, any student could build their castle as tall as they wanted without

THE SCHOLARSHIP

fear of it collapsing under them. It was the students' job to improve their position every day.

Though the drills were allowed until six A.M. the following morning to complete their punishments, Sarah was still a recruit and subject to a midnight deadline. This gave her six hours less to complete her work. If she failed, she would get regretful sleep. If she succeeded, she would get blissful sleep. For now, sleep didn't matter. It was her turn to sacrifice herself for Gloria.

After shoveling a mountain of food into her stomach without tasting a bite, she sped toward the mountain to grab another boulder and start back up the hill. After hours of hauling the monotonous boulders, thunder clouds rolled in over the academy. The afternoon sun disappeared, and rain took its place, watering nature's garden. The hill became slick with mud and her struggle to stay upright was increasingly difficult. The pounding rain washed the mud off her until she replaced it with her next slip and fall. Lightning flashed and thunder followed only a second behind.

A small, tin building stood atop the hill. and Four drills huddled inside, hiding from the lightning. Sarah only cared about one thing: finishing what her drill had started. She didn't know how many boulders she would have to haul to the top. She did know that every moment counted, and she wasn't going to stop until it was finished. The drills took six-hour intervals watching her. except for one. Drill Hawkins was there every time she sent the trolley down the cable.

Sarah figured that Hawkins was counting, and when she took a one-time glance back, she caught the drill making a mark in a notebook. Sarah thought it was amazing that she could still look fresh and alive after fifty- plus hours of watching over her. Sarah thought that if there ever was true magic, Drill Hawkins must possess some to appear that radiant even after the lack of sleep, searing heat and pounding rain.

The wind increased as the head of the storm came to ravage the landscape, and all who stood to defy it. Sarah grunted against the wind as it tried to rip the breath from her lungs. Slipping and stumbling up the hill she plodded, one foot after the other. She didn't care. She had to keep going.

Trees strained and bowed against the wind, rocking back and forth as the storm took out its vengeance on the docile landscape. Branches broke and leaves were ripped from their tender connections and blown far away. Sarah looked up to where Drill Hawkins stood her ground waiting for Sarah to top the hill. The winds screamed through the darkening sky. Lightning flickered to illuminate the grounds but did a poor job as the heavy rain hammered anything it could into the ground.

Gust after gust of wind kept Sarah from making a swift climb to the top. Time was against her. Not knowing how many more trips she needed was killing her. She began to fear that she wouldn't be able to complete the task and the dread of failing again sickened her to death. Hammered by a gust, she fell to one knee. She looked up to see Drill Hawkins staring at her, daring her to get back up. The woman seemed to be unmoving, as if the wind did not affect her at all.

A loud snap caught Sarah's attention. She looked to the trees behind Drill Hawkins. A large hickory tree snapped at the root tipping toward Drill Hawkins. Sarah screamed a warning, but her voice was carried away as soon as it left her mouth. She dropped the boulder and sprinted toward the drill. Drill Hawkin's eyes grew wide as she prepared to defend herself from what appeared to be an attack. Just inches away, Drill Hawkins saw the fear in Sarah's eyes, not anger.

THE SCHOLARSHIP

The blow to Hawkins midsection knocked the air from her lungs as she was driven backwards, down into the mud. The hickory tree pummeled the ground where she had been standing. Sarah rolled off the drill as others came rushing up to help the two to their feet.

"Are you alright, Drill?" Drill Hollister asked.

Hawkins looked around at the tree and where she had been standing. "Yes. I'm good. Take her to sit in the lean-to." The drills helped Sarah to the shed and sat her down. They looked her over for any injuries and gave her some water and a protein bar.

Sarah didn't listen to the chatter from the drills: she was too numb to understand their gibberish anyway. Two days of constant hazing had dulled her senses to anyone speaking to her. She stared out through the rain where Drill Hawkins had disappeared over the edge and out of sight. She was gone for only a moment when she reappeared again, carrying Sarah's boulder.

"I think you dropped something." Drill Hawkins held out the boulder to Sarah.

Sarah smiled and stood up to accept her boulder. She paused for a moment, realizing that the simple gesture was an immense one for Hawkins. With a stern voice, Hawkins poker face turned to a mean glare. "Are you going to finish this or what?"

"Yes, Drill Hawkins. Moving, Drill Hawkins." Sarah tore out through the puddle-laden ground. She hung the trolley on the cable and sent it sailing down to the bottom where she would pick it back up. Without hesitation, she scrambled down the hillside to grab the stone and start carrying it up again.

She kept working as darkness fell. Sarah knew that she was running out of time: the midnight deadline was approaching fast. Her muscles screamed to rest as drill after drill taunted her. She dodged their attacks at her spirit, yet the attacks still wore her down, along with the painstakingly slow climb. Her own energy reserves had hit bottom, and the strength she had before was replaced by pure willpower to continue to put one foot in front of the other.

"You filthy slob. Pick your feet up!" Drill Hollister stepped in front of her, blocking her path. Sarah paused and altered her course trying her best to keep moving and to pick up her feet.

"Sorry, Drill Hollister." Sarah moved up the hill, ready for next insult. She knew her feet had blisters that had started the day before. The double layer of socks helped but did not prevent the blisters from forming. Her muscles ached, and her left calf muscle was in an almost-permanent state of cramping. The thunderstorm fizzled to a steady drizzle. She was soaked to the bone and beginning to shiver.

The night wore on as she continued to lug rocks up the hill. It seemed that she could follow the trail blindfolded now. She had been around it constantly for weeks. The familiar trail had become more than a ritual: it had become an obsession that she knew could lead to Gloria's freedom. She knew it was only one obstacle, but it was one she could do right here, right now. She slipped, falling face first in the mud. She tried to bring her arms underneath her, but they refused to move.

Clinging to the edge of consciousness, she tried to focus on her breathing. She had to pull energy from somewhere. The thought of prison seemed a tropical paradise compared to what she was doing now. She would be more than willing to surrender to prison, so long as she completed the debt for Gloria.

THE SCHOLARSHIP

She sniffed muddy water up her nose, sending her brain into panic mode. The grainy, salty sensation caused her to sneeze. Blowing out the nasty substance, Sarah rolled onto her side where she could get a better breath of air. The rain had picked up again, cascading its heavenly moisture down to clean the mud off Sarah's face.

"Why, God?" Sarah whispered to the heavens.

"Why? I'll tell you why." Drill Dawson knelt in the mud. She put her face down close to Sarah's. "Because you don't deserve a friend like Drill Witcom. She should have passed you over like the other five who didn't get to meet a wonderful opportunity. You wasted your time here."

"No. I didn't waste my time." Anger stirred within Sarah. They were just trying to get inside her head.

"You wasted your time. You deserve to go back to that prison and rot for what you did to a saint."

"Yes, I do, but not yet." She struggled to her feet and started to walk again.

"Why not?"

"I'm not finished here yet. I have to finish."

"You are finished. You were done the moment you walked into the academy." Drill Hollister followed her up the hill, taunting her every step of the way.

Drill Hooks stepped out from where she had been hiding from the weather. "You should quit, Twelve. Go and be a bigger number in the state pen. You'll end up there anyway."

"No. I won't. She taught me that I'm better than that."

"She didn't teach you anything. You're too damn stupid to learn." Drill Hooks blasted Sarah with her insult. Sarah gritted her teeth to keep from backhanding the drill. She knew she wasn't stupid. She knew that they were trying to get a rise

235

out of her, trying to make her fail, testing her to see what she was made of.

"I may be stupid, but I am loyal to my mother and I will not fail her. There ain't a damn thing you can say to stop me from finishing this," Sarah said more to herself than to any of the drills whose voices were nearly drowned out by the raging storm blowing through Missouri. She ducked her head as she forced one foot to drag up behind the other. Side-stepping up the steep and slippery terrain, she plodded on, hauling the boulder to the top of the hill.

Wind ripped leaves off the trees and tore Drill Hooks' rain jacket hood from her head. Her neatly wrapped bun was soaked now and coming undone. The storm ripped strands of hair loose until the pins gave way and released a flood of blonde hair to whip at her face.

Sarah's foot slipped in the mud as rain pounded her face. Her ankle twisted, and she dropped the boulder that she carried. Sarah cried out from the pain in her sprained ankle and from the pain of watching as the boulder rolled back down the hill. Her clothes were slick with mud and torn from holding the rough earthen rocks against her body. She sobbed into the mud from the pain and from failing the woman who taught her how she wanted to live her life.

It was over. She had failed. She had failed herself and Gloria. She didn't give a damn about failing herself, but she did give a damn about failing Gloria. She slid down the hill to the boulder that had stopped in a pile of dead brush and thorns. She reached in to retrieve it but quickly withdrew her hand at the sharp stab of the thorns ripping her skin. She looked toward the sky, toward a god that she didn't believe in, toward anything that would guide her into her next move.

THE SCHOLARSHIP

Rain continued to beat down on her as if to punish her for every wrong decision she had made in her life. Wind ripped at her hair and chilled her to the bone. She started to shiver uncontrollably as hypothermia began its invasion to claim her life. She thought it was fitting that she leave this world on a cold and miserable day since so much of her life seemed to be just that: cold and miserable.

She curled up in a ball, hunched her shivering shoulders against the storm and gave permission for death to come and take her. She had tried. She had given everything. It was time to sleep for good, a sleep that didn't require her to open her eyes ever again.

Chapter XXIV

"Get up!" Drill Hawkins' booming voice seemed to send the storm reeling away. She stood over Sarah looking for a response. "Get up, damn you."

"I can't." Sarah said, slightly louder than a whisper.

"You can, and you will."

"I can't."

"This coming from a woman who nearly ran me into the ground because she had a point to prove, from a woman who has pushed through every task most times pulling double duty, and you can't haul a damn boulder up a hill."

Sarah shook her head and buried it back in the mud, hoping that she would be too weak to raise it again and so drown herself in the rainfall.

Drill Hawkins grabbed a fistful of hair, holding Sarah's head up out of the ground. "Then you ponder these words as you lay there feeling sorry for yourself. You completed a marathon because you hated me. You hauled the heaviest plate of lies, because you hated us. You fought us tooth and nail because your heart was full of hate. You would have graduated long ago, but Gloria held you back. She held you back because she knew that you weren't ready. She knew that there was something buried deep inside you that needed to be fixed, otherwise you would be doomed to repeat this pattern of faking to get by.

"She sacrificed her freedom to save you. She sat up hours at night, praying for a way to get through to you. She agonized over you like a parent does for their terminally sick child, begging and seeking a way to save that child. Her bed did not get the luxury of her company for the last four nights she was here. She loved you so much. She would have given anything to see you succeed.

"I've seen what you can do when your heart is filled with hate. What will you do when your heart is filled with love?" Drill Hawkins released Sarah's hair and let it fall back into the mud, then stomped off down the mountain as if she had given up.

Sarah heard the words. She didn't know that Gloria had invested that much time into her, that much dedication and that much love. She wept at being an embarrassment to Gloria. She wished she would have opened up sooner and saved her from all those nights of anguish. Helping someone should not have been this hard. She opened her eyes and stared at the stone through the pounding rain. "Until it explodes," she said to herself thinking of her heart and the love that she had for the best mother she could think to have.

Boiling together a mix of love and hate, she shoved her hand into the prickly tangle. She cupped the heavy stone and rolled it out of its entrapment. She tried to stand but her ankle screamed its protest. From her knees she began rolling the stone up the hill, inching along as fast as she could. She thought about everything that Gloria had said to her, about all the lessons learned and the Army acronym that symbolized everything rolled up into one. She understood the groundwork that the program was designed to instill in each student. It wasn't just for business: it was for life as well.

She thought about her life. She didn't feel that she had a future in anything. She couldn't think of what she would do after this, but she did know that she had to finish. Maybe then she would have a clearer picture of the different possibilities that would be available to her. She rolled the stone again and dragged her twisted ankle behind her. She had almost made it back to where she had fallen. Her ankle throbbed fiercely. "If it's gonna hurt, let it hurt." Sarah stabbed her foot down on the wet ground. Pain shot up her leg, exciting every nerve to its maximum capacity. She gritted her teeth and forced one step, then the next.

She glanced ahead up the hill to find the rest of the drills waiting to give their verbal assaults. She knew it would be a gauntlet. She ducked her head to the charge, placed her good foot on the lead and dragged the other behind. Step after slippery step she plodded forward, making slow but steady progress. Zigzagging up the steepest part of the trail she met the first group of drills ready to hound her into submission.

"You're nothing. A little whore like you isn't meant to live. You should just go kill yourself." Drill Hook started the attack with a level of cruelty that none had ever witnessed before and set the stage for others to follow suit. "Go home. You're nothing and never will be."

"You're nothing but a coward. You'll never be able to face real fear. This ain't real, this is make-believe, happy-time. The real fear is outside those gates in a world that's unforgiving. Do yourself a favor and squash your time."

Sarah ducked her head and tried her best to ignore the ridicules, yet each one still stung. Turn after turn, she met with each drill whose student had long ago graduated to the next phase. A phase she was wondering if it was even worth entering. But she wasn't going through all this pain to prove her worth to these people. She wasn't trying to prove anything to them. In her mind, there was only one person to prove worth to, one person whose opinion mattered. It was clear that a lot of hatred had built up against her because her stone-hardened grudge against any authority figure had sentenced an innocent woman to prison for many years. More belittling rants came at her, seeking to tear her down. She knew she deserved no less than what they were doing, but she had to see her work through. She had to finish.

A rock rolled out from under her foot and her ankle twisted again sending her crashing to the ground. Pain shot through her leg and up her side. She clutched at her boulder to keep it from rolling back down the hill. She couldn't afford to give an inch when Gloria's reputation was at stake. A cold concrete bed in prison seemed quite welcoming compared to the brutal assignment she had placed upon herself.

"You're all alone. There's no one here to help you. No one here to say 'Oh poor pitiful number Twelve. No one likes her, and she will never amount to anything.'" Drill Abernathy said. "Who could love someone as self-centered as you?"

Pain and exhaustion belted at her soul like the rain did at her skin. Everything around her seemed to want to kill her. She knew that if the laws were different, she would have been tasting her own blood right now from the angry mob she was facing.

The words from Drill Hawkins resonated back out of the screaming wind. *She loved you so much, she would have given anything to see you succeed... What will you do when your heart is filled with love?* Sarah grabbed every ounce of love

241

she could find in her soul. She pulled it from the trees and the rain. She pulled it from the animals hiding from the storm and she pulled it from her real mother. The one mother who fought tooth and nail against a rebellious child. The one who believed in her when most believed that she was not worth the time to glance at.

She rolled all that love into a fiery red ball. Like a forest fire burning out of control within her, she rolled all the hate she ever felt toward anyone into the driving force that propelled her forward. She started taking each step a little faster even as the drills attempted to bring her back down. She turned that hatred into fierce love, a love that gave her all the energy that she needed.

She blasted through the remaining drills to carry her boulder to the top of the hill where the cable awaited her trolley, with a sling that would carry her boulder back down to the bottom. The path was clear to her destination. No more drills stood in her way. It was time for the home stretch. She had no more energy. Everything was spent. She was running on all the hate she had pulled from every ounce of her past. All the mean words from her school days. All the times her mother came home drunk to beat her and tell her it was her fault for her parents' divorce. All the hate she had for herself for being inadequate and a disappointment. She took all that hate and fed the one thing she knew she had. She had the love from a woman who didn't know her, who didn't understand the task she had signed on for, who blindly pulled her name from the bottom of the stack where it should have been left buried.

She was not worthy of this woman's love, but she wasn't going let that love go down in vain. She had to finish for her. Sarah looked at the cable and saw that one more drill stood there. It was Drill Hawkins. Sarah had thought that Drill

THE SCHOLARSHIP

Hawkins had gone back to the barracks, but here she stood next to the cable, staring at her. She was getting ready to call time. Sarah hurried her step.

The wind picked up and rain turned to hail as an icy front twisted around to batter the compound. Marble-sized hail shot down out of the sky, creating a welt and bruise on whatever it hit. Sarah ducked her head toward the barrage and shuffled her left foot ahead while dragging the sprained right foot. The storm winds increased, ripping more leaves and branches from the tree trunks. Sarah moved toward the cable despite all the falling debris. The trees swayed, leaning hard away from the wind.

"Look out!" Drill Hawkins screamed.

Sarah didn't see it coming. Another tree toppled. Leaves and branches hit her, pressing her forward into the mud. She didn't have the strength to pull herself out of the tangle. She stared forward at the boulder that needed to get on the trolley, but she couldn't breathe. The weight of a heavy branch pinned her to the ground, crushing the air from her lungs. Hail continued to beat down on the forest canopy, decimating the leaves and pulverizing everything except solid rock.

She had failed. She hoped she would die right there so that she wouldn't have to face Gloria and say that she failed. She couldn't pull a breath. The tree would soon suffocate her, and her worries would be over, she would soon be able to see her baby and tell her she was sorry for not being the mother she had deserved.

She suddenly felt light as a feather. She looked at the boulder then at the movement at her side. Drill Hawkins stood there with several others lifting the tree and allowing air to circulate back into her lungs. She looked up into the face of the drill. She wore an expression that screamed *finish it*. Sarah turned back to the boulder and clawed her way forward. She pulled her feet under her and heaved the rock up out of the mud. Step by step, she inched closer to the cable. She closed her eyes and forced her feet to move the last few steps. Opening her eyes, she found the cable and with the last bit of strength, heaved the trolley onto the steel wire. Her legs buckled, but her arms gave it one last push before she fell to the ground, striking her head on a rock.

Chapter XXV

W here is the line supposed to be?"

Master Drill Ietel surveyed the scene after the storm. From the heavy rain and footprints, the line that each boulder coming down the cable was to cross had been erased. If a boulder did not cross the line, it did not count and had to be redone. The pile of boulders at the base of the hill were concentrated in one area except for one. That one stood alone, just two feet short of the others. It was the last boulder Sarah had sent down the cable before falling and hitting her head. A tree had toppled and derailed the boulder letting it fall just two feet short of the original line.

Drill Zefon held a can of spray paint. Drill Hawkins and all the rest stood looking at the results of the previous night's onslaught. "The line was here," Drill Hooks said, pointing to a spot just behind the lone boulder. Drill Zefon sprayed a line where Drill Hooks pointed.

Master Drill Ietel looked at the faces of the drills searching for any sign of a dispute. "I want a concrete line topped with steel right here. Master Drill Ietel pointed with his toe to the orange line. "Ten feet across, two feet deep, and topped with steel so that we don't have this confusion in the future. I want it done by the end of the day."

"Yes, Master Drill," the drills said, in unison.

"Good job, drills. We didn't succeed with everyone, but we still did good work. Group attention." The drills snapped to attention. "Continue the clean up and build this concrete structure, next formation will be at the barracks at eighteen hundred. Fall out and continue your work." Master Drill Ietel turned and walked back to the barracks. His detail at the academy was almost done and he would return to Fort Leonard Wood to start basic training with a brand-new group of Army volunteers.

****

Sarah opened her eyes. Dim light from the hallway spread across the room she was in. It was the infirmary. An IV drip was fastened to her arm and a heated blanket covered her. Her head throbbed, and she felt like a group of thugs had beaten her with sticks. Warm sunshine beat against the shade-drawn windows. A warm icepack was affixed to her ankle. It had long ago lost its effectiveness. The swelling had gone down, but her ankle still hurt. Her thoughts turned to her unfinished task. She still had to haul boulders. She had to clear Gloria's name.

Scooting to the foot of the bed she sat up and jerked the plastic IV tube apart leaving it to drain onto the floor. She had to get to the boulder field. She tested her foot. It hurt, but she could still put weight on it. Shuffling out the door in the hospital-style gown, she walked to the students' barracks, to her closet and fished out a fresh set of clothes. Instead of taking the time to go to the latrine to change like they were supposed to do, she changed right in front of her locker.

246

THE SCHOLARSHIP

The building was eerily quiet, and she might have noticed if her brain was turned off of autopilot. Her only thought was to finish what she had started. Finish seeing that her mother's reputation was as untarnished as her heart was. She stuffed her feet into her second pair of boots, quickly laced them up, and ignored the pain in her muscles. She had grown so used to the pain that it seemed a part of life now.

She was met with a blinding light when she walked out the barracks door. The sun was high overhead, shining down like a proud father. Sarah continued her march across the asphalt and on to the damp ground. She had slept through the morning and into the afternoon. Vapor rose off the earth, evaporating some of what was delivered the night before. In the shadowy areas, pockets of hail still hid from the overpowering sun. The grass was matted to the ground. Leaves and branches littered the area. Sarah stepped over and around them, making her way to the pile of boulders.

She picked up the boulder she had last flung down the cable, adjusted the rope that held the boulder and slung it over her shoulder. She grasped a trolley lying nearby and started up the hill. The words from Drill Hawkins invaded her mind. *She sat up hours at night praying for a way to get through to you.* Sarah thought about the woman who had set her soul free, and she smiled up at the mountain that had helped turn her into a woman who was free from any demons.

"Good afternoon, Miss Twelve," Drill Abernathy said, shocking Sarah out of her trance. Sarah looked to see a pristinely dressed drill moving branches and debris from the path. A smile graced her face as bright as the sun that shone down on them.

"Good afternoon, Drill Abernathy." Sarah continued up the hill. Her pain began to fade away from the warm greeting.

Sarah pushed ahead; she still had her job to do. She had to complete her mother's task. If Sarah ever had the chance to see her again, she would certainly ask Gloria if she wanted a daughter.

"Good afternoon, Miss Twelve." The voice of another drill called out to her. Sarah looked up to see another blue uniform pause from sawing on a fallen tree. This tree had fallen on the cable and derailed the boulder a moment before crossing the original line.

Sarah nodded and continued up the path. One by one the drills greeted her warmly and addressed her as Miss Twelve. Topping the rise, she followed the path with only a slight limp. Before her lay the tree that smashed her into the dirt. Drill Hawkins and three others stood up to watch her advance with the boulder. They wore leather gloves and carried the simple tools for dismantling the tree and hauling it out of the way. Sarah walked up and stopped before them.

"Good morning, Miss Twelve," Drill Sanders said.

Sarah was stunned. She was expecting a bombardment of insults and demeaning remarks. "Why is everyone being nice to me? Why are you calling me Miss Twelve?"

Drill Hawkins walked around the tree that they had lifted off Sarah the night before and stood before the student.

"It is because you've earned their respect," Drill Hawkins answered. Sarah stood dazed, not understanding what Hawkins meant. "You completed Gloria's task and in doing that, you also graduated."

Sarah looked to the other drills behind her. They nodded their agreement. "I finished for Drill Witcom?"

"Yes, you did."

Sarah's knees buckled, and she collapsed to the ground. The boulder hit with a thump at her side, sinking into the mud.

THE SCHOLARSHIP

Tears streamed down her face as joy and relief overcame her and sapped her energy and willingness to stay up right. She had worked day and night to complete her task and exhausted herself to a point where she lost track of the days and could only remember that she must continue until her heart gave out. Minutes streamed by as she knelt atop the mountain and let her emotions overtake her. She didn't know why she was crying; she just knew that it was necessary. It was a release of everything bad leaving her and a breath of everything good waiting to become part of her life.

"Come on, Twelve. Stand up." Drill Hawkins said and hooked a hand under her arm. She and Drill Sanders helped Sarah to her feet. They helped wipe off and straighten her clothing, so she looked more presentable. "Since you appear that you don't need any more rest, why did you bring the boulder to the top of the mountain?"

Sarah looked at the boulder next to her feet. Her mind drew a blank. She had done so much work for Gloria to clear her name, now she didn't know why she had hauled the boulder up the hill. "Why did everyone make the journey so hard last night? Why did everyone yell at me and call me names?"

"That was your test. It was our job to make that journey as difficult as we could. We had to test your resolve to push forward or quit. The rules say that when we test you, we must be the world against you. We must be the ones to hold you back just like things in the real world do. We have to push you until you break. Gloria did that. She broke the rules by giving you the butt-kicking that you needed to break through that thick skull and find out why you had such an issue with authority.

"What we did was test you to see if you had the resolve to put your feet where your heart is. You pissed off a lot of people when Gloria was sent away and some of them may still be mad at you for it, but you have earned the respect of all of us. That is why we are calling you Miss Twelve. Our job is to be the resistance you may face in life by trying to tear you down. We're not allowed to encourage you."

"But you said you saw love in my heart."

"I saw it, but I did not say that. I asked, 'What will you do when your heart is filled with love?'"

Sarah understood. Drill Hawkins didn't build her up or tear her down. She just got her to think. To think of the possibilities on the other side of the fence and to think about the potential of what life could be like. She looked at the gathering drills as they all made their way up to the top of the hill. She looked at the boulder putting together the reason why she had packed it to the top of the hill. "I guess if it's not for Drill Witcom, then I guess it is for me?"

Drill Hawkins smiled a warm and friendly smile. "I see now what a heart full of love can do. It is time to finish."

Sarah nodded her head. "Yes, Drill Hawkins." Sarah lifted the stone back up on her shoulder. Drill Hooks dragged a fallen branch out of the way, so Sarah could have a clear path to the cable. She looked down the zip line and could see that the fallen tree had been cut and removed from obstructing the boulder's descent. She hung the trolley on the cable, the rope holding the boulder on its hook and sent it back down to the bottom.

She now saw the purpose of the obnoxious task as a character-building exercise. It represented all the stupid things in life that made no sense, but we are made to do them anyway. Whether it is sitting in jail or watching cement dry, it's a task that builds character. She understood that each day and each boulder was one given to her to build something, whether it was a bottomless pit or a grand castle. The choice was hers.

THE SCHOLARSHIP

Turning, she found Drill Abernathy standing behind her. With tears in her eyes, she embraced Sarah. Sarah returned the endearment for a moment and then she was passed on to the next drill. Some gave her a hug, while others gave her a solid pat on the back. Drill Hooks was the last to give her a hug and turn her toward the gate where Drill Hawkins waited. She unlocked the gate and motioned Sarah to follow.

Through a narrow path that led to the back side of the hill, they stepped over fallen trees and branches. Soon a grand compound appeared that was void of any tall fences with razor wire. It was surrounded by lush crops and various outbuildings.

"I'm one of the few who doesn't like you," Drill Hawkins said. "Drill Witcom asked me personally to see that you had every opportunity to succeed. I gave her my word that I would do what it took without breaking the rules. If you didn't finish, it wouldn't be my problem. It would be yours. Life would go on for the rest of us and you would see the outside of prison, eventually."

Drill Hawkins turned to a locked, waterproof box. Pulling the keys out of her pocket she opened it up. Three harnesses remained in the box. Two of them would not get used from the original class of twenty-five. "We prided ourselves on one hundred percent success rate. Now we are down by three people."

Sarah knew the three people she was talking about. The first was the girl who didn't get off the bus on day one. She had gotten pregnant by one of the guards who was supposed to oversee her safety and well-being. He himself was now serving jail time for his act. The second harness had been for Fern, whose mental instability had gone unnoticed by everyone in the system. After the initial charges on her for her attack on Sarah, more charges were brought as evidence unfolded in a

251

missing persons case. The case was about a young man who had gone missing three years prior, after he had rejected Fern during her senior year of high school. The boy's body had been found during the excavations for a new residential development with a greeting card pinned by a knife to his chest. The name on the greeting card and a forensic lip-print match pulled from Fern easily tied her to the scene. The print was detailed enough to substitute for a good fingerprint. She was now currently being held in a psychiatric ward awaiting a review of her mental condition.

The third harness would be Sarah's. Due to her determination to clear Gloria's name and allow her to graduate the system, Sarah also ensured her graduation into the next phase. Gloria was one who was sorely missed by everyone because she had been an angel all along. She was one who had built the most pristine castle. She had helped others complete their tasks. She had given good advice on helping fellow students. She had gotten first dibs to pick any student out of the thirty files on the table and she picked the one who was least likely to succeed. She had set a standard so high that anyone else could only hope to achieve half the accomplishments that she had. Although it cost her freedom, she succeeded in her mission.

"Everyone screws up. Everyone makes bad choices. Everyone has a moment of weakness where things fall apart. It's in those times where we are given a choice to make it right or to run away from the mess we have created. One of the rules we have is that the drills are not to talk about or discuss the reasons that brought us to this facility. Not to anyone who hasn't graduated phase one, that is. I was sent here because I beat my boyfriend to a bloody pulp. They placed him in the I.C.U., and he stayed there for nearly four months. They still don't know how he survived. They settled on a less severe punishment for me since he was driving drunk and killed our daughter in a wreck outside my house, which is why I beat him up. They gave me a simple battery charge.

"I spent many months in therapy to get past everything that happened. I'm still not sure what I will do once I leave this place."

Sarah gulped at the realization that all the drills had some sort of dark past that had been their own demon that they had to contend with. "I'm sorry for your loss."

"It's mostly alright now. I still have issues at times, but most of the water has passed under the bridge and I'll find peace with it someday. Seeing you try so hard and succeed has helped me get over some of it as well, especially yesterday. You had such determination; it was like watching a soldier go through a war zone. I still don't like you, but I know you are worth the effort we have put into seeing you succeed."

Sarah was stunned at Drill Hawkins admission of respect. It took her a moment to find words. "Wow. I don't know what to say. I didn't expect you to reveal something like that."

"I've found it better to be upfront and honest than to bottle things up. It will take a bit more courage to do that in the beginning, but the rewards are better when you do."

"I see."

"Remember, you're still not done. You still have a long road ahead of you, but I believe you have already climbed the steepest part of your journey." Drill Hawkins handed the harness to Sarah. Sarah looked down at the complex below. A zip line stretched out just above the trees to a small, fenced area with a gate open to the main building.

"This spot is meant to symbolize that you have climbed the mountain and that everything in your life from here on out should be easier than what you have gone through in the past.

"Drill Witcom was right to hold you back. I didn't see it at first and I don't think anyone else did either. She had that mother's intuition that told her there was something more and to keep digging until she found it. Now I see that she was right. She has given you the best chance of being free from the plagues of your past. It's up to you to forge your future. Now, if I see you on our side of the fence again, we are going to have serious problems."

Sarah wrestled into the harness and pulled the straps tight, then looked into the proud face of a woman who was as close to tears as she would ever allow herself to be. "I'm going to talk to the Dean about making you Master Drill. I think they need you to be here where you can make the most difference in this world."

Drill Hawkins' face soured. She snapped the carabiner to the loop of Sarah's harness and shoved her off the platform.

Dear reader,

Thank you for allowing me to entertain you with this novel. I also hope that it was enlightening for you as well. As with most all writing there are lessons to be learned from the words scribbled on a piece of paper or characters hammered out on a keyboard. For you who have your lives figured out and are on a good productive path, congratulations! You are among the lucky few whom hardship has overlooked. Keep doing what you do and enjoy all the successes that you achieve. You needn't read on if you don't want to.

For you who are staring at walls of concrete and steel, or a stack of overdue bills, or any other insurmountable task that makes you feel imprisoned, this novel was written for you. After graduating high school, I thought I was the shit. I knew enough to survive. What else did I need? I was taught to work and became very good at it and the trades at which I applied myself.

It wasn't until a series of really tough life lessons that knocked me down over and over barely giving me a chance to catch my breath, when I realized that I didn't have a clue about this game called life. Once I diagnosed this problem, I became a student again. I became a perpetual student and learned a lot about myself and the path ahead of me.

Now let's talk about you. What put you in the hole that you're in? What caused cold steel to wrap around your wrists? What caused the need to buy the useless crap on the infomercials? What caused you to key your cheating spouse's vehicle? Do you feel betrayed by the promises of another? Do you feel inferior next to the social standings of your friends or family? Do you disagree with the system you are currently living under? Did your parents present a false or biased view of how society works? What is the core feeling you have when you face the problem that sits before you?

Now imagine that you are on the other side of the fence from where you sit. Is it fair to you if someone stole from your store? Should you pay for your nose which someone else had broken? Should someone manipulate you into doing something which you know is wrong? Should you be killed due to someone else's stupidity or mental breakdown?

Yes, these are tough questions, but also necessary questions. Our society includes you. You are a relevant part of this game. There are rules but there are also a lot of freedoms that allow you to be happy. I want you to focus on the root cause of the problem you face and come up with a legal and at least mostly fair solution to it. It may be as simple as waking up on the right side of the bed, or as complex as writing a thesis paper on quantum physics. I assure you that there is a positive answer to your problem.

One of the greatest career decisions I enjoy is being a dad. It is tough. It is stressful, but it is immensely rewarding. For you, a solid parental figure may have been lacking in your life. If you need one, I am right here. I will be that parental figure or valued friend. Time changes things and opinions vary. Counselors come and go causing you to tell your life story over again. In a sea of shifting waters, I will be that rock which you can cling to. I will be that parent who never gives up and shuts the door on you. I will never die on you, because I am right here immortalized in these pages. I am Dean Vickery teaching you to be respectful to the janitor and the CEO. I am Drill Hawkins lifting your head out of the mud showing you that you're worth more than you realize, and I am Gloria dishing out tough love when you need it most, sacrificing myself to help you become a better person.

I am right here in these pages to help you become the amazing person that I know you are.

Take care and I'll see you in the next pages,

Alex R Price
P.O. Box 593
Green River, WY 82935

P.S. Once you overcome the core problem that you face, I encourage you to read Jonathan Livingston Seagull written by Richard Bach. Once you understand the message in his book, there is no way to imagine how high you could fly.